C000161657

Too
Many
Scars

SHARRON E TOWNSEND

PublishingPush

Copyright © 2021 by Sharron E Townsend

All rights reserved. No part of this book may be reproduced or used in any manner without written permission of the copyright owner except for the use of quotations in a book review.
For more information contact sharront75@sky.com

FIRST EDITION

ISBN 978-1-80227-302-1 (paperback)
ISBN 978-1-80227-303-8 (ebook)

Prologue

"This has to be the best holiday I've ever had!" Meg remarked as she gazed at her fiancé.

"Of course! That's because you are here with me!" came the proud response from Tim, flashing his beautiful white teeth as he smiled at her.

Meg smiled as she gently lapped the warm water with her hands. The Caribbean Sea stretched endlessly in front of the two of them with the sun bouncing off the water making it shimmer.

They could see the fish swimming beneath them, darting around their tanned legs. Crabs scurried along the sand underwater, occasionally disappearing beneath it.

Tim swam towards his stunning lady, his bronzed, athletic body easily seen beneath the clear water.

"Can we move here? I never want to leave Jamaica," Meg asked as she wrapped her body around Tim, interlocking her fingers behind his neck. Tim just rolled his eyes at her. Meg kissed his lips. They lingered, blissfully unaware of any holidaymakers.

The aroma of cooking on the huge barbeque on the beach behind them caused Meg to pull away.

"Lunch!" she proclaimed with a huge smile, her emerald eyes lighting up.

"You and your stomach!" Tim remarked. "I don't know where you put it all; I mean – look at you!" Tim looked up and down Meg's tiny body.

"Do you ever think of anything else other than food?"

1

"One or two things…!" Now it was Meg's turn to look up and down Tim's body. Meg slowly glided out of the ocean, revealing her bright orange bikini.

They strolled hand in hand towards the small crowd gathering around the Jamaican chef who was standing behind the barbeque smiling at his audience. He was dressed in shorts. His thick dreadlocks tumbled over his shoulders, and he was singing along to "Three Little Birds" which was playing loudly in the background. He was flipping the burgers over to the beat of the song. Before they knew it, they were at the front of the queue. They selected some delicious-looking food and went to find some seats.

The swimming pool shimmered to the side of them with a bar in the centre. A few couples were sat on the seats there, laughing away whilst sipping their drinks.

Meg was delighted the resort wasn't too busy and overcrowded. It was a couples-only resort, one of Tim's requests. Meg wouldn't have minded hearing the sounds of children laughing and enjoying themselves, but she had to admit, this was nice too.

"Hello…where are you?" Tim asked.

"Right here!" Meg replied grinning. She began tucking into her food.

"Drinks!" Tim announced. "What do you fancy?"

"Sex on the beach!" came the cheeky reply.

"Too much sand going everywhere," was Tim's response.

Meg just rolled her eyes at her fiancé, who stood up and went to the bar.

Meg sat back and relaxed, soaking up her surroundings. It really was stunning - the sun, the ocean, the palm trees and the hotel. It was so nice to be away from all the hustle and bustle of life at home.

They were planning their wedding; well, Meg and her mum were planning the wedding. She also had the added stress of the hospital appointments. So, this was nice, just the two of them, enjoying their holiday.

Tim returned with the drinks, the blue sky and the golden sunshine making a beautiful backdrop for his fantastic-looking body.

Later that evening, they were in their large hotel room getting ready for their evening meal.

"I can't believe I am going parascending tomorrow," Tim suddenly announced as he admired his reflection in the mirror. He glanced at Meg.

"I know you wanted to go too sweetie, but I really don't think you would enjoy it and we are running out of cash."

"Well, I am sure I WOULD have liked it and that's why we brought the credit card!" Meg said indignantly. Tim walked over to her and stroked her face.

"We are saving for a wedding, you know." He paused.

"You look beautiful," he complimented her black dress which skimmed over her small frame.

Meg knew he liked that particular dress but the compliment meant nothing to her. She really had wanted to go parascending. The exhilarating feeling of being high up in the air, floating across the beautiful blue Jamaican sky... It would have just made her holiday complete.

The following day, whilst Tim was enjoying himself, Meg decided to take a stroll along the beach and visit the small shop which was about 500 meters away.

The shop had many carved objects. Meg took her time and looked around, seeing giraffes, elephants, and many other cute little creatures.

The shopkeeper was very friendly, giving her a big smile when she looked his way. Naturally, he seemed to be trying to sell her everything in the shop! In the end, Meg decided on a small but beautifully carved giraffe. The shopkeeper offered to carve the year on one of the legs. Meg nodded and watched as he expertly carved the year.

Meg ambled back to the hotel and was surprised that Tim was already there.

"Where have you been?" he demanded with a slightly annoyed tone in his voice.

Meg told him where she had been, showing him her purchase.

Tim showed no interest all but said, "I had a fantastic time!"

"Great," was all that Meg could say in response.

The last two days of their holiday flew by with Tim on cloud 9 and Meg feeling rather cheated.

Their flight home seemed even longer than the outbound one, probably because they were heading back to reality. In a couple of days, Meg would be back at work, back to learn what the future held. To say she was concerned was an understatement. The hospital appointment was only a few days away…

Chapter 1

Meg Walker crossed her long, slender legs beneath her desk, bored at the fifth meeting that week. She looked out of the window at the terrible weather; it was raining and had been almost non-stop for days. Anita, Meg's boss, was holding the meeting. Her voice droned monotonously, which didn't help matters. Anita had been Meg's manager since Meg had joined Insurefirst over four years ago. They had got on well over the years, had their little disagreements like anyone else, but their working relationship had been fine. Anita was firm but not bossy, Meg thought, and always very fair. Meg did, however, make a point not to talk to her too much. She had her own circle of friends and didn't want to be branded 'teacher's pet!'

It was fair to say that Meg had always enjoyed her job there. But it didn't stop her from feeling bored now. She should have been really interested in the meeting today though, after all, it was about the new positions that were going to be made available in the upcoming months.

Insurefirst was expanding and had bought out another company, leaving promotional prospects for many of the employees. One of the positions was one that Meg, herself had applied for. She had always loved training other staff members when they had joined the company, but as she only did it on rare occasions, there was not enough work to warrant it being a full-time thing for her. But now, as new staff would be joining and staff from the other company were being transferred, that would change. There was a post available for a training coordinator. Today's meeting was to announce the new positions. Meg would have preferred to have been told either way in private, beforehand, which to her was common sense, but then a large company and common sense didn't always go hand in hand!

Meg tried to keep her eyes open and concentrate on the meeting, but the lack of sleep wasn't helping matters; she had a lot on her mind now, and as much as she did want this job, that was the least of her worries.

There were three positions to announce, and typically the training coordinator was the final one to be announced. Meg had already seen the disappointed faces of the unsuccessful candidates for the other two positions and was getting very nervous, but the moment had arrived, "And finally, after a lot of discussions, we are pleased to announce Meg Walker as the new training coordinator!"

Meg was overwhelmed with the news but was a little saddened at the faces of the others. There was no need however, as Jenny, one of the other applicants, came up to her and congratulated her.

"We all knew you would get it really; you are the best person for the job."

"Oh, thanks for your support! I am surprised at the way it was done though," exclaimed Meg.

"What do you mean?"

"Well, you all find out like that, that you didn't get it…"

"Oh no, we already knew. They called us into the office earlier - only the ones who had the jobs didn't find out. We were sworn to secrecy. Oh, hell no, they wouldn't tell us like that. I know they can be dumb sometimes but give them a little credit!"

"I see."

"Well, anyway, enough about work, how is everything else?"

"Tim or the hospital?"

"Both."

Tim was Meg's boyfriend, well, fiancé, in fact. They had been going through a few problems over the past couple of months.

"Oh, Tim's the same, dismissing everything and saying I am totally over-reacting, and tomorrow…I am worried sick about tomorrow!"

"Is he going with you to the hospital?"

"Don't be so stupid! Tim? Take time off work to go to the hospital? Ha!"

"I'll take that as a No then! He'll come round. He's got to appreciate it's your health we are talking about and not something and nothing. Don't worry, he'll come round," she repeated as if trying to console her friend.

"I hope so. I can never weigh him up. Sometimes, I couldn't wish for a better partner and then he goes and acts like this; it's like he's…I don't know, Jekyll and Hyde, I guess!"

Jenny just smiled at her friend.

"Sorry! I am going on, aren't I?"

"Not at all; I asked, didn't I?"

Jenny was one of Meg's closest friends, so close in fact, that Meg worried whether the promotion would jeopardize their relationship. She was always there for her; in fact, they were always there for each other. Meg remembered all too well when Jenny was having trouble with her boyfriend, now ex. He had been seeing someone else behind her back.

"Kick him out!" Meg had advised her friend. Jenny just needed someone to tell her that was the right thing to do. She had known in her head, but her heart was somewhere else. They had, after all, been together for years. She had eventually plucked up the courage to send him packing.

"What are you thinking about?" Jenny asked her friend.

"Just that we have been through a lot together," Meg said warmly.

"Yeah, remember that holiday we went on together? How old were we? 16? 17?"

"17, I think; it was great, wasn't it? Remember that waiter? He really liked you…"

"Ladies, I hate to break up the reminiscing, but we are at work here…"

Anita's voice startled the two.

"Oops! Sorry, Anita, we were just…"

"I know, well, please get back to work. The training coordinator of all people… I'm starting to think I made a mistake."

"Anita, I…" Meg was worried at this comment but as she looked at Anita, she saw she was smiling and winked at Meg.

"Oh!"

Both Meg and Jenny went back to their workstations.

Their department was situated on the top floor of a busy office in the centre of a bustling city.

"See you at lunch," Meg said.

Lunchtime seemed to take ages to arrive, but it eventually did and the two girls were back together, walking into town to their usual shop for their food, chatting about their morning, and Meg's new position. Meg was so excited and had many plans for her training.

"Have you told anyone yet?" Jenny asked as they sat in the café waiting for the coffees and sandwiches.

"Believe it or not, no!"

"I can't believe you! The job you have been after for months, and now you've got it, who do you tell? No one!"

"I have been too busy with the phones and everything. I had the most obnoxious caller, and besides, Anita has had her eyes on me since we spoke this morning."

"OK, I forgive you." The conversation seemed to stop abruptly when the food arrived. Meg had ordered a healthy sandwich of ham and salad in a granary teacake, whereas Jenny had gone for a burger! They sat at their table and tucked in. They had always liked 'Isabel's Café' - the homely surroundings and sofa-style seating. The staff were friendly and polite. Naturally, the food was good too.

Jenny looked at her watch.

"Oh no! Two o'clock already! I guess we'd better get back."

"Yeah, see you at 5." Meg and Jenny shared the driving as they lived relatively close to each other. They could chat more when they met up at the close of their working day.

Later that afternoon, when Anita was at yet another meeting, Meg seized the opportunity and picked up her phone to call her mum. Tim would have been her first call but she knew he was very busy at the moment, and besides, he didn't like her calling him at work.

"Hello," came the reply when she dialled the number.

"Hi, Mum, it's me."

"Who's me?" her mum joked.

"Yeah, yeah, very funny! You remember what I told you about today?"

"Remember? I've been throwing up all morning thinking about it! How did it go?"

"Bad news, I'm afraid. I'm going to be spending more time here since… I GOT THE JOB!"

"Oh, love, I am so glad! I am very proud of you!"

"Thanks, Mum, look I will have to go, you know what it's like! I just thought I would let you know."

"Sure, thanks for ringing me; I can eat now!"

"See you tomorrow."

Meg put down the phone.

'How funny,' she thought. 'Such good news today and tomorrow I could be hearing the worst news of my life!'

The afternoon was finally over. Meg and Jenny were back together again! They said their goodbyes to their colleagues and were on their way.

Meg said very little on the way home.

"You ok?"

"Yeah, just nervous I guess."

"I can understand that, but you know where I am if you need me tonight, and ring me when you find out, ok?"

"Sure."

Jenny dropped Meg off at home. She waved as she saw the car speed off down the street.

Meg was surprised to see Tim's car in the drive. She walked into the house and could immediately hear that he was in the shower. She dropped her bag and looked in the fridge to find something for tea.

"I knew there was something I forgot to do last night, get that meat out of the freezer."

A short while later, Tim walked down the stairs, his hair wet, but looking as sexy as ever, Meg thought.

"Hi, baby," he said to her, giving her a long, beautiful kiss.

"Hi, gorgeous," she replied.

"How did it go then?" he asked her; he knew today was the day of the announcement.

"OK, I guess. I had the most annoying customer on the phone; he…"

"That's not what I meant; I meant the promotion!"

"Oh that, well, yeah, that went ok too…I GOT IT!"

"Oh, wow, I am so pleased," he said, picking her up and spinning her round the room then giving her another huge kiss.

"Yeah, me too."

"How about we go out and celebrate, for tea, even?"

"Great idea. I'll just go and shower and I'll be with you in ten."

"Yeah, course you will."

"OK, maybe twenty."

And that was that. She had her shower and they went out for dinner.

Tim had chosen the restaurant, which didn't bother Meg as he had impeccable taste. On this occasion, he had chosen Bistro Capri, an Italian restaurant quite near their home. Italian food was Meg's favourite and this restaurant was lovely. It had recently been refurbished and looked better than ever. They were sat in the conservatory which had a nice view of the stream and waterfall outside.

Throughout the whole night, Meg couldn't keep her eyes off Tim; after all, he was stunning!

"How about we have dessert at home?" he suggested, raising his eyebrow at her.

"Whatever do you mean? I was looking forward to the crème brûlée. I hear it's really good here!"

"Oh, ok."

Meg leaned over to him and whispered, "I am only joking! Yes, I would love to have dessert at home with you." Tim paid the bill and led Meg out to the car.

They went home and ran straight upstairs, laughing like a couple of schoolchildren.

At 6.30 am, the alarm had awoken both of them. Meg had followed Tim out of bed, washed and gone downstairs in her nightdress.

She put on the kettle.

"Toast?" she asked, still buzzing from their romantic evening the night before.

"Ok." Tim obviously didn't feel the same way; it was like he was a different man.

'I wonder if we have Mr Hyde this morning,' Meg thought.

Breakfast was eaten pretty much in silence with only the odd pleasantry being passed by him.

"Doing anything else today?"

"Not really. I just thought I'd have a nice long soak in the bath and prepare myself."

"I'm sure there will be nothing to prepare for. You're just going over the top, jumping to conclusions as usual. Everything will be fine, trust me." His tone was annoyed, almost aggressive.

Meg was not convinced.

Tim continued, "Why are you setting yourself up for bad news anyway?"

"Because then I won't be as upset if the worst happens."

Meg knew this was not true. She was expecting bad news, but nothing would prepare her.

Tim didn't respond to her comments this time, but Meg wasn't stupid; she knew, or maybe hoped, that no matter what he said, he was worried too.

"Well, I'll have to go, otherwise I will be late for work. Have a good day."

'Yeah, right,' she thought.

"Maybe you should go out for lunch with your mum when you get back."

"If I feel like it after…"

"Oh, stop it, for goodness' sake. You're so pessimistic. Look, I really have to go; good luck, ok?"

"I love you, Tim."

"Ditto; see ya."

And with that, he was gone, leaving Meg alone to think of the day ahead. He had been like that for quite some time, ignoring the issue. That, she thought, was his way of dealing with it.

The two of them had been together for six years. They met at a club but really got together because of the local gymnasium. Tim had been going for years. Meg had taken advice from her friend and joined. She had wanted to get in shape for quite some time but like every other teenager, either she couldn't be bothered or just never got round to it. She had finally joined and was very pleased that she had done, if only for the fact that she had got together with Tim there. He was a fitness fanatic. Their relationship had taken off from their very first meeting really. Although it was obvious what she saw in him, his fantastic body, charm and good looks, to name but three reasons, she had absolutely no idea what the attraction was for him, but there had obviously been one because here they were, in their own house together and soon to be married.

Meg cleared the dishes, smiling at the memories. She took her bath.

She then proceeded to dress, carefully choosing an outfit that made her feel good.

"The trouser suit, I think," she said to no one in particular. From the wardrobe, she took out the deep green outfit, which complimented her hair beautifully, and dressed.

She sat at the dressing table and put on her make-up.

Her hair was fiery red in colour and very long. She put it up in her favourite clip and smiled. She always felt better when she had made an effort to look good. She walked down the stairs and left the house.

Meg shivered as she stepped out onto the snow-covered path.

As she turned to lock the door, she smiled. It hadn't been a white Christmas for, well, she couldn't remember for how long, but it looked very much like it was going to be one this year. It was the 17ᵗʰ of December and the weather had been very cold, so the weathermen all across the country were predicting a white Christmas.

This year was very different though, not only due to the weather; in fact, that was the least of the abnormalities of the annum.

Despite the worries though, she was looking forward to Christmas; at least she thought so. This year was going to be the first for a long time that all the relatives would be together. No doubts they would get into the usual petty arguments over which games to play and who cheated the most by knocking over the Monopoly bank just by sheer coincidence into their own savings and then miraculously inheriting a few extra £500s. Ah well, I guess that's what Christmas is all about.

But now to more serious tasks; enough reminiscing. Christmas was a week away and there was a lot to consider and deal with before then.

Meg walked carefully along the path and left the lovely house behind. It looked as pretty as the Christmas cards that stood on her mantelpiece in the living room. She walked to her car and carefully scraped the ice from the windscreen.

Stepping into the car, she thought of everything that had occurred over the last few months - the good, but mainly the bad.

'Ah, not to worry,' she thought as she turned the ignition key.

'All will work out for the best.'

The car started first time, which didn't surprise her. The car may be old but it never failed her. Startled motorists were furious as they tried in vain to start up their cars.

The houses were so close together and they all looked alike apart from the obvious personal touches of their owners. As much as she loved her home, there was very little privacy. Everyone seemed to know everyone else's business. The fact that in the living room was a huge window didn't help. People couldn't help but look in when passing.

Meg loved her house though. She had fallen in love with it at first sight. They had decided to move in as soon as the decorating was done. It had taken a while though, as both Tim and Meg had specific and very different ideas as to the look of all the rooms. However, they had received many gifts for their engagement party, so didn't have to buy an awful lot.

Just as she was about to leave, Meg's neighbour came running out of the next-door house to talk to her. Meg turned off the ignition.

"You ok?" the concerned neighbour, Jane, asked.

"Of course!"

"You're not worried?"

"About what?"

"You know what! What are you trying to prove, that you are happy with all this?"

"Don't you just love the weather like this, all cold and pretty and…?"

"Meg, I hate it, but that's not the issue or the answer!"

"Look, I'm fine." Meg was totally dismissing the problem in hand.

Jane raised her eyebrows at Meg, who had by this time got out of her car and walked closer to her neighbour.

Jane had been a pretty good friend to her in the few months Meg had lived next door to her. They got on well together. Jane was married and had three children, Ben, Matthew and her newborn, Chloe.

The two friends had spent many nights with each other, chatting about the usual things, men, kids and all the rest of it. Many a night was spent crawling back to their own houses, after sharing numerous bottles of wine.

"Meg, oh Meg…?"

"What?" Meg was getting very agitated and just wanted to get out of the street.

"Don't be like that. I know you are worried; today is the day, isn't it?"

Meg, eventually realizing that she could no longer hold back the emotion or avoid the issue, broke down in tears and replied, "Yes, today is the day."

Chapter 2

"Today is indeed the day," Meg said as she pulled out of the driveway. What was today? The results…

The MRI scan had been quite something else.

Evie, Meg's mum, had gone with Meg to the hospital as she always did. They always did so much together. They were incredibly close and always had been. They had been through thick and thin together. Meg looked at her mother not only as a terrific parent but also as a great friend. They would talk to each other about everything, never having any secrets from each other.

They arrived at the centre in plenty of time. The building had only been open for 6 months so they weren't sure where they were supposed to go. Meg thought it best to allow plenty of time to find it. As it turned out, it was just adjoining the normal hospital building so hadn't been a problem.

They walked into the plush centre, which had the look of a private health centre rather than the NHS building that it was. It was spotless with magazines neatly placed on the tables which matched the comfortable chairs. Flowers stood in a beautiful vase on the reception desk.

The lady at the reception smiled at Meg.

"Can I help you?"

"Yes, I have an appointment at 10 am," Meg replied politely.

"Meg Walker?" the smart lady enquired.

"That's me!" she replied with a smile.

"Ok, please take a seat; we will be with you shortly." The lady looked immaculate. Her hair was tied in a somewhat stern ponytail. Meg estimated her age to be mid-thirties. She had a very warm, friendly face and nails beautifully manicured as she typed on the computer, which sat upon the desk.

"Have you had an MRI before?" she asked.

"No."

"Don't worry about it; the doctor will come out and explain everything to you. Are you claustrophobic?"

"No, not that I know of." Meg knew the scan entailed laying in a cylindrical-shaped apparatus, so presumed from the question that it wasn't roomy.

Meg sat next to Evie taking in all her surroundings. There were tasteful prints on the walls and a plaque mentioning the sports celebrity who had opened the building earlier that year.

"Ooh, tea!" her mum exclaimed, noticing the machine, which was behind Meg.

"Look's nice," Evie commented.

"How can you tell what tea is like from the machine?" Meg teased.

"I don't know, it just looks like it will be a nice cuppa."

"Help yourself; it is nice, actually," the receptionist offered on hearing them talk.

"I'm no good with modern technology!" Evie looked puzzled.

"I'll do it for you, Mum." Meg walked over and put a tea sachet in the machine which snatched it away from her hand. After a lot of noise, the tea was produced. Meg took the cup and got some milk for Evie.

"Hmmm, lovely," Evie exclaimed, impressed with the brew. Meg had been told not to eat or drink before the scan and was getting rather thirsty at the sight of the drink. However, after a few moments, the doctor approached out of the door that was opposite Meg. He had a warm face as he looked at Meg.

"Just a few questions for you," he said, smiling. He ran through the various questions about whether Meg had any metal in her head, or a pacemaker, just the standard questions that preceded such examinations. After confirming everything was in order, Meg was instructed to follow the gentleman to the examination room.

It was fair to admit that Meg was nervous, particularly after seeing the possible illnesses that MRI scans can detect. She was dressed in a tracksuit for the occasion purely because the leaflet had requested something like it. It had instructed her to avoid wearing anything with zips or metal objects which could affect the results. She had already removed all her jewellery, all except for the naval bar.

"I have my belly button pierced; do I need to remove it?" she asked the doctor.

"No, they show up clearly on the scan, so we are used to that kind of thing." He sounded as disapproving of the bar as her mother had when she'd had it done.

"Please take off your clothes; you can leave your pants and socks on and put the gown on." He pointed to a little room for her to change, which contained a selection of gowns. Meg wondered what the point in had been wearing the most unflattering item in her wardrobe if she was going to strip it off! She changed into one of the gowns and went into the room that contained the MRI scanner. It looked like something from a sci-fi movie. She was asked to lie down and told that she would be slid into the machine.

"Lie as still as possible. You will be able to hear me inside and the microphone is two-way, so I will be able to hear you, ok?"

"Yes, fine." She was given ear plugs. Meg looked puzzled.

"It gets noisy in there," the doctor advised.

As Meg lay on the mortuary-like slab, she slid into the machine.

She knew at once why the receptionist had asked her about claustrophobia. She was relieved of her small build as she probably had a little more room than most people. Her arms were tightly by her side as that was all there was room for. The roof of the contraption was only a couple of inches above Meg's nose.

She heard the voice of the doctor.

"Noisy for four minutes now, ok?"

"Ok," she replied tentatively.

Click-clack, the noise began, click-clack, and then tick, tock.

'Oh God,' Meg thought, 'there's a bomb in here!' she joked

to herself if only to calm herself down as she was getting a little panic-stricken.

The noise, as the doctor said, went on for about four minutes and then silence.

"Meg, are you ok?"

"Fine, thanks." And this was how it continued for the next thirty-five minutes. The noises sounded like a badly conducted orchestra. Trying to pass the time away, Meg tried, under her breath, to sing her favourite songs to the beat of the noises.

She thought that this must be what it was like to be in a coffin.

As the scans went on, Meg grew more and more panic-stricken, suddenly thinking that maybe she was claustrophobic. At this point, she heard the doctor's voice again.

"Just one more now; about four minutes of noise again."

Click-clack, click-clack, the scanner rattled on, giving Meg a terrible headache. Finally, the four minutes must have been over as Meg heard the footsteps of the doctor. She slid out of the machine.

"Right, that's your spine done; now we will do your brain."

'What brain?' Meg thought with a smile. She thought about telling him that he need not bother as they wouldn't find one but decided against it.

"Please step off the bed as I need to arrange it for your head."

She did as instructed and watched as what could only be described as a cage was placed on the machine. He opened it and instructed her to get back on the bed.

As she lay down again, the cage was placed over her head.

"Hannibal Lector, eat your heart out, ha!" she uttered, not realising what she had said - 'Eat your heart out'.

She was once again slid into the scanner, but only the top half of her body went in this time. There was a mirror on the cage, which was positioned so she could see what was at the front of the scanner. This was the little room with the doctor and the computer, which was taking all the information from the scanner. At least she had something to watch this time. Before very long, the scanning was over, and Meg was out of the machine and advised that her consultant would arrange an appointment for the results.

She got dressed and joined Evie in the waiting area. Still thirsty, she helped herself to a coffee and replaced all her jewellery. After a few minutes, Evie and Meg left the MRI centre.

"Now I am nervous," Meg announced.

Evie just smiled and touched Meg's arm.

"Come on, let's go for some lunch."

"Is it time already?"

"Well, are you hungry?"

"Yes, I am very, actually."

"Well, it's time then!" They walked to Meg's trusty old car and Meg drove to the café, which was near the hospital.

Meg and Evie didn't speak of the scan really; instead, they mainly spoke about David, Meg's dad, and how his job seemed to be taking him all over the country. But he would be home for Christmas. 'He never misses Christmas,' Meg thought. 'No matter how busy he is, no matter how much he works, he is always back for the important holidays.'

"He is fine, just worried about you though. It just seems like you are having such a bad year health-wise. We both worry about you, but your dad particularly, as he's not here."

"I know. The next time he rings, ask him to give me a ring. I am fine and I will put his mind at rest!" As soon as Meg had said that she wondered why, if anyone's mind needed putting at rest, it was hers…

The rapping sound of Jane's knuckles on the car window startled Meg, bringing her back to the present. Realising she was sitting daydreaming in the driveway; she waved to Jane and drove off.

Meg was nervous. She drove to Evelyn, her mother's house, her music booming through the stereo speakers. However, Barry Manilow was not everyone's taste in in-car entertainment, particularly a woman barely out of her teens. Even though her favourite track was now playing, she wasn't in her usual good voice, singing at the loudest decibel possible; she had too much on her mind.

She reached to turn off the stereo.

"Oh, shut up, Barry!"

Tim had been the last one to drive the car, although Meg had no idea why he couldn't use his own. However, looking at the petrol gauge and seeing it was empty, it made sense. 'Why use your own petrol when you can use mine?' He had also left it dirty. Meg took a slight detour and stopped at the garage. She filled up the car and walked into the kiosk to pay. She couldn't resist picking up a bar of chocolate, which was naturally at the side of the paying desk. She got a token for the car wash.

"Good morning. Lovely day, isn't it?" said Meg.

The lady at the desk just smiled, puzzled. It was freezing and snow covered many of the roads. After saying that, the winter sun shone brightly over the paths, making the roads and trees glisten. She passed the car token to Meg.

"Well, I made the effort so the car might as well try to look good too!"

When she had been through the car wash, she drove on the few miles to her mother's house.

She parked her car at the house she used to share with her parents, the house with many fond memories.

She had grown up in this house with her parents, Evelyn, or Evie as most people called her, and David. They had moved here as soon as Evie found out she was pregnant with Meg. The house they were living in before hadn't been large enough for the three of them. Then when Meg's brother, Jack, had arrived on the scene, their decision to move had been an even better one. Jack had been an unexpected but very welcome addition to the Walker family, weighing in at 7 pounds 5 ounces, exactly 7 years after Meg on the 1 July 1982. Meg and Jack had always been very close siblings, maybe on account of the shared birthday, or maybe just for the simple reason that Meg had always wanted a younger brother to look after.

Now, at 17, one of the oldest and certainly most mature of his year, Jack had recently left school receiving 10 excellent GCSE results. The

'A' man as Meg liked to call him (affectionately, of course!) had just broken up for Christmas after his first term of college. Meg hoped he would be home as she got out of the sparkling clean car to enter her mum's house.

Meg had loved the neighbourhood and had many friends there.

She had only just moved out of the house to live with Tim. They hadn't intended on moving out of their parents' home before the wedding, but they had found the house of their dreams and completed the decorating, so there seemed no point leaving it empty. It hadn't been difficult for Meg though, as they had not moved too far away; on the outskirts of the same village, in fact. Meg had always said that she didn't want to leave because she liked it too much.

As she looked over the snow-covered garden, she remembered how beautiful the flowers had looked that year. She only hoped they would be as striking for her wedding the following June. It would be perfect for the pictures.

Meg walked carefully down the path, knocked on the door and walked in.

"Hi, Mum, it's only me." Her voice was tentative, nothing like her usual self. She wasn't the most outgoing person in the world, but this wasn't her at all.

"Hi, love! Just give me a minute and I will be with you," came the voice from upstairs.

Jack, on hearing the voice of his older sister, walked into the kitchen to join her, much to Meg's delight.

"Now then, 'A' man," she teased.

"I wish you'd stop calling me that," he said with a chuckle.

Meg was trying to keep her spirits high, so seeing Jack was just what she needed. He usually could cheer her up, whatever was wrong with her.

"So, going for the test results then?" he asked with obvious concern.

But then, seeing the worried look on his sister's face, he added, "Finally going to get confirmation that you're a nutcase!"

"Something like that!"

Meg walked up to Jack and hugged him much to Jack's disgust!

"Eughhh!" he said with a smile.

Evie appeared a few moments later and smiled warmly at her son and daughter.

"What's going on here?" she asked.

Meg and Jack just smiled at their elegant mother.

"I'm off," said Jack.

"I thought I could smell something!"

"Ha, ha, the old ones are the best!"

"Get lost!" said Meg, smiling, and with that, Jack left the room, but not before wishing his sister good luck.

Evie and her daughter were left alone in the kitchen.

"You look nervous; beautiful, but nervous," Evie said, turning to her daughter.

"Well, I guess I am," Meg responded.

"Don't be; think positive. We will be ok."

"That's what Tim said, but I am not convinced."

"Your dad sends his love and said good luck."

"How is he? I haven't seen him for ages with him working away so often. Where was he last time, Scotland?"

"Yep, he came back yesterday, late-night, and he is going to London just after Christmas for a few days. I was thinking of going with him this time. We could maybe go to a show or something, that's if everything is ok with you." Evie turned to her daughter as if for approval.

"I think you should; you never see him."

"Good, right, should we go now?"

"Yes, I think so."

Evie drove them to the hospital quietly; they both felt too uncomfortable to speak.

Upon arrival at the hospital, they reported to the desk and were asked to take a seat.

As they sat in the waiting room, Meg looked round. Apart from the occasional nurse walking by, it didn't look like a typical hospital. The walls weren't the usual clinical white. The wallpaper may have been a pale shade of cream but there was a border of a pretty floral design.

"Everything will be fine, don't worry." The soft voice of her mother was in response to the look on her daughter's face.

Meg smiled; they both knew it wasn't true. Meg had already guessed what was wrong; it was obvious now, looking back. It had been a week since her MRI scan and just before she had been booked in, the nurse had given her a leaflet. It detailed what was involved and what an MRI scan detected. There it had been in black and white.

A friend from work had phoned the same day as the scan. Meg had thought it was to wish her luck. She had been off work on and off for weeks and everyone knew about the scan. She remembered the call as if it were yesterday.

"Hi, Meg, it's Rachel. How are you doing?"

"Not so great; I'm nervous."

"About what?"

Mmm, so she hadn't called to wish her luck, Meg thought.

"The scan. I've just read a leaflet and I could have…"

"Oh, give over; don't overreact. It will be something and nothing."

"Yeah." Meg was unconvinced.

"Anyway, enough chit-chat. The reason I called was that Janet says your stuff has arrived from the catalogue and you owe her £7.99."

"Oh, em, yeah, no problem; I'll send a cheque."

"Okay great. Bye then."

The phone had gone dead. She couldn't believe she wasn't well and was very worried and Rachel was calling for money with no interest in her at all.

"What are you thinking about?" The voice of her mother brought her back.

"Just Rachel last week."

"Oh, forget about that. You dwell on things far too much. You know, she was probably right; everything will be ok and you'll wonder what all the fuss was about."

'Who is she trying to convince, me or herself?' Meg pondered, sick of hearing those words - "Everything will be alright."

Meg only had to look back at the incidents leading to today to see there was something drastically wrong.

It had all started about five months ago. She had been driving home from the train station. It was a beautiful summer's evening. The flowers were blooming; the sun shining brightly.

She was straining her eyes to see clearly; the glare of the summer's evening sun had been annoying her on a number of occasions. Fortunately, there were trees shading most of the road. There was a parked car on her side of the road so she pulled around it. She never saw the car approaching on the other side of the road and almost had to mount the kerb to avoid a collision.

The exchange of words that followed was not one she had cared to recall, but the whole incident had frightened her enough to realize that a visit to the opticians would be wise.

From then on, she had been wise enough, if the sun was too bright, to phone either her mum or boyfriend to pick her up. They would then go to pick her car up later on in the evening when it was dark.

Meg had paid a visit to the opticians, only to be told that her eyesight was very poor and that no lenses appeared to improve it. She was referred on to a hospital optician, who, after various examinations (one of which made her pupils huge and made her look devilish, according to her mum!), said that there was nothing really wrong with her eyes, but it was, in fact, the nerve behind her eyes. The colour of the nerve, she was told, was usually a healthy pink, but Meg's were so pale they were almost white. More referrals.

This whole episode of Meg's life worried her so much, she had no idea what was going on.

There had been other warning signs. Work had become increasingly more difficult - the early mornings, not getting home until late and nearly falling asleep in her tea, or just being too tired to eat, which was not really Meg. The problem would also be sleeping; she couldn't. This was bizarre to Meg with her being so tired.

One particular morning, after having had no sleep the previous night, she was at her desk at the insurance office. She was on the telephone to a rather irate customer who was complaining about the huge increase in his premium. Although she really felt for the customer and personally agreed with his grievance, she was supposed to give reasons for the rise. She'd rehearsed, a thousand times, in anticipation of such a situation, but when she opened her mouth, not a great deal came out.

"Have you been drinking, young lady, or do you not speak English?" the voice responded in anger to her slurring and stuttering.

"Of course not!"

Meg tried her hardest again to explain the reasons for the increased premium, but the caller grew tired of not being able to decipher her words. Insurance was full of jargon to him anyway and this young lady was not helping.

He hung up.

Strangely enough, the more she thought about it, that was the same week as she was having difficulty walking too, stumbling and staggering all over the office.

"Heavy night?" Rob had asked.

"Something like that, or that elusive invisible dog!" was all that Meg could say in response.

At that time, she had just put it all down to sheer exhaustion, but now it was all piecing together. All she needed now was the doctor himself to confirm her fears; the final piece of the jigsaw.

It was at that point that she heard her name being called out, jolting her back sharply from her memories.

"Meg Walker, the doctor will see you now."

Chapter 3

Earlier that morning, Tim had left Meg alone in the house and driven to work. To say that he was apprehensive would be an understatement. He was petrified.

He knew he had reacted badly when Meg had told him of her fears. He knew what she thought was wrong with her and he had dismissed it. There had been two reasons for that. For one, he really did think she was overreacting. He was fed up with her constantly getting worked up about something that might not happen. The other reason was that he was a man, and his father had always taught him that men shouldn't show their emotions.

"It couldn't really be that though, could it?" he said to himself as he turned the ignition key.

"Nah, she has always been a drama queen! It's not fair though, she is trying to worry me when she knows there is nothing wrong with her. Not only is she a drama queen, she is also a hypochondriac!"

It was almost as if Tim was trying to convince himself that everything was going to be alright, but it really wasn't working. The trouble was he was more worried about what would happen to *his* future, not hers.

'It never used to be like this,' he thought to himself. 'It used to be fun.'

He sat and remembered the time they had first got together. The day after they had met at the club and exchanged phone numbers, he had telephoned her to arrange a night out.

They had agreed to go bowling, so Tim had picked her up and taken her to the local bowling alley. They had chatted away on the way. He had done most of the chatting as he had noticed she had seemed a little on the shy side. This had been quite an attractive feature to him though. She was very sweet and had a beautiful smile. Tim had thought, even on that early encounter, that they had been an ideal couple - he with his undeniable good looks and tall perfectly toned body, Meg being petite and stunning. Yes, they had certainly looked the part.

All through their evening together, they had gotten on very well and this had continued for a long time. Tim had always found her to be so sweet and caring. He had fallen in love with her. So, what had changed? Although he hated to admit it, he knew something was wrong with her.

The real worrying sign for him though, was when they had been out shopping. They had visited the local shopping centre, which Meg loved. She loved to shop. Usually, she enjoyed this with either Evie or Jenny. Today, however, it was Tim's chore to take her to the shopping centre. Well, he did need a few things; a designer shirt and new jeans, to name but two. He wasn't entirely selfless!

The drive itself was a beautiful run. Meg loved to take the scenic route.

Tim drove through the countryside with its various beautiful shades of green, the trees, and the lush fields, which surrounded the two of them like a giant patchwork quilt. The sun was shining brightly, bouncing from the road and occasionally disappearing for a brief moment behind the trees, as if it were playing a game of hide and seek.

"Don't you just love the countryside?"

"It is beautiful, but it would have been much quicker to take the motorway," Tim had said in a disapproving tone.

"I know, but as Louis Armstrong said, we have all the time in the world!"

"Ha, ha, very droll. You know, that song fits you perfectly, so calm and laid back."

"What's wrong with that?"

"Nothing at all, Meg, it's a rare quality."

They arrived at the shopping centre eventually and the two of them were looking for clothes for their honeymoon. It was late summer, less than a year before the wedding. They knew they would probably be too busy (well, she would be busy, it wasn't really his idea of fun!) with the wedding plans and the big day itself, so they had decided to go at this time.

Meg had been trying on clothes all afternoon and although Tim was fed up as he hadn't found anything decent, he was gallantly carrying on for her sake.

"Do you like this?" she had asked, appearing out of the changing rooms with a blue flowing dress.

"Beautiful," he had replied.

At that moment, she turned round and simply passed out.

"Oh, my God," Tim had exclaimed.

The shop assistant had gently tapped her on the face to bring her round and demanded that the other assistant go and fetch a glass of water.

Meg had come round after a short time had elapsed, wondering what all the fuss was about.

"Are you ok, Madam?" The assistant's voice was clearly worried.

"Of course! I'm fine, I guess I've just done too much shopping! It is very hot in here, isn't it?"

"Yes, it is a very warm day."

After the crowds, gathered by curiosity and concern, had dispersed, Tim had spoken.

"You had me worried there!"

"I'm ok, really," Meg reassured him.

Nothing more was thought of it. Tim had agreed that she must have simply been too hot. He took her to the coffee shop and she had seemed fine.

Not wanting the incident to spoil the afternoon, Tim had suggested they continue with their shopping. Meg had agreed.

Later that afternoon, it had happened again. This time, Tim was most definitely worried.

"Why didn't you say you didn't feel well enough to carry on?"

"I knew you hadn't found anything you wanted to buy," Meg had replied.

"And you think I would want to carry on with you in this state? You make me out to be a monster!" Tim had been most upset.

What did she take him for? Surely, she knew that he would have been quite happy to go home, with her feeling so unwell. There were plenty of times to shop for their honeymoon.

The sound of a beeping horn brought him back to the present.

He noticed that the traffic lights were at green so pulled away.

He arrived at work around half an hour later with Meg still on his mind. He was quickly cheered up though, at the sight of his colleague, Rose. They had been good friends for almost seven years, ever since Tim had started working at the graphic design centre. Rose would have liked them to be more than friends though, but Tim had never made any secret of the fact that Meg was the only one for him. However, he never saw the harm in the occasional flirting with her. He thought it was good for him. 'Look but don't touch' had always been his motto.

The two of them had spent a lot of time together. Rose had started going to the same gym as Tim a few months earlier.

"Morning, Tim, how are you?"

"Not bad. Meg gets the results of her scan today."

"Oh." Rose wasn't really interested in Meg. She was making no secret that she had set her sights on Tim; it was only a matter of time before he came round.

Tim was seated at his desk a few moments later, coffee in hand. His mind was now clear of thoughts of Meg and ready to tackle the day's work.

That was until Rose's sister Sue came into the office to see her. She was in a wheelchair.

'I wonder what's wrong with her,' he thought. After he watched Rose and her sister chat for a while and arrange lunch, he saw Sue leave.

A few moments later, Rose came into his office to check if everything was ok.

"Yeah, I guess so; just trying to get these designs done as soon as

I can. I want to leave early today as I am really tired. I seem to be working overtime a lot these days!"

"You are always working overtime," she said as she sat on his desk.

Tim wasn't oblivious to Rose; he knew what she wanted. But he was faithful to Meg; after all, he was marrying her in a few months.

Tim thought nothing else of it as he watched the slender figure of his friend leave the room. He continued with his work and was so absorbed in it that he totally forgot about Meg and her visit to the hospital. He didn't even think to call her to see how it had gone.

Chapter 4

Meg took a deep breath as she rose to her feet and followed the nurse into the small room, which was the consulting room of Doctor Sharpe. The nurse smiled warmly and pointed her arm towards the chairs, indicating for the two to be seated. The nurse herself then turned to sit down on the chair behind them. The coldness of the room sent a shiver down Meg's spine. It was so much different to the waiting area. It was all white with a small window looking out onto the cold, wintery day.

Doctor Sharpe himself was sitting slouched in his chair, a short, plump-looking man with greying hair and a beard. He looked either worn out from his long day or totally disinterested in Meg and her situation. He offered no gesture of greeting to either Meg or Evie.

They smiled gratefully at the nurse, but both seemed apprehensive at Doctor Sharpe's apparent lack of emotion or affability. He simply scratched his chin, rubbed his forehead, and slipped further down his chair. He yawned, stretched his arms out and spoke.

"So, you wanted the results quickly then," he asked, seemingly unaware that Christmas was approaching and that the thought of waiting for the results until after Christmas may prey on her mind.

"Well, yes, I don't want to be worrying over Christmas. It may not matter to you, or it may not be important. I'm sure I am just another patient to you but I am worried and want to know as soon as possible!"

"Meg, there's no need to speak to the doctor like that," Evie reproached her daughter.

"I'm sorry, I've just been a little tense about today." Meg looked at the doctor with obvious remorse but again, there was no offer of empathy made by the doctor; in fact, he didn't seem to notice her rude remark to him.

"Well," he began. Meg took a deep breath yet again.

"As you know, we do have the results of your Magnetic Resonance Imaging Scan."

Doctor Sharpe paused to stand and place the x-ray he had been holding on the projector for them all to see.

"As you can see, this is the scan of a skull, your brain…"

Horror dawned; Meg could see obvious marks on her brain.

The doctor was acutely aware of the fear in both Meg and her mother's eyes.

He showed no sign of sympathy but simply took a pen out of the breast pocket of his very rumpled grey suit and placed it on the marks on the x-ray.

"As you can see, there are blemishes on your brain, which, although small, should not be there. Multiple Sclerosis can show up on an MRI scan in this way but is more commonly diagnosed in a lumbar puncture. Now, MS is a disease of the nervous system…" he paused as the tears welled up in Evie's eyes.

Meg herself just stared blankly at the doctor who was now finally showing signs of sympathy. It appeared that the doctor was going to go on but the sound of the sobs was making it difficult for him to be heard. The nurse, who had been sitting behind them quietly the whole time, reached forward to pass a box of tissues.

"Did you just tell me I have MS?" she asked.

"Yes."

'I knew it,' she thought. 'But there was surely a better way to tell me, not just slip it into the conversation as if it were nothing!'

Meg turned to her mother who was sobbing and broke down.

"I'm very sorry, Meg, but I think the best thing you can do is go home now and rest. You have taken in all the information I feel you are able. I think you should try and relax for the rest of the day, then write down any questions you may need to ask and we will schedule an appointment for after Christmas. Again, I am truly sorry."

Doctor Sharpe rose to his feet to say goodbye to Meg and Evie.

"Please come this way." The nurse's tone was sweet and caring. Meg and Evie followed her out of the consulting room and back into the waiting area.

"If you would just like to sit here for a second…" The nurse disappeared round the corner, leaving the two, in a busy waiting room, devastated. Concerned onlookers waiting to go to see a doctor just looked at the two.

"Meg, please come this way." It was the voice of the nurse again. She escorted them into a small room with no doctor, just chairs and medical equipment.

"If you would just like to sit in here for a few moments, I'm sure it was a horrific shock for the both of you. Do you know anything about the illness?"

"Well…" It was Meg who spoke. "No, not really."

"Well, I think the doctor is right; just go home and cry; get angry if it helps and then sit down and think of anything you may need to ask."

The nurse continued.

"We also need to get the lumbar puncture organised so we will send you an appointment through soon."

"Thank you, nurse," Evie managed to say.

The nurse smiled a sympathetic and warm smile to the two women and left them, but not before touching Meg gently on the shoulder.

Meg didn't see the point in waiting any longer so she stood up and walked out of the room. Her mother followed her closely.

Meg didn't cry, she just stared at her mum in astonishment as they walked into the hospital waiting area. Evie, on the other hand, was inconsolable, her beautifully made-up face moist with tears. Her waterproof mascara, obviously poorly named, now formed a smudged black line beneath her eyes. Meg couldn't see the point in tears. She knew nothing about the illness really. Ok, she had pretty much predicted this outcome, that she had MS, but what did this mean? She knew of people with the illness and they seemed to be ok every time she saw them. It wasn't such a bad thing, was it? In any case, she was glad there WAS something wrong with her. All this time she had suffered many different medical problems, at least she could now put a name to them. She knew, at long last, that she wasn't overreacting, or being a hypochondriac, like she knew other people thought. Of course, they would never admit it to her face but she knew. Every time she had rung in sick to work, people thought things like, 'She's off again!' but she had to admit, she would have probably thought the same. Every time she had rung in, it had been something different; there was no consistency. Many people were off a lot of the time, but they had a known medical problem. Meg's mind was running wild, thinking of the strangest things. What difference did it make what other people thought? She had a very serious illness. But other people's thoughts were to plague Meg for a long time to come. She had always been the same, constantly worrying about other people's thoughts of her.

The sound of sobbing made her realise where she was. She looked round to see the red face of her mother.

"We had better go; the ticket will run out on the car soon," was all she could think to say.

"How can you even think about that?" her mother shouted at her. "Do you realize you have just been diagnosed with MS? Don't you know what this means?" Her voice was getting louder and louder and was raising the attention of other people waiting at the hospital.

"Yes, I am aware of what I have been told and no, I don't know what it means; do you? What is the point in getting upset about it when we don't know anything about it? We don't know what it is. It's not like I have a brain tumour or anything; it's not like it's going to kill me."

The two women were getting more and more annoyed with each other, showing how alike they were, getting angry at a situation that neither of them knew how to control.

"Meg, don't even say that!"

"It's true; it won't kill me …will it? Come on, let's go; people are staring at us."

They left the hospital in a quieter fashion, watched by the same onlookers, the patients waiting to go and see the doctors. They had obviously seen and heard the whole thing; the two women being escorted out of the doctor's office and into another room. They had to be wondering what news these two strangers had just been told; news that was so bad that the older woman was in floods of tears and the younger woman just looked in total shock. They would be left wondering as the two figures appeared smaller and smaller, walking down the long corridor, round the corner, and eventually, leaving the building.

Meg and Evie walked slowly back to Evelyn's car, climbing into it in silence. Evie turned on the engine, turned off the radio and drove away from the hospital. Eventually, Meg, who could no longer stand the silence, turned on the radio and, upon hearing one of her favourite songs, began to sing as joyfully as if she had just heard some good news. She was oblivious to the truth, the fact that this illness would change her life forever, whether she liked it or not. But then something dawned on her - how would she tell other people? The rest of her family, her friends, work, what would this mean at work? Would people look at her differently? But the worst part of this whole day… how would she tell Tim? He had dismissed her whole worrying as overreacting. He had always been like that, very dismissive, never taking anything too seriously She guessed that was because nothing bad had ever happened to him. He'd had nothing serious to deal with in his life.

Sitting in the car as Evelyn drove home, Meg remembered how she had first met Tim. She had been out with the girls from college and the group of them had been admiring the view of the young men across the dance floor. Meg herself had spotted one, a tall slender man with fair hair immaculately styled and he had the perfect physique. Dressed impeccably, to Meg there were no other men in the room.

"What do you think of him?" She pointed the tall dark stranger out to her friend.

"Yeah, I guess he's ok, but I'd prefer him if he looked more human!"

"Nah." Meg was not impressed with the shorter man with the tousled hair.

"But let's face it, why would somebody like him like me? I mean, let's be honest; he's absolutely gorgeous! What could he possibly see in me? I bet he wouldn't even look at me!"

Then, as if by some magic force, the man looked directly at Meg and smiled.

'Wow!' Meg thought.

'Bet he won't speak to me.' Again, the force urged him to walk over to where Meg was standing; many of her friends had left the two of them to dance.

Meg was nervous. He introduced himself.

"Hi, I'm Tim."

"I'm Meg."

"Would you like to dance?" he asked the young woman who felt like a younger teenager, not the eighteen-year-old she actually was.

"Well, ok, but I must warn you, I have two left feet!"

"That's fine; I have two right feet, so we should be ok!"

From that moment on, the girls' night went to pieces.

Towards the end of the evening, Meg noticed how easy-going he had been. She found him very easy to talk to, and this was saying something, as Meg was a very nervous person. But then, disaster struck - someone tripped over and spilled their drink all over Tim's outfit, soaking him from head to toe!

"Oh, I am so sorry!" the lady said.

"Don't worry, it will wash out," he replied, obviously not in the least bit perturbed at the mishap.

Meg was quite amazed! Most men, she thought, would have been livid.

"I'm sorry," he said as he turned to Meg. "I guess I will have to cut our evening short! I will have to go home and dry off, but I really would like to see you again."

Once again, Meg was surprised, wondering how, or more to the point why, someone like him would want to see her. But she was happy to exchange phone numbers with him. That had been the start of their long-term relationship.

"Beeeeep!" The sound of her mothers' car horn jolted her back to the current situation.

"Stupid fool, what do you think you are doing? You can't do that…" Her mother was overreacting to someone who had edged slightly over into her lane.

"Mum, calm down, it's no big deal; no harm done!" Meg tried to appease her mother who wasn't going to take any nonsense from anyone; not today! She was not in the mood.

"It's ok, Mum," she continued to reassure her.

"No, it's not ok."

"Mum, please don't get so upset about everything; we don't know enough about it to worry so much. What is the point of overreacting like this?"

Evelyn knew exactly why her daughter was doing the opposite; she was dismissing the whole thing, denying anything had happened. Maybe that was her way of dealing with it or maybe it hadn't sunk in.

She tried to calm down and change the subject slightly.

"Shall I take you straight home and wait for Tim with you?"

"But my car is at your house."

"Well, we can sort that out later, get someone to take you for it; let's not concern ourselves with that."

"No, Mum, really it is fine."

"Well, stay at our house for a cuppa, until we have calmed down a little."

"I'm perfectly calm. Besides, I want to go home; I have got tea to prepare."

Evie was still waiting for Meg to get to grips with the news, but whenever that time would be, she would be there for her daughter.

Evie pulled into her driveway a short while later. Meg walked around the car after they'd both got out and gave her mum a hug.

"Don't worry," she said. "Everything will be fine." The roles had reversed; for the past few weeks, everyone had been trying to reassure

Meg that things would work out alright, but now it was Meg doing the reassuring. Despite this, reassuring was not going to be of any help; everything was not going to be all right. Far from it, in fact.

Meg drove home, leaving Evie in total despair.

Chapter 5

As she drove home, Meg couldn't help but feel guilty for leaving like that. Maybe she should have stayed a while longer and talked it all over with her mum, but then again, what good would talking do? It wouldn't change anything, would it? Even so, she really ought to have stayed with her mum, but she couldn't face her mum in that state. She had to remain calm and compose herself for her to be able to face Tim.

She pulled into her drive to find her neighbour doing the same thing. They both alighted their cars at the same time. Meg was fearful of Jane's words to her after their exchange earlier that morning, but her neighbour seemed to have much more on her mind as she just gave a wave and said a simple "Hi" to Meg and was gone. Meg slowly locked her car door and walked to her house, unlocking the door and entering. The first thing she did was to put on the kettle. She looked blankly into space whilst waiting for it to boil.

At that point, the phone rang.

"Hello?"

"Hi, Meg, it's Jenny. How did it go?"

"Good timing. I've just walked in…not too good, I'm afraid."

"It's not what you feared though, is it?"

"Afraid so."

"Oh God, Meg, I am so sorry. What has Tim said? You must both be devastated!"

"I haven't told him yet because he doesn't like me phoning him at work."

"Well, it's not just your normal phone call saying hi, is it? It's important; I am sure he would have wanted you to phone him."

"I am not so sure."

"Hasn't he rung you anyway?"

"No, and besides, I don't really want to tell him over the phone."

"I can appreciate that, Meg. I don't know what to say; I am so sorry."

"Thanks. Look, Jenny, thanks for ringing, but I am going to go now. I'll phone you later, ok?"

"Yeah, sure, well, take care. I'll speak to you soon."

Meg put the telephone down. She decided to wait in their living room. She sat down, looking at her surroundings, her beautiful cream sofa, and curled up in a ball. It was the same sofa that both parents had advised them against buying…

"What are you going to do when you have kids?" was Evie's response when Meg showed her the suite in the showroom.

"Mum, I'm not thinking that far ahead, and besides, you know our feelings on that subject; we don't really want children."

"You mean Tim doesn't want them," Evie had responded.

"No, not at all. I'm too bothered about my career. You know I love my job, and my promotion prospects are so good at the moment; the company is expanding and there are going to be more senior positions."

"You always wanted children!"

"Well, I can change my mind, can't I?"

"Of course, if it's YOU who has changed your mind and no one has changed it for you." Meg knew that Evie was concerned about her daughter and naturally wanted the best for her. She didn't want to see her daughter sacrificing what she wanted out of life for Tim.

"Honestly, Mum, I am really enjoying my job. Children are not a priority for either of us." And that had been the final word said on the matter. Meg had managed to convince her mum that this was what she wanted…

What did the future hold now? Meg thought as the sound of the door opening broke her chain of thought…

She looked at her watch and glanced out of the window to see

Tim's car. He was early. Meg had hoped for a little longer to gather her thoughts and find a way to break the news to him.

"Meg?" Tim called out.

"In here!" Tim walked through the hallway after placing his coat on one of the hooks.

"You are early."

"Well, I was tired, so they let me go! I have been working so many hours lately."

"I know; you must be tired."

"What's for tea?"

"I don't know. I haven't thought about it yet, as I wasn't expecting you."

"Shall I make it?" Tim offered.

"That would be nice." Meg hadn't been expecting that.

Tim walked up to Meg to embrace her. He kissed her lightly on the cheek and then walked into the kitchen to see what he could prepare.

Meg remained seated, amazed that he hadn't mentioned the hospital appointment.

As if on cue, Tim called out, "How did it go then, was I right? Nothing to worry about, was there?"

Meg, to avoid having to shout back, walked into the kitchen to join Tim.

"Well," she began… She hesitated, not having the first clue how to break the news to Tim.

"Well, I was right, wasn't I? I knew it, you were getting all worked up about something and nothing. I said to everyone at work that you were frantic and there was no need. You know what they usually say, it is stress, but this time, I could believe it, you do get so stressed about the tiniest little thing…"

"Tim, stop, please!" It was as if Tim were the doctor, diagnosing Meg and quite content with his decision.

"You weren't right at all; it's bad news, I'm afraid. Sit down for a minute."

Meg walked up to Tim and placed her hand on his arm. She led him to the pine breakfast bar and pulled out a chair.

"Sit down." Tim did as instructed and was shortly followed by Meg herself.

"What's wrong then?"

"It's what I thought; it's MS."

Tim was speechless for a few moments.

"What does that mean? What exactly is it? It's not that bad, is it? There is something they can do to get rid of it, right?"

He, like most people, knew very little about the illness; like Meg herself, in fact.

"I don't know a great deal about it myself; I will have to find out, but I know it's incurable and there is very little they can do for me."

She told him about the x-rays and the spots on her brain. She also explained that MS was a disease of the nervous system, which affects the coating around it.

"It's called the myelin sheath. Mine frays, so it means that messages can't get to my brain when I want to do certain things, like walk."

"But you can walk, and what does that have to do with your brain?" Tim just did not seem to understand anything he was being told.

"Look, they told me bad news, it was horrible, but they thought that was enough for me to take in, so they told me very little about the illness. I am going to look it up myself and find out more about it. The doctor told me to write down any queries or questions I have for the next time I see him."

"But it's not that bad…is it?" Tim still refused to believe it was anything serious.

"I don't know, but I know I need a hug."

Tim stood up and pulled Meg to her feet. They stood in the kitchen for quite some time, just holding each other, fear running through both their minds.

"We should tell your mum and dad," Meg commented.

"Yeah, I'll ring them, and we'll call up and talk. Do you want something to eat first?"

"Whatever." Meg was deflated at that response.

"Go sit down and I'll make us something."

"They do know about all the problems I have been having and your mum is really worried. She knew I had the appointment today, so she is probably panicking."

Tim touched Meg lightly on the face and spoke.

"Calm down, baby; I will tell her. I will ring them up just as soon as we have eaten."

"Thanks for being so understanding about it all."

"Don't be worried about it; everything will be ok. We'll be fine."

Meg smiled, unconvinced but relieved at his more than understanding attitude. The truth was, it hadn't really sunk in, the same as it hadn't with Meg. It was at that point that the phone rang.

"Hello, love." It was her father; his voice was trembling.

"Hi, Dad, nice to talk to you. How are you?" It was as if nothing had happened.

"I'm ok but I just heard about you. How are you? Have you told Tim?"

"Fine, I guess, and yes."

"Well, I am here if you need anything. How is Tim?"

"A bit upset, but I guess he has taken it really well."

"That's good. He loves you very much, you know. I am sure he will always be there for you like we will."

"Thanks, Dad." Meg was touched by her father's affection, and his support of Tim, but then he had always liked him.

"Is it ok if we come over and see you?"

"Yeah, of course! We were going to see his parents but we can go after you've gone. Just a sec, I'll check with Tim."

Meg turned to her fiancé, who was looking rather pale and shocked.

"Is it ok if Mum and Dad come over? I mean, 'cos we were going to your folks."

"Fine, we can go and see them a little later." If the truth be known, Meg was aware of the fact that Tim didn't really want to break the news to his parents. He had already spoken of the possible outcome and Meg's fears and his father thought the same as Tim had thought, that she was a drama queen and overreacting as usual. But what he didn't know was that Meg was right. His mum was really fretting over the whole affair.

Meg turned back to the phone, "Yes, Dad, come over. We haven't got round to making tea yet so…"

"We'll bring something."

"Great; see you soon."

And with that, the conversation was over.

"Dad is bringing us some food, so you don't have to bother."

"I am capable of cooking." Tim was rather offended at the offer.

"Well, they obviously haven't eaten either so that's that!" Meg thought the offer was nice and it would be good to eat with her family, something which they seldom did.

A short while later, Meg's parents had arrived along with her brother and a takeaway, which smelled delicious!

"First, let's eat!" Her brother was the one who spoke.

"Typical!" his sister retorted.

The food was served up and eaten by the five with very little conversation passing between them. No one really knew how to even start.

"I am honoured," Meg said, "my favourite Chinese food with my favourite people!"

Meg's parents just smiled; they didn't think she was in the least bit honoured, not after today. The Chinese food, which was now totally gone, was the least they could do to try and lighten the mood and cheer up their daughter.

"I brought you this," Jack said rather sheepishly and produced a large box of chocolates.

"They're my favourite!" Meg exclaimed.

"You think I don't know this?" he joked.

"Thanks, 'A' man!"

For once, Jack didn't complain at the name; it didn't seem appropriate.

The hospital visit and the diagnosis were not discussed in great detail except for Jack saying, "My friend's mum has MS and she is fine; we never hear of anything really wrong with her. I think she just has a few bad days every now and then. She looks fine; in fact, she is gorgeous!"

"Jack!" Evie exclaimed.

But Jack had said the perfect thing - everyone, surprised by this comment, started laughing - it was just the tonic needed! Before long, discussions were in full flow.

"How's work, Dad?" Meg hadn't seen her dad since he got home.

"Oh, fine, I guess; busy as usual."

"How was Scotland?"

"Bloody freezing!"

The evening went by pretty quickly. Jack spoke the most, as usual, mainly about his first term at Argrave College. In fact, it was very difficult for anyone else to get a word in! He talked of tutors he liked, ones that he didn't like and the new friends he'd made.

"I didn't really have a choice," he said, "as no one I know is in any of my classes."

"I'm sure you manage," his mum said.

Jack had always been the outgoing chatty one, like his father, He never had any problem getting to know people or being the first to break the ice in a new situation, unlike Meg who had always taken after her mother in being very shy and reserved. The two were not alike in many ways.

"It's great though; I really like college."

"I didn't like college very much; too difficult," Meg said. "Too much like hard work!" she continued.

"You made it through, though. Loads of people drop out, but you didn't, you went all the way!" Jack spoke with a giggle.

"Only by dropping one of my subjects and even then, it was too hard!"

"Yes, but look what you gained from it," Jack interrupted, "2 Bs; that's great!" There was no way that he was going to let his sister undermine her achievements.

"Didn't you say your grades were much lower before you dropped chemistry?" It was her father who asked the question.

"Yep."

"Well, there you go then, you got further than any of us." He was also in support of Meg. "You are the first Walker to get such excellent grades," he continued.

"But you won't be the last," Jack teased.

"Yeah, I know, 'A' man!"

All the family were keen to make Meg feel better, except for her mum, who was too devastated herself to be able to offer any support to her daughter. Evie remained quiet.

"Aren't you doing well in your job too? Mum tells me you are now in charge of the training."

"Training co-coordinator, if you please," Meg said in a very superior voice which made everyone smile.

"How did that come about?" her father asked. With him being away so much of the time, he found it difficult to keep up with the achievements of his children.

"Remember I told you about the company expanding a few months ago? Well, it has all happened now, so new staff is needed. Naturally, they need training and I went for the interview and got it."

"That is fantastic, love, I am so proud of you; we all are," her dad said.

"Thanks, Dad, it's what I have been waiting for. You know how much I love training people."

"You would never believe it to look at you, on account of you being so quiet, and you are not bossy at all," Jack teased his sister. If the truth be known, the only person she was bossy with was her little brother. But isn't that what big sisters are for?

For the first time in a long time, Meg felt good about herself.

Chapter 6

It was the morning after the diagnosis. Meg quietly left the bedroom in her nightdress. She had already spoken to her mum to see how she was.

"It should be the other way around," Evie had said to her daughter, "but you hardly gave me the chance. I was giving you plenty of time for a lie-in!"

"Well, no need; you know me, up with the larks!"

"Did you sleep ok?" her concerned mother had enquired.

"Fine, and you?"

"Not really; I was too worried."

"I'm sure there is nothing to worry about. It's not like I feel ill or anything!"

"I know, but it's the future I am thinking about."

"Oh stop fussing, Mum. I'm thinking positive; everything is going to be alright! No one really knows about their future, do they?"

Evie did not respond. Instead, she said, "I told a few people; I hope you don't mind."

"Why should I? Who though?"

"Well, your Aunt Ellen called to see how everything went so I had to tell her, and your Aunt Jackie also called, oh, and I called Cathy."

Cathy was one of Evie's closest friends and Evie had really needed someone to talk to.

"I think your Aunt Jackie and Uncle Pete are calling sometime today to see you."

A few more words were spoken and the conversation was over.

Tim was still in bed, so Meg dressed quietly after carefully going through her wardrobe to find her grey jogging suit. Not that she ever went jogging but it was the most comfortable outfit she owned. She didn't look glamorous by any stretch of the imagination but as she had no plans to go anywhere, what did it matter?

Meg crept soundlessly into the bathroom. She looked at her surroundings. The bathroom was small but beautiful. White tiles enclosed the room with white bathroom furniture. The floor tiles were black and had a subtle sparkle to them. A vase of dried flowers stood on the windowsill, flowers which Meg had chosen very carefully despite Tim making the comment that they looked like dried grass.

Meg stood at the washbasin and looked at the emotionless reflection that stared back through the mirror. The sound of Tim's resonant snoring caught her attention long enough to pause her thoughts and wash her face, brush her teeth, and brush her striking long hair.

Meg decided to tidy the house a little and get ready for Christmas. 'Christmas,' Meg thought. 'It's next week - I normally have all this done by now.' With all the worrying and countless trips to the hospital, there had hardly seemed time to think about Christmas. She wasn't anywhere near as excited as she usually was. Of course, she was looking forward to seeing everyone, but this year, Christmas didn't have quite the same sparkle.

Meg seemed to be in a very confused state of mind. With everyone else, she was positive and very decisive that this 'minor' setback wasn't really going to change her life in any way, but deep down inside, she was petrified. It was true that she knew very little about the illness, but she knew enough to be worried. She knew it could, and probably would, get worse. She may have to use a wheelchair at some point. How on earth could she, or, more to the point, Tim, cope with that. The thought of Tim wheeling her around, his young wife, really frightened her... But the worst thing about this whole illness, the one thing she knew for certain - there was no cure.

All kinds of questions buzzed round in her head. 'What about work?

My promotion? Children?' Even though they were not a priority at present, later was always an option, but now? At least before she knew she had the choice, but now? Then, more thoughts of Tim came into her mind, the wedding, and their lives together. She really didn't think this would be a life that Tim would be able to or even want to cope with. Then, as if on cue, Tim walked down the stairs.

"What are you up to?" he asked, seeing her staring blankly into thin air. "Daydreaming?"

"No, well, I guess." Meg couldn't be bothered with an explanation.

"I was thinking of getting ready for Christmas. It is, after all, just over a week away."

"I see. Do you want me to get the tree and the decorations down from the attic for you?"

"Good idea, thanks! Do you want to help? It being our first Christmas here together and all…" Meg looked at Tim who still seemed half asleep, rubbing his eyes. He looked as impressive as ever. His hair was perfectly groomed. His teeth were dazzling white. He was casually dressed in jeans and a blue shirt. She could still see that his body was in perfect shape.

"I should get to work really."

"But it's Saturday; you never work on Saturday."

"I know but we are so busy, and I did leave early yesterday."

Meg's face showed obvious signs of disappointment as she was really hoping that their first Christmas would be special. She already knew she had spoilt it somewhat with her news, but she was really trying to make the best of the situation. Tim, not oblivious to the look in her eyes, said, "I'll get the stuff from the attic and put the tree up for you, but then I really should go."

They were both doing a terrific job of avoiding the situation. It was almost as if yesterday had never occurred; like they had both skipped a day.

A few minutes later, after some cursing, Tim came down the stairs, arms filled with the Christmas decorations. They had been in the loft for almost a year. Meg had insisted they bought them after the previous

Christmas rather than rushing around this year. Also, it had the obvious advantage of being cheaper, an idea Meg knew would appeal to Tim.

"Great, thanks. This will be fun; I can't remember exactly what we bought."

Tim just smiled and commenced the task of putting up the tree.

"Tim…?" Meg began.

"Hmm…?" came the reply from behind the tree.

"Have you rung your Mum?"

"No, why, should I have?"

"Are you serious?" Meg thought Susan had been kept in the dark long enough.

"What do you mean?" Tim seemed more preoccupied with the tree, while Meg just stared at him, astonished. Tim eventually turned round to see Meg's face.

"Oh," he said, realizing the problem. "Sorry, no, I haven't spoken to her yet. I will phone her as soon as I get home from work." He didn't sound too convincing.

"Don't you think she will be worried? She knows about the hospital appointment."

"I don't know that she did," Tim exclaimed, "I can't remember if I told her."

"Oh Tim, honestly!"

But Meg was sure that Tim had spoken to his mother about the tests, the whole story in fact of how it all started and all the health worries. Meg knew, in fact, because she herself had told Susan about the shopping trip, work, the narrowly avoided car accident; yes, she knew all right. Meg felt sure she would be worried.

"Where are you?" Tim asked at the dazed expression on Meg's face.

"Nowhere, really. Are you going to ring her?"

"I said I was, didn't I? Now stop nagging me!" Tim sounded annoyed. "Look, the tree is up so I'm going to the office. I shouldn't be more than a few hours; it may be around 3 when I get home."

"Ok," came the deflated reply.

"Bye."

"Bye." And with that, he was gone. No kiss or embrace, no smile. Just leaving Meg alone in a living room full of Christmas decorations but no Christmas cheer.

"Right," she said to herself, trying to find her own Christmas cheer. "Let's get to work!"

She found a Christmas CD and put it on. Meg seemed to think that by getting on with something cheery, like decorating the tree, that it would take her mind off Tim's unusual, if not appalling behaviour. It didn't work; many thoughts went through her mind like…

'Is it really his way of dealing with it…? Does he realize what this means…? Does he care…? Will he still want me?'

She interrupted her own thoughts.

"Why the hell shouldn't he? I am still the same person. Nothing should change the way he feels about me; nothing like this, at any rate." Meg couldn't decide if that's what she really thought or if that was what she hoped. After all, she still couldn't help but think that marrying him may be a big mistake for him… So many thoughts, so many worries.

"Damn it!" she said out loud and then threw down a bauble in anger, smashing it to pieces.

"Oh shit!" she said, standing up and consequently standing on another.

Most of the decorations were silver because that's what Tim had wanted.

"But that will look boring," Meg had protested.

"No, elegant, stylish," he had replied. Meg had looked very disappointed in the Christmas shop, seeing so many colours and beautiful decorations, but as usual, Tim had got his own way. Meg had been very sly though and sneaked back to the shop to get a few of the decorations she had wanted, just to break up the colour slightly.

Meg sorted out the decorations and began to trim the tree. However, it wasn't as much fun as she thought it would be, probably because she was alone.

Before she knew it, it was one-thirty. Looking at her watch, she commented, "No wonder I'm hungry!" She walked over the decorations, carefully this time, and went into the kitchen.

"Now, what to have… leftover potatoes, a few peppers, eggs, cheese, ham…perfect, a Spanish omelette!"

The kitchen was very large and spacious and had only been fitted a few months before they had bought the house. It had black and white décor. In fact, it had been one of the selling points for Meg, who loved to cook. It was not only spacious, but it had a breakfast bar, which was one of those silly little things that Meg had always dreamed of when she was a child.

After making her lunch, she sat herself at the breakfast bar looking out of the back window at the lovely view of the countryside, white all over.

'What Christmas cards are made of,' she thought There was a knock on the door. It was her Aunt Jackie and Uncle Peter. Meg opened the door and immediately put on the kettle.

She smiled at them both and moved aside to let them in.

"Hello, love!" said her uncle, giving her a warm hug.

"Hi!" she replied to them both.

"How are you?" asked her concerned aunt.

"Fine, I guess."

"I am so sorry to hear your news." Her uncle looked quite distraught in fact. They had always been very close, since the day Evie and David had brought her home from the hospital. She had always been able to talk to him about anything from school friends through to boyfriend troubles. Peter was Evie's older brother.

"Thanks."

She made them both coffees and got out some biscuits.

"Sorry they are not homemade, but I have been a little busy," she tried to joke. They all walked into the room. "Oh, and it's a mess in here too. I'm decorating the tree."

"So I see!" Aunt Jackie replied. "Looking good, don't you think so, Pete?"

"Sure does, Hon! Where's Tim, Meggie?"

"He had to go into work."

Jackie and Peter just looked at each other with a disapproving gaze. Upon seeing this, Meg said, "I know, he doesn't normally work on Saturdays, but he should have worked late yesterday but he came home early. He said he was tired but I think he was really worried about me." Meg wasn't sure if she believed this herself but it seemed to convince her relatives.

"How has he taken it?"

"I don't know really. Ok, I guess, but I don't think it has sunk in."

"That is more than understandable." Her uncle looked at Meg with very gentle, caring eyes.

"More to the point, though, how are you?" he asked

"I'm alright; I guess it's just the fear of the unknown. I wanted to go to the library and check it out, but I don't want to worry myself unduly."

"Well, it affects different people in different ways. No two people are the same and the symptoms vary greatly from person to person. Some are the same though; there are common ones. But even if you do have one symptom one day, there's no certainty that you will ever have it again. You may even only have one or two relapses occasionally, and then nothing for years. Apparently, though, a change in temperature can cause a relapse, like hot weather or a hot bath, so don't you be running off all the hot water!" he joked.

"How come you know so much about it?"

"My friend Shaun is a doctor, so I took the liberty of asking him about it. I hope you don't mind."

"Not at all; that's a really nice thing to do." Meg looked at Peter gratefully. He looked devastated. She had never seen him this melancholy. Was this really such bad news? Was he overreacting? Maybe he was but she had never seen anything affect him like this. He was pale; gaunt even. Tears welled up in his eyes.

"Oh, by the way, he said if ever you needed anything, a question answering or someone to talk to, call him."

Pete produced a card from his wallet with the telephone number.

"Thanks." Meg was somewhat relieved that someone had a little more knowledge about the illness.

Pete had decided not to hold his thought about Tim any longer, and, after a moment of silence, he said, "Tim should be the one you talk to though, not us or Shaun. Don't get me wrong, I don't mind at all, I am always happy for you to talk to me about anything; you know that we are always here for you." He looked over and smiled at his quiet wife.

"Definitely," she said reassuringly.

"Tim really did have to go to work..." Meg began but Pete interrupted her.

"I'm sorry, love, but at a time like this, work should go to hell. You really need to talk things through together and soon. I'm sure you want to; I am sure you will feel better after having a good long talk to each other."

"What are we supposed to talk over though? What is there to say? There's nothing that talking can do to change things."

"He should just be here for you, that's all your Uncle Pete is saying, love."

Meg knew they could both see that she wanted to talk to him. She knew they were right.

"What has he said exactly?" Pete continued, "Not a lot, really." Meg began to open up, "I have no idea how he feels about it all. He hasn't really spoken to me, and when I try to talk, he just avoids the situation. But it is early days yet; it's not like we've not been talking for weeks. It was only yesterday, after all."

"Just don't forget this affects the both of you, so he can't just ignore it like it's not happened to him you know!"

"I know. I will talk to him, I promise."

Jackie looked at her watch.

"Goodness, where did the time go? It's gone half-past three!" She looked at her husband. "We need to go - we are going to the neighbours for tea, so we'll have to be getting ready."

"Ok, love," Pete replied. Meg could see that going to the neighbours for tea was the least of his concerns. Peter would rather have stayed with his niece who meant the world to him.

"Well, have a nice time and thanks for stopping by."

"A pleasure; well, you know what I mean. Under different circumstances, it would have been a great pleasure."

"Uncle Pete, it's fine, I know what you mean." Meg smiled.

"I will get on with the tree. Tim should be home any minute."

"You haven't put the angel on the top," Jackie noticed.

"I was leaving it for Tim to do. I thought he might like to; besides, I can't reach!"

"Get the angel," Peter ordered. Meg did as she was told, puzzled. Peter took her by the waist and lifted her until she reached the tree's tip. It was easy for him - besides the fact that he was a regular at his local gym, Meg had only a tiny frame. She gently placed the angel on the tree and waited for her uncle to put her back on solid ground.

She took a step back to admire the angel.

"Perfect!" Pete commented.

"Meg turned to face him.

"Thank you," she said. She put her arms around him and hugged him very tightly. The gratitude wasn't really for the lift but he knew that. He returned the smile.

"No need for thanks; that's what we're here for. Right, we're off!" Meg smiled.

"Yeah, yeah, you can smell us from there," he mimicked.

"I never said a word!"

"You didn't have to!"

"See ya," Jackie said.

And with that, they were gone, leaving her alone again, alone in too many ways. Peter and Jackie had been right though, this was the time she needed Tim to be here for her. Where was he anyway? Didn't he say he'd be home by three?

Peter had always been Meg's favourite uncle, ever since she was a small child. He had always been there for her, ever the voice of wisdom, but a great listener too. He had always made her feel grown up, including her in every conversation, but never talking down to her. Peter and Jackie were a childless couple but not by choice. They had tried for years but found out only a few weeks after Meg was born that they could not conceive. This could have explained their close relationship with her.

An hour or so later, just as Meg was trimming the tree and wondering where on earth Tim had got to, he breezed through the door with apparently not a care.

"Perfect timing," Meg said to herself. He said very little to her as he walked into the living room. No word of how nice the tree looked, but at least he wasn't complaining about the colour change she had implemented. More important though, he didn't ask her how she was. She had to keep reminding herself that it had only been a day since the news, but Tim was acting as if it were just part of their lives and had been for a number of months; years, even. It was clear to Meg now, if not before, that he was avoiding the situation big time. Meg wondered what had changed his attitude since the previous day. He had been understanding and sympathetic with her, but not anymore. Tim interrupted her thoughts.

"What's for tea?" he asked.

"Not sure. I haven't really had the chance to think about it, to be honest. I have been busy, you know!"

"It's taken you since I left to trim the tree?" he asked with great surprise.

"Not exactly. Aunt Jackie and Uncle Pete came over."

"What did they want?"

Meg's temper was fraying like a rope being rubbed up against a rock, leaving the climber dangling, not knowing what was going to happen next.

"They didn't want anything, they just called to see how I was! God, you are unbelievable!" The rope snapped! "I'm going through a crisis here, and there you are, not helping, and more bothered about work and your tea, for Christ's sake!"

"Don't be so over the top! You're basking in this really. You've always been the drama queen, always wanting to be the centre of attention. Well, it won't wash with me; maybe with Mummy and Daddy, and maybe with dear old Uncle Pete, but not with me. We both know this is nothing really serious. You know deep down you are going to be alright." Tim looked furious with her.

If Meg wasn't confused before, she certainly was now.

"I really wish you'd make your mind up," she snapped. "One minute you are with me all the way, acting like you really care, and the next minute you are like this."

Meg, quite naturally, was annoyed with Tim, but deep down, she could understand. This was a very confusing time for him. He must have been having the same thoughts as her, thinking about what this meant for the future. Or did he really mean the things he had just said? Only Tim himself knew but his attitude towards her had changed. Had something been said to him to either frighten him or make him think that this dreadful illness wasn't as serious as Meg thought? Meg wanted him to open up to her and tell her what was going through his mind. She looked at him, trying to forgive the dreadful things that he had just said, putting it down to him being scared. He just stared blankly at her.

"Tim…?" she said; no answer.

"It's ok to be scared, you know. I am." It was as if she had flicked a switch. She must have said just the right thing because the response she got was very unexpected.

"Meg, I…I am sorry. I didn't mean those things I just said. I am scared, you're right. I guess I thought I could avoid the issue; stupid, really. I am so sorry, Meg." Tim's voice was almost breaking. He looked mournful.

"There is no need to be sorry; I feel the same way. I'm glad I know how you really feel. It's no good having this all boiling up inside you, but we can get over this, you are right. It might be alright; I may never have another problem with it. If we stick together, we can get through this. We are both strong enough, aren't we? We love each other - what else do we need to get through this?" Meg walked over to him and put her arms around his muscular frame. He returned the gesture.

Tim didn't look as convinced as Meg but at least she had found out how he really felt.

"Uncle Pete was telling me about it. I am going to be ok. We have to think positive; some people can go months, even years without having any problems. We can cope with that!" Meg was trying to convince Tim, who by now had tears in his eyes.

"I'm so sorry. I have been so selfish, I have just been thinking about me, not you."

"Well, don't worry about it; we are sorted now, right?"

"Right, but I think we should go and see my mum. I never rang her."

"Ok, but can we eat first? I am really hungry!"

"You and your stomach! You never stop eating and look at you…"

Tim looked at her slender figure.

"I know, fat, aren't I?"

"Positively obese!" Tim put his arm around her.

"Right, what are we eating?" she asked with a smile.

Meg went into the kitchen, feeling a little better now everything was out in the open.

Chapter 7

Tim's parents, Susan and Jeff, lived in Chesleton, which was a small village about forty-five minutes' drive away from their only son. The couple had lived there since before Tim had been born. Susan was a petite, thin, almost frail-looking woman which matched her less than confident personality. She had short, greying wavy hair which had remained in the same style for longer than Meg had known her. She was a very houseproud wife and even prouder of Tim. She was fastidious about her home. It was always spotless, not a speck of dust or a thing out of place. She was very fond of baking and was extremely good at it.

She was very fond of Meg and was very pleased about their upcoming wedding. Meg, Susan and Evie were often to be seen together having lunch. Jeff, on the other hand, was the total opposite of his wife in almost every way. He was a burly man, a fireman and a very arrogant man. He was also very chauvinistic. He didn't think very much of Meg; he thought she was changing Tim too much. He felt his son's wife ought to be more like Susan, there at his beck and call.

Tim and Meg knocked and walked through the door of his parents' house. The kettle was boiling away, cafetière was waiting to give out the aroma of fresh coffee. Beautiful coffee cups with their matching flowered saucers were sat on the tray with homemade cake and biscuits.

"You didn't have to go to all this trouble!" Meg exclaimed with a grateful smile. She walked over to Susan embracing her.

"No trouble at all!" said her future mother-in-law.

"Mmmm, chocolate cake, my favourite!" Tim walked over to his tiny mother and gave her a kiss on the cheek.

Meg helped carry the tray into the living room followed by Tim, hesitantly, knowing the task ahead would not be easy.

Jeff was already sat down watching the television.

Susan found the remote control and turned it off.

"Hey, I was watching that!" commented Jeff indignantly.

"I know, love, but we have guests," Susan said softly.

"It's only our Tim." Those three words spoke a thousand; Not – "It's only Tim and Meg" or "It's only these two"; it summed up his feelings for Meg, not really acknowledging her existence.

"No, Dad, we need to talk to you."

"About what?" Susan enquired, her husband despondent at his son's words.

It was Meg who spoke.

"Two bits of news, really," she began. "Did I tell you about applying for the training position?"

Susan nodded hopefully.

Meg went on to tell them that she had got the job.

"That's great news!" She looked at her husband. "Isn't it, love?"

Jeff just nodded, not hiding the fact that he really wasn't interested. He was lifting the sofa cushions up, looking for the remote control.

Meg then looked at Tim, hoping he would help her with the other news. When Tim just looked at the floor, she could see no help was forthcoming.

So, Meg began. She had already told Susan about the initial symptoms and the hospital visits, so she began with the last hospital visit and told them about the consultant showing her the scan of her brain.

She looked at Tim again. His face was blank, almost bereft of emotion.

"I have MS."

"Oh my God, how? Why? I don't understand, this is awful, you poor thing!" Susan's concern was obvious. She stood up to embrace Meg, crying. Meg caught a glimpse of her future father-in-law. He looked horrified and glanced at his son, who was still staring blankly into space.

And that was that. Tears and looks of horror shadowed the scene, the previous sense of excitement about the promotion gone. For minutes, the room was quiet with no one knowing what to say. Jeff managed to break the silence by asking his wife for another drink.

"Of course." She looked at Meg offering her another drink.

"No, Mum." This time, it was Tim who spoke. "We should head home."

"Yes, son," replied Jeff. "You go home and get some rest." Tim stood up and offered his hand to Meg who was now seated again.

Jeff, noticing the gesture, shook his head and turned on the TV, unhappy to see the credits rolling on the program he had been watching.

Susan walked Meg and Tim to the door and before long, the house was back to two occupants.

Susan waved through the window as Tim drove away. She looked at her husband and spoke.

"Well?" she said, turning to Jeff.

"Well, what?" came the disinterested reply.

"It's terrible, isn't it?"

Jeff didn't respond.

"Poor Meg."

"It's not just Meg this affects. Tim is going to have to cope with her. He will have to look after her for the rest of his life. He might as well say goodbye to his own life."

Susan was horrified by her husband.

He was about to speak to his wife, but she didn't want to hear any more.

She walked into the kitchen and washed the cups and plates up. She walked straight past Jeff when the task was complete and walked up the stairs to go to bed, her mind full of thoughts about poor Meg and Tim.

At around the same time, Tim was unlocking the door to their home. Neither of them had really spoken much in the car.

They both headed upstairs exhausted.

Chapter 8

It was Monday morning and Meg had decided to go back to work. She had chosen a short skirt that complemented her figure. Her blouse was white and fitted to her torso. Although she had been given bad news, she didn't feel ill, so why not? It would only be for a few days; Christmas was at the end of the week and she had booked a whole week off. She was starting to look forward to it more than ever now, a big family get-together. She only hoped no ones' attitude would be different towards her. The last thing she wanted was people's sympathy. Besides, if she stayed at home, doing nothing, her mind would be left to wander, to think about what might be, about what the future may or may not hold. At least if she was at work, she would be too busy to think about such things. Besides, she had only just started her new role as training coordinator. She had lots to do; training plans to organize, decisions to make as to who needed what training.

Tim had spent most of the previous day at the gym leaving Meg by herself, yet again. Nothing had been discussed with either of them or by either of them. The whole issue had been avoided yet again. She didn't feel like staying home alone for another day. The company would do her the world of good.

Jenny pulled up outside her house, ready for the journey.

"Morning!" Meg greeted her, stepping into the car. Jenny was wearing a dark blue trouser suit with her blonde hair tied back. The little make-up she wore looked perfect on her pretty face. She smiled at Meg.

"Good morning! You are either very brave or very stupid." Her friend looked at her warmly and gently touched her leg.

"How do you figure?"

"I couldn't believe it when you rang yesterday. I am amazed that you are going back to work so soon after…"

"But I feel fine; why shouldn't I be at work? I am not ill. Besides, I would only be stuck in the house on my own with nothing else to think about."

"Maybe, but are you sure you feel up to work?"

"Look, I appreciate your concern but really, I am fine. Can we just forget about it all and talk about something else? I have had about as much as I can take with all this, and besides, I just got a promotion, remember? I can't let everyone down by calling in sick on my first day!"

"Ok, you are the boss!"

"Not yet but there's time," Meg winked.

"Watch out, Anita!" Jenny joked.

"You said it!"

Meg said very little else on their journey to work; she had to admit that Jenny was right. If she thought about it, she didn't really feel up to going to work. But it had to be done, and today seemed as good a day as any.

"Besides," Meg said to herself, "I need a distraction." She was trying to repeat this thought over in her mind to convince herself.

They walked into the office together. Jenny gave Meg a warm smile as she left her to go to her own desk.

"You know where I am if you need to talk," Jenny said, gently touching her friend's arm.

"Thanks, I'll be fine."

Everything was exactly as it had been when Meg had left work the previous week. But then, why shouldn't it be? The office was a large one with Anita's desk at the far end. There was a clear path leading to her desk with the rest of the staff's workstations on either side. Meg made her way past them all and approached her manager who was smiling towards her.

"Morning, Meg, or should I say training coordinator!"

"Hi Anita, good weekend?"

"Yeah, pretty good. Ben took me out for a meal on Saturday which was a little unexpected but great and then we watched Dean at football. He is in the school team you know, he's a good little footballer."

"That's great!"

"Right, to business; no rest for the wicked, I'm afraid, everything starts today. First of all, I know you already have some training prepared; let's face it, you were doing this job before it even existed! So, we need to check on it all, and expand on it to include all the new stuff…"

Meg was quite surprised at Anita's absentmindedness. She knew she was at work and personal problems should be kept personal… and at home, but that attitude usually didn't bother Anita. She had always been there for her staff and appeared concerned if they ever had a problem. As if Anita had read Meg's mind, she interrupted herself and said, "Oh, Meg, I forgot, I am so sorry. What with all the changes and everything, I've been so busy…how did it go at the hospital?"

"Not so good."

"Why? What happened?"

"Bad news, I am afraid," Meg replied.

"Do you want to talk about it? We can go into the little office if you like?"

"Please. I don't really want to talk about it in front of everyone else."

Anita led Meg past all the desks into the small office at the back of the room. The two sat down and Meg began to tell her the bad news.

"I can't believe you are here! I am so sorry, Meg."

"It's ok, and I am here because I just got a new job and I am keen to get started."

"Your passion for this job is very compelling but really, I would have understood."

Meg just shrugged off the attention.

"Shall we get back to it then? I know there is a lot to be done!" It was obvious that Meg was ignoring the problem, even acting as if nothing had gone on. It was a classic case of denial. She hadn't really got upset about it. This was to be understood as she really did feel all right. All she wanted to do was get back to life as it was before the diagnosis. She wanted to forget it all and look forward to Christmas. She could think of no better way of spending it than with her family. Then, it suddenly dawned on her, she had not bought all her Christmas presents yet. On her way back to her own desk, she stopped by Jenny's.

"Do you fancy going shopping at lunch? We could see if we can have an extra half hour. I'm sure Anita won't mind."

"Sure, if you feel up to it."

"Why not? Retail therapy never did anyone any harm!"

"Right then, see you at lunch!"

Meg cleared it with Anita, who seemed only too happy to oblige.

Jenny and Meg were soon together, dashing round the bustling shopping centre which was only a few moments' walk away from their office. It cheered Meg up a little to see all the shops decorated in their own styles for the season, but with the same annoying Christmas song blaring out.

Meg was really glad of Jenny's company, today more than ever. They had stuck together through thick and thin, and the current situation was no exception. She watched admirably as Jenny elegantly walked by the side of her sifting through the various novelty gifts on offer.

"What are you smiling at?" she was asked as Jenny caught the grin.

"Just you, and how glad I am that we are still so close after all these years!"

"Yeah, it's been hell, but I figured you wouldn't have any friends if I abandoned you!"

"Yeah, yeah, though you are probably right at the moment; most people would be scared off!" For a moment, Meg looked perturbed, her voice wary.

Jenny caught sight of the expression on her old friend's face.

"Don't be like that; I don't think I am doing anything any other decent person wouldn't have done. We are friends, right?"

"Of course we are!"

"And would you run off if something like this had happened to me?"

"Of course not!"

"Well, shut up and shop then!"

Meg managed to find everything she needed and miraculously, before long, she had completed the list.

After stopping off at a café for a bite to eat, they were back at the office.

"Looks like you had a successful trip," Anita said, catching sight of all the shopping bags in Meg's hands.

"Yes, it was." Meg smiled. She sat down at her desk and was surprised to find that she was absolutely exhausted. In fact, she almost fell asleep at her desk.

That afternoon, a few people who were aware of the situation Meg was in had popped over to her desk to see how it had all gone. Most were very shocked to hear the news that Meg broke to them. They all had the same thing in common though - no one really knew how to react to it. They all knew very little about it, so for the main part, they just said how sorry they were and went back to their business.

The day was finally over and Meg and Jenny were on their way home.

"So, how did it go?" Jenny enquired.

"Ok, no one really said anything, but they didn't really know what was going on. I only told a couple of people, and, as you would expect, they didn't really know how to react."

Once again, Jenny pulled up outside Meg's house and waved goodbye to her.

Meg walked slowly to her house, still aware of traces of snow and ice on the path. She walked into the house and was suddenly overcome by sheer exhaustion. She had incredible pains in her legs and her feet were twitching uncomfortably. She put the bags on the floor and collapsed in a heap on the sofa. She was asleep within a few short minutes.

About an hour later, Tim walked through the door, the sound waking her up. She got to her feet quickly and went into the kitchen to prepare the tea.

"Hiya, Meg," Tim greeted her, walking over to kiss his fiancée.

"Hi!" Meg was concerned that he would wonder why there were

no signs of food in the kitchen, but he seemed too preoccupied with his day, complaining about this, that and the other. Meg was having difficulty concentrating, not only because of her sleepy state but Tim's work was very boring to her. She didn't really understand it all.

After a few very arduous days at work, it was finally Christmas Eve lunchtime. The office closed at 12 and the tradition was that everyone gathered in the local public house and saw Christmas in with a few drinks. Meg and Jenny had caught the bus into work so that they could participate in the festivities. But Meg didn't really feel in the joyful mood. She was far too tired, yet again. She went home quite early on in the afternoon, after wishing everyone a very merry Christmas. She arrived home a few hours before Tim was due so decided that the best thing she could do would be to take a nap. She needed to be alert for the evening to come as Tim always wanted to party with his friends on Christmas Eve.

The sound of Tim walking into the house awoke her. A little worried about what he would think of her sleeping, she dashed into the bathroom and splashed cold water on her face.

She joined Tim downstairs and after greeting him with a kiss, prepared something for their tea. They were ready to go out a few hours later and Meg realized that the nap had been a wise choice. She managed to get through the evening without being too tired.

Meg awoke on Christmas morning to find Tim bringing her in a tray with coffee, toast and cereal.

"Good morning, baby! Merry Christmas," he said

"Oh, Tim, you are so sweet; Merry Christmas." They kissed.

When Meg had finished her breakfast, they exchanged presents. Meg opened hers first and was not surprised to see, yet again, sexy lingerie.

"Put it on then," Tim said excitedly.

"Steady on, boy!" but Meg did as requested and slipped into the underwear. She looked at herself in the mirror and had to admit it was a beautiful set. In a beautiful shade of purple, the bra, briefs and suspender belt were a perfect fit. But then Tim had always known exactly what size Meg had been and took great pleasure in seeing her slight build in the underwear.

Meg had bought Tim a casual shirt by his favourite designer. After all, Meg knew Tim would wear nothing without a label!

Meg had dutifully dressed in the underwear which Tim had bought her, along with one of her favourite dresses, a maroon fitted one with black panelling around the waist. It was very flattering. Meg had put her make-up on and been wise enough to put extra colour in her cheeks since she looked rather pale. Naturally, Tim had worn the shirt Meg had purchased for him. He wore designer jeans along with it. Later, they drove to Meg's parents' house.

Tim pulled up outside Evie and David's bungalow and Meg took a deep breath. They walked inside and were greeted with an embrace and Christmas good wishes. The bungalow looked beautiful in all its festive cheer. The Christmas tree was alive with colour, bold and beautiful, standing tall in their lounge. Tinsel was perfectly draped around the fireplace. A poinsettia plant was placed in the centre of the bay window.

Meg looked around to see which family members had arrived before them.

Meg spied her Aunt Jackie and Uncle Pete, and Jack, minus his girlfriend Scarlet, whom Meg loved to tease him about. Meg was told that she was spending the day with her own family and Jack may join her later. A few of Evie's friends were also there.

All the usual party games were played, and a lot of delicious food was eaten. Meg was pleased to note that there was no mention of her illness throughout the evening, but then there had been no need. Everything that had needed to be said, had been. The mood was good and even the slightest mention of the condition would spoil it. As the evening went on, the guests departed to be with other members of their family.

Tim and Meg were the next to leave. They went to see Tim's parents. As they lived quite far away, they had agreed to stay overnight. It was fair to say, for that one day, Meg forgot her troubles and had the perfect Christmas.

Christmas and New Year passed all too quickly and before she knew it, all signs of the festive season had gone.

Meg awoke a few mornings later and decided her ignorance of the illness should change. Tim had gone to the gym… for a change! So, Meg sat at her laptop and went on the internet. She had a pen and paper at the side of her to take the necessary notes. As she typed in the letters MS, she wasn't surprised to see several web pages with information about the disease. She read and read and made the notes as she was reading.

"Inflammatory disease of the central nervous system…damage to myelin, which is the coating around the nervous system, causes lesions/scars…stops the messages getting to various part of the body. People with MS can experience partial or complete loss of functions.

SYMPTOMS: fatigue, balance problems, pain, vision problems, difficulty walking, communicating, muscle stiffness or spasms…"

The list of symptoms went on and on… Meg continued to write.

A RELAPSE where old symptoms may resurface and new symptoms may appear. A relapse can last days, weeks or even months.

Meg decided she had probably had enough of a scare for one day and decided to turn off the computer. She was sure she had heard Tim's car pull up anyway so she felt sure that he would certainly not want to see all this. Besides, he would probably be wondering what she had made him for tea.

She went downstairs to look through the cupboards.

Chapter 9

A couple of weeks later, Meg awoke to find a letter in the post. The envelope was marked with a hospital stamp.

"The lumbar puncture," Meg said to herself, dread in her voice. She opened the letter to find she was correct. The appointment was for a few days later. Meg tried to calm her thoughts of why the appointment was for so soon; maybe there had just been a cancellation. Reading the letter further, she found she would receive an injection in her back with an anaesthetic, followed by a needle, which would go around her spine to draw the fluid from it. She read on to find that after this, she would have to remain as motionless as possible to allow the fluid to re-circulate into her spine. If the fluid didn't go back into her spine, there would be a risk of severe headache and dizziness. This prospect didn't appeal to Meg as she couldn't sit still at the best of times!

Meg telephoned her mum to see if she would be available to take her. The idea of her being on her own for such a procedure filled her with more dread than she was already feeling. Evie had seemed more than happy to take her to the hospital. If she hadn't already known, Meg was feeling very lucky to have a mum as wonderful as Evie.

When Evie had replaced the receiver on the cradle, she sat and cried, her beautifully manicured hands cradling her head. By the sound of Meg's voice, she hadn't seemed too unnerved by the news of the lumbar puncture. Evie, however, felt very differently. She hadn't told her daughter that Evie herself knew of someone who'd had the procedure and had told Evie how horrendous it had been.

The days passed with the anguish and anticipation building up inside. The night before the appointment, Evie couldn't sleep. She didn't have her husband to hold her. David had been working away again. Evie lay awake with the wind howling as a background to her sorrow. She knew her daughter would be suffering a great deal the next morning. There was nothing she could do other than be there for her, holding her hand.

The day of the lumbar puncture arrived. Evie drove her to the hospital, ever the faithful friend and loyal supporter. Meg had really been hoping that, on this particular occasion, Tim might have taken the day off work to be with her. She felt she needed him at this time. He had been his usual self and declined to take her, saying it seemed to be a routine procedure and that she would be fine.

Evie and Meg arrived at the hospital, and, shortly afterwards, were joined by another patient awaiting the same investigation. Meg felt it best not to ask her if she had MS; after all, this test was to confirm that Meg herself had it. Maybe this other lady didn't even know herself yet.

Meg was called first and was instructed to lie on the bed on her side. The doctor, who was a young, very statuesque, slim lady, was very nice, talking and comforting Meg while she carried out the procedure. Unfortunately, it was of no help. Meg screwed up her face in agony as the first needle went into her spine to numb the pain. Meg winced. The only thing Meg was glad of was that her mum could not see this look of distress on her face. The doctor seemed satisfied that the anaesthetic had worked and inserted the other needle into Meg's spine to begin the process of drawing out the fluid. Evie was sitting watching the whole procedure. Meg wondered how her mum was bearing up, looking at the whole thing. She decided it was probably best that she couldn't see her; she was suffering enough without seeing the worried expression on her mum's face. It seemed to take forever and at one point, the doctor commented on how long it seemed to be taking, and that this was not normal. Meg was trying to distract herself, doing her usual trick of singing under her breath. Nothing was helping, not even her favourite singer. The trouble was, a work colleague, who hadn't even gone through the ordeal of this, had told her it wasn't painful. She shouldn't have listened to her. Meg had gone into the hospital with some apprehension, but she hadn't expected it to hurt quite so much.

Meg tried her utmost to take her mind off this sheer agony, thinking she was a big softie and must have a very low pain threshold. That was until the doctor said yet again, "It doesn't normally take this long; I am so sorry. Are you alright?"

"Yes," Meg tried to utter, hoping she had at least convinced her mum if not the doctor.

Eventually, the procedure was complete, and Meg was at last relieved of the pain. She was instructed to lie on her back and move as little as possible. As she did so, it was as if she could feel the exact point where the needle had been inserted, as she felt a sharp, stinging sensation. Evie walked around to sit beside her beautiful child. She took her hand and stroked Meg's face with the other.

"My poor, brave baby," she said, her eyes filled with tears.

"That hurt!" Meg said mournfully.

"I bet it did; the other lady started after you and was finished a long time before."

Meg looked over to the other lady and smiled. She looked back at her mum.

"So, I wasn't just being a baby then?"

"No, love, it took such a long time that it had to hurt." Evie's voice was filled with love and devotion. "But I always thought you were generous..."

Meg looked puzzled and said, "I don't follow."

"You seem so tight you won't even part with your spinal fluid!"

Meg tried to smile but was too disturbed. She was having a difficult time dealing with the whole situation. She lay on her back with very little but the ceiling to look at. The television was on with angry voices shouting at each other. Why the television had even been put on Meg had no idea, as the only people in the room were the three of them, and two of those weren't allowed to move and watch it! At least she had her mum to keep her company. The other lady was by herself.

She chatted with Evie about various things but mainly about Tim, Jeff and their attitude.

"Oh. let it go over your head."

"I know, Mum, but it's Tim we are talking about. How can I let that go over my head? And my future father-in-law, he has always wanted an excuse not to like me, and now he has the perfect one!"

"I am sure he is not all that bad; maybe he just doesn't know how to handle it all."

Meg looked thoughtful. "Yeah, I guess I can understand that. I don't really know how to handle it myself. I can't really expect him to."

There was a jug of water beside her which she had been asked to drink, so she began sipping away with great difficulty given the position she was in. Evie was her usual caring self and offered to help the other lady, for which she was very grateful. The lady's name turned out to be Elizabeth. She was 25 years old, single and with a small child.

After what seemed like days, Meg was eventually allowed to go home but instructed to take it easy for a few days at the very least. She took the rest of the week off much to Tim's disgust. She returned to work the following week.

Weeks and weeks passed with hardly anything else said about Meg's health. In a way, Meg could understand this, as she did not seem to have suffered from any problems. Then again, it seemed that no one seemed to care how she felt about it all. Tim had gone back to his usual routine of going to the gym nearly every day. Everything seemed to be normal. But it didn't feel so normal to Meg. She still hadn't really got terribly upset about the whole affair. Was that normal? Should she have sat and cried or got angry...something?

It was a Saturday morning. Meg looked out of her bedroom window. It was very cold and the wind howled through the bare trees. However, winter was almost over and spring was just around the corner; in a few days, in fact. She was alone. Tim had gone to the gym, as usual.

The bedroom was very tastefully decorated in peach and cream. Well, it was tastefully decorated as far as Meg was concerned. When they had been decorating, Tim had stated in no uncertain terms that he wanted either green or blue.

"But it's so masculine," Meg had protested.

"And pink isn't feminine?" he had responded.

"I don't want pink, I'd like peach."

"Same thing."

On this one occasion, Meg had got her way and so the room was peach. The stripes were the compromise, rather than the flowered paper that Meg had liked.

That hadn't been the only compromise though. The spare bedroom had been decorated in a very dark blue shade, much to Tim's approval.

As she sat on the bed with its beautiful bedding, cream with a self-coloured pattern and a lacy trim, Meg decided that now was the time. It had been over a month since her lumbar puncture and the consultant had confirmed that it was Multiple Sclerosis. He also told her that a good way to relieve the stress and tension of the situation would be to write down what she felt.

She thought she had now come to terms with the news, so she wrote and wrote.

"Before I found out I had MS, I had read a leaflet – for my MRI Scan. MS was one of the illnesses detected with such a scan.

The day my results came, I had already convinced myself that it was MULTIPLE SCLEROSIS - wow, I can spell it! So anyway, when I was told, I was upset, of course, but I wasn't as shocked as I could have been. Everyone else was. They were all shocked, but they didn't know what I had guessed; they hadn't read the leaflet.

They just thought it hadn't hit me!

I had convinced myself that the reason I took it so well and had not reacted so hysterically, was because I had prepared myself. Everyone seemed worried about me because I had not broken down and got upset. I mean, it is shocking news, isn't it? I don't know if I managed to convince everyone, but I was acting like I wasn't surprised but was well-prepared for the news.

I'm sorry to say, nothing was further from the truth. I was just trying to be brave for everyone else's sake. I am good at that.

But why should I? Why should I try and go on as if nothing was wrong, trying to protect everyone else? It was a week before Christmas and it was terrible, shocking news. Everyone else was devastated, but devastated for me, or for themselves, wondering how it would affect their lives? No, that's not very fair, but why should I be the brave one? No disrespect to everyone else, but it has happened to ME, not them. Yes, it may affect their lives, but not as much as it will affect mine. I'm the one with the illness - have some people forgotten that?

Meg paused for a few moments then put her head down and continued to put pen to paper.

No one has said they know how I feel, which I am relieved about; they can't know. I still don't know how I feel, but here are a few words, no explanation, just words:

EMPTY, ANGRY, CHEATED, UNFAIR.

WHY ME? WHAT DID I DO WRONG? DO I DESERVE THIS? DID I DO SOMETHING SO WRONG SOMEWHERE ALONG THE ROAD?

These words may not make sense but they just spring to mind. They seem to sum up everything at the moment. This is a very difficult time for me and I don't know how long it will take for me to get over it, or come to terms with it. How long should it take? Weeks, months, years? Oh, I hope not. Does it matter? Should I take as long as I need? Why should I be rushed?

This is why I am writing these words, in the hope that they will help me, help me release how I feel, and hopefully, help me deal with it all.

The difficult things to cope with are:
Not knowing how I am going to feel each day.
Not knowing if a part of my body will work from one day to
the next.
Being positive is difficult. I have been told it is essential, but how
can I be positive?
Having to rely on people is not a prospect I am looking forward to.
Not being able to cope with work, will I have to stop? I love my job.
Not being able to cope with little tasks.

Meg stopped to read what she had written, feeling drained and exhausted.

'God, that sounds so over the top and dramatic,' she thought.

She decided that she had drained enough emotion for one day and left the diary for a while. The one thing writing in the diary did, though, was to make her cry, the one thing she hadn't really done. The tears flowed and flowed for quite some time.

Over the past month, she had spent a long time looking into the illness, and what it meant, particularly at the library. In some ways, she wished she hadn't. It was frightening; all the possibilities, the disabilities, the problems, however insignificant, that may or may not happen.

She had spoken about it to Janet among other people. She had been her usual self and ignored the problem, ignored what Meg was trying to do.

"You shouldn't read that stuff. It will make you worse. Before you know it, you'll end up suffering from something you've read about when there's nothing really wrong."

'Typical Janet, not looking at it from my point of view; ever since the diagnosis, she has been trying to ignore it as if it is a cold that will just go away.' Meg wasn't happy at all with Janet's change of personality.

But in her own way, she was right, she had to be positive about the whole thing. There, she was making a start, being positive. All the problems that she'd read about may not occur. In every book that she had read, she had noted that no two people with MS suffered the same symptoms. Even if she did suffer from a lot of them, it didn't mean she would always suffer from them. She could have one for a week or so and never have that same problem ever again.

'That's the spirit,' she thought.

'Now we are talking; this thinking positive lark is easy.'

It was easy while she was calm and in reasonable health. There would be many times to come when being positive wasn't so easy.

After a week or so, Meg decided that she was ready to tackle some more emotions. She removed her diary from the bedside table. She hadn't dared to tell Tim about the diary as she knew what he would say.

'Funny,' she thought as she found a pen, 'I always meant to keep a diary; it's just a shame that it has taken something like this for me to finally write one.'

She got to work.

From what I understand so far after reading all those books, I just have to be careful and not overdo things; know my own limits. What am I talking about, my own limits? I am 22 years old - I shouldn't have any limits! I used to be very active and fit, so how am I supposed to suddenly accept that I have limits?

I guess on a good day, I will just have to make the most of it and do things I want to, and on a bad day, relax and take it easy. Some people say I should try to get on with things and I will feel better, but I know what I should and shouldn't do. If I try to exert myself when I am not feeling too good, then it will make me feel worse. There is one major problem I foresee - where does that leave work?

Well, I guess I will have to cross that bridge when I come to it. I've not had such a bad time with it…yet.

Another thing I have found out about the illness - you get remissions, (a time when you may not even notice there is anything wrong) which can, if you are lucky, last months, even years. Some people have had one attack, as they call it, and have never had any problems since. Maybe I'll be like that, but then again, as I know, no two people are the same. This is pessimism, which is no good.

I have just had some treatment which the consultant says may take a few weeks to get into my system but once it does, I should be ok for a long time. There, how's that for being positive?

Another problem I foresee is that I don't want anyone thinking I will use my MS for my own gain, as an excuse if you like.

I guess what I am saying is I need people to be patient with me. It will take me as long as it takes me, to get to grips with the whole thing, to come to terms with it and to deal and cope with it as best as I can.

I think that's all I have to write for now. Maybe I'll come back if I need to write more.

With that, Meg put down her pen and smiled. It was much easier getting down her feelings on a piece of paper, rather than having to bore people with her depressed state. Maybe counselling would help; she would have to discuss it with Tim.

At that point, he walked through the door.

"Good time?" she asked

"I suppose. What's for tea?"

"Typical, thinking of your stomach!"

"I've worked up an appetite."

"I was hoping we could get a takeaway; I'm a little tired."

"I thought we were saving up. We seem to have had nothing but takeaways for ages. Whatever happened to a good home-cooked meal? I thought you liked to cook."

"But… never mind, I'll find something."

Tim didn't seem in the least bit sympathetic, so Meg decided maybe now wasn't the time to discuss her day's events.

She straightened the bed and went downstairs while Tim unpacked his bag.

As usual, he arrived in the kitchen just as she had finished preparing the dinner.

He used to help her with things like that, but lately, he didn't seem to care. He worked for a living, so it was up to his partner to cook for him. At least, that seemed to be how he felt as far as Meg was concerned. He seemed to be showing signs of being more like his father every day.

The following day, she decided not to wait to discuss her feelings with Tim.

"What do you think about me going for counselling?" she asked him.

"Whatever, but don't you think you are being a little dramatic? You haven't been that ill and it is weeks since you were told."

"What do you mean?" Meg was puzzled. It wasn't an everyday thing being told you had MS, and other people had suggested counselling to her.

"Well, you've come to terms with it all now, haven't you? You've read up about it and decided that you don't suffer from a lot of the symptoms, so you are ok, aren't you?" Tim didn't seem in the least bit concerned about her, Meg thought.

'Maybe that's because he hasn't looked at what could happen.'

Meg decided to avoid any more negative feelings from Tim and just agreed with him.

"Yeah, maybe you are right. I guess it wasn't the best thing to do, reading up all about it?"

"Yeah; it's like my dad says - don't bother with things like that. They will only make you feel bad, thinking what may or may not happen."

"I've written down all my feelings in a diary as the doctor advised," Meg commented in the hope that he may take an interest and want to read it, to get an idea of how she was feeling.

"Oh." This was Tim's only word on that.

And with that, he left the room.

'Ah well,' thought Meg. 'Maybe he will come round in time.' Was Meg trying to convince herself?

A few days later, Meg had an appointment at the hospital. It was kind of like a follow-up. Meg knew it wouldn't be made long after the original appointment. She had, after all, not been told too much about it all yet. She was learning more and more every day though. Everyone seemed to know someone with it.

The few things that had stuck out the most about the appointment were the instructions, one of which was not to get too tired out. Fatigue was a major problem in MS and was to be avoided at all costs, even by taking a nap in the afternoon.

'Fat chance of that,' Meg thought.

She was told of various symptoms that were present in MS, such as trouble with walking, memory loss, difficulty in speech, dizziness (she didn't have to have MS to know that she was dizzy!), pins and needles in limbs...the list went on. She was, however, assured that she would not necessarily suffer from all of these symptoms, and even if she had, it may only happen once or twice. She could be blind one day, and absolutely fine the next.

'That's reassuring,' Meg thought dismally.

"Oh, and one other point," the doctor had concluded, "try to avoid stress!" Like that was possible.

Meg decided to keep the appointment and its contents to herself. No sense in worrying anyone else. Besides, she really had been fine. She had only had a few little problems here and there; nothing to really get herself worked up about.

One morning, not too long after that, Jenny picked Meg up for work and announced, "My cousins' cat had kittened a few weeks ago."

"Aww, how sweet!" Meg had always been very fond of animals, particularly cats.

"I wondered if you wanted one of them. She had 9 and I think Bobby is having trouble finding homes for them all."

"Wow, I'd love one! I have been wanting a cat since we moved in, we've just never, well, I've just never brought up the subject with Tim yet..." Meg's voice trailed off.

"What?"

"Tim, I don't even know if he likes cats. I think if anything he's more of a dog person."

"Too girly for him, a cat? Do you think he'd prefer something a bit more butch?"

"Why do you say that?" Meg looked at her friend, almost insulted.

"I can't see him owning up to having a little kitten. I think it would spoil his macho image!"

"Hey, that's my fiancé you are talking about, if you please!" But Jenny had known Meg long enough to be able to speak her mind.

"Go on, have one, you know you want one. I am sure he'll come round when he sees one…maybe? I can ring Bobby up today and tell him we will call in on the way home from work so that you can pick one."

"Hold on, let me think about it." Meg smiled at her friend. She had to admire her persistence. Jenny had changed so much over the years from being a shy overweight child who wouldn't say a word out of line. Meg looked at her now. Her hair was in a chic style with blond highlights, and her puppy fat had gone to reveal a very slender figure. She took pride in her appearance. Her nails were beautifully manicured all the time.

Jenny caught Meg's gaze.

"What are you staring at?"

"Just you, thinking how gorgeous you are."

"Thanks, honey I know, but you ain't my type!"

"Really? That's not the impression you've been giving me!"

The two girls smiled at each other, and Meg fluttered her eyelids at Jenny which made her friend laugh instantly.

Over the morning, Meg thought long and hard about the kitten, and decided, what the hell? She was sure she would be able to bring Tim round to her way of thinking, one way or another. She told Jenny her decision at lunchtime, so the phone call was made to Bobby, her cousin, saying they would be there that evening. They stopped by at a pet shop to get some supplies first, a bed, some food, a bowl and a litter tray.

When they arrived at her cousin's, Jenny walked in, closely

followed by Meg, peering over her shoulder, looking in anticipation for the kittens.

"Hi, Bobby! You remember Meg?" Jenny walked over to her cousin and gave him a kiss and hug.

"Of course, I do! Hi! How are you?"

"Fine, thanks!" Meg was not really interested in small talk; she just wanted to see the babies!

"Come through." Bobby invited them both into the kitchen. A large box full of grey fluff lay on the floor. Little heads emerged at the sound of voices and 2 or 3 kittens jumped out of the box and scurried around the room. Meg was totally in love!

"They are just about old enough to leave their mum so go ahead; pick one."

Meg crouched down and put her arm out.

"Madison!" she called out. Bobby and Jenny looked at each other, surprised.

"You named one already?" Jenny asked. "Why am I not surprised?"

"Well, I love that name, and I figured if I shouted it, whichever kitten came to me, then that's the one I would have."

"Sounds like your kind of logic."

She looked at the babies again.

"Madison!" she repeated. A couple of cats loomed around but one in particular scampered towards Meg and nuzzled her hand. Meg picked the kitten up and held it close to her face. The kitten licked her cheek.

"I'll take this one!" she announced.

After thanking Bobby, the two headed home and Meg was delighted with her new friend.

"Now, I just have to tell Tim!" Meg announced as they arrived at her house.

"Good luck!"

"Think I'll need it! See ya!" Meg watched as Jenny sped away.

Tim had left a message on the answerphone announcing that he was going to be late, again. He was going for a drink with his friends.

That was fine by Meg; not only did it give her a little more time to think of how to tell him, but it was also a little bonding time for her and Madison.

Tim arrived home an hour or so late and his reaction surprised Meg. He saw the litter tray and the food bowl as he walked through the kitchen.

"Ok, where is it?" he called out affably.

"In here!"

"Very cute," he announced as he walked into the room, seeing the cat on Meg's lap. He walked over to stroke it and picked it up from Meg's lap.

"Girl or boy?" he asked.

"Girl, I think. Madison, I thought..."

"Good name!"

"You don't mind?"

"Of course not! I'll make her a scratching post if you like, save the wallpaper!"

"Good idea, thanks."

"Yeah, you'll like that, won't you, Madison?" he touched the cat affectionately. Meg just watched, amazed, not expecting this reaction. She got up and walked towards Tim hugging him.

"Steady on," Tim said, "you're squashing Madison."

Chapter 10

It was now exactly 5 months since the diagnosis. It had been a particularly traumatic day for Meg. Her doctor had recommended that she should enquire about the possibility of having a wheelchair. She had been shocked at the suggestion. He had told her that he knew she didn't need one at that time, but it could act as more of an energy-conserver. She had to admit that long walks around a shopping centre were starting to wear her out. If she had a wheelchair, she could go round in that and feel well enough afterwards to enjoy the rest of the day. But the shock of the wheelchair had been nothing in comparison to the evening that followed. She was concerned as to how Tim would react to the suggestion…she was soon to find out…

…As Meg sat amongst the broken glass, some of the gifts for their engagement party, she was struck with fear and sadness. The cuts and grazes across her face and arms were causing her great pain. She sobbed, reflecting on happier times.

Tim had decided to take Meg out for a nice romantic evening, although she had no idea where they were going. She had been instructed to wear the little black dress she loved so much, mainly because of how flattering it had been. The restaurant had to be the most beautiful place she had ever been to. It had taken them some time to get there as it was in the middle of nowhere, amongst beautiful countryside. Meg had thought they were lost as the road leading to the restaurant, although beautifully scenic, had been very long. But then the trees had parted, and there it had been; it looked like an old country mansion. They were met by a very smartly dressed man and led straight to their table, which had a beautiful view of the countryside they had just driven through.

"So, why have you brought me here?" Meg asked, staring into Tim's eyes.

"I wanted to ask you a very serious question," replied Tim, those same beautiful eyes twinkling at her across the table.

"Oh…?"

"Yes, which do you think I should go for, the stroganoff or the Chef's speciality?"

"You never brought me here to ask me that!"

"Of course I did; this place came highly recommended."

Tim was being his usual self and teasing her. He was that type of person. A joker, towering above her at 6ft 4 with piercing blue eyes.

Meg thought he was incredibly attractive, his blond hair loosely falling over his face. He promptly flicked it back.

"What are you thinking?" Tim caught the thoughtful expression in Meg's eyes.

"Just how gorgeous you are!"

"Hmm, if you say so…" Tim caught his reflection in a nearby mirror and smiled, admiring himself.

"You know you are."

They ordered their meal and chatted whilst waiting for it to arrive. When the meal had arrived and they had finished eating, Tim spoke; "There was something else I wanted to ask."

"Aha!"

"Yes; which dessert?"

"Give it a rest, Tim," she said, laughing.

He smiled at her, and rising from his chair, he reached into his pocket and pulled out a small box.

"You know I love you, don't you?"

"Of course, and I love you."

Well, what about making it official?"

Meg looked puzzled, foolishly.

"I thought you were an intelligent young woman."

"What are you talking about?"

"Don't you get it? Ok, fine."

Tim knelt on the floor by the side of her chair which attracted the attention of many of the other diners.

"Meg, will you marry me?"

"What…?"

"You heard!"

"I heard but I don't know what to say."

"I believe yes would be a good word."

"Of course, yes!"

He opened the box and placed the ring on her finger.

This had to be the best moment of her young life.

It all seemed to be a distant memory now though, as Meg was brought back to the present, as the pain in her face grew worse.

It hadn't been right since she had told him the news. He had promised her that nothing would change the way he felt about her and that they would always be together. That had been before that fateful day at the hospital. Quite a lot of events had occurred which led her to believe he may not keep his promise, but nothing could have prepared her for today. Today was the final nail in the coffin. Today, Tim had changed a great deal.

She hadn't been to work because her illness had flared up for the third time that year, and it was only March, 5 months before their wedding.

Tim had come home from work to find her sitting in the chair in the living room watching their enormous television.

"Are you ok?" he asked with obvious concern. Her eyes were very dark and she looked to be in a great deal of pain.

"I haven't been to work."

"What? Why?"

"Because it's really bad today. I can hardly walk. the doctor came to see me and said it sounded like I was having a relapse. He shocked me by suggesting I should have a wheelchair; he is trying to get me one as soon as possible."

Meg could see that Tim was horrified, so she said more to try and reassure him.

"He said I may not need it often, but I should have one just in case."

"What do you mean wheelchair? You are never that bad! What does this mean for me? I can't have a wife in a wheelchair; how will it affect my life?"

His attitude towards her had totally changed after hearing that word, wheelchair.

"I thought you told me you probably wouldn't need a wheelchair. Remember, when I told you about Rose's sister, you said you wouldn't get like that." Tim's voice was getting louder and louder and seemed to be more panic-stricken with every syllable.

"I was trying to be positive. Don't you understand? That's what this whole damned illness is all about; it's unpredictable." Meg was furious! He was acting like it was all her fault, like she had some say in the matter.

"Anyway, how can you be so selfish - how will it affect you? For God's sake, you don't have to live with it knowing it's there 24 hours a day!"

"Stop being so dramatic!" She couldn't believe she was hearing this. She was being dramatic? What was he doing?

She could see that he couldn't handle this situation anymore. He reached into the cabinet, grabbed a glass and smashed it to the floor with great fury, and then another, and another. Shards of broken glass flew across the room.

"What the hell do you think you are doing?"

Meg was powerless to stop him.

"I hate you; you promised this would never happen!"

"How can you say that? It's not like I've done it on purpose."

He picked up another glass and hurled it at Meg, making her wince with pain. Ignoring her cries, he threw another glass, which just caught her face.

"You bastard! You evil bastard! How could you do that to me?" Meg pleaded.

"I haven't even started yet! I bet you can walk; you are just trying to get my sympathy. Well, it's not going to work, you vicious bitch! You have been playing me for a fool right from the start of your diagnosis; you've read up on this illness and been pretending you have every symptom in the book!"

"I would never do that to you; I love you. How could you think that?" Meg was now fighting back the tears - tears of pain, frustration, and disbelief. Regardless of all the fighting, the tears fell down her blood-soaked face.

Tim marched across the room crunching glass beneath his feet. He yanked her out of her seat, dragged her across the room and let go.

Meg fell to the floor like a rag doll.

Tim threw more glasses until the whole cabinet was empty. He then went upstairs and returned a short while later. He was carrying two suitcases.

"What are you doing? Where are you going?" Meg's face was a bright crimson colour from the cuts and the crying. She was still sitting in a minefield of glass which by now was cutting through her clothes and into her buttocks and thighs.

"It's over; I'm leaving!"

Meg could not stop him, so just sat there, weeping the tears of a condemned woman, condemned to living a life of misery, without the man it had taken her years to really love and minutes to despise.

Chapter 11

When Meg had stopped crying and shaking, she tried to pull herself together. She took a few deep breaths and dragged herself into the kitchen. Looking at the face that stared at her in the mirror made her wince. She looked horrific. She tried her best to clean up her face, despite the sheer agony it was causing her. She could feel tiny shards of glass. She did her best to remove what she could. When she was reasonably satisfied, she hobbled back into the living room to telephone her mum.

She didn't tell her too much over the phone, only that she'd had a bit of an accident. She asked her, if it wasn't too much trouble, if she would call over.

Evelyn ran straight into her daughter's house after dropping everything to drive over. She found all the glass, scattered across the floor, but was more concerned at her daughter, sitting in the middle of all the debris, blood pouring from her face.

"What on earth happened?" Evelyn was horrified at the whole scene.

Meg broke down yet again, relieved to see a friendly face but heartbroken and in obvious pain. She told her mum everything; the seemingly nice Tim who changed into the monster who hurled the glasses at her before abandoning her.

"I don't believe it! Tim, the nice, sweet young man I met 6 years ago, did this to you? I'm speechless!" If it was possible for Evelyn to look more distressed, then she did at this point.

"I know. Me too; it was just the mention of a wheelchair that freaked him out," explained Meg between sobs.

"That's enough to freak anyone out but that's not the way to react. Come here, my poor love!" Evelyn reached out and Meg sobbed into her mother's loving arms, comforted by the smell of her mother's scent, the one that always reminded her of home, of security and safety.

"I think we should pay a visit to the hospital," said Evelyn, realizing there was blood all over her pretty pink blouse.

"Oh, Mum, I'm sorry."

"Don't be silly; it's my fault, I should have taken you to the hospital as soon as I got here."

At that point, Jane, Meg's neighbour, knocked on the door.

Evelyn went to the door and let her in.

"I heard a lot of noise but didn't know what to do, and then I saw Tim leave. What on earth happened?" Jane looked shocked to see the state of the lounge, but more so, the sight of Meg.

It's too long a story to go into now; we have to go to the hospital." It was Evelyn who spoke; she was anxious to get Meg treated.

"Was this Tim?" her concerned neighbour questioned.

"How did you know?" Meg was stunned. 'How could anyone predict him doing something like this?'

"I don't know. There was just something about him; I had a feeling, that's all."

"Look, I don't mean to be rude, but we really need to get Meg to the hospital, so if you want to chat, get in the car with us."

After Evelyn and Jane helped Meg, who was still struggling to walk, into the car, they drove to the hospital and although Meg was obviously in pain, she seemed quite prepared to talk about how she had got into this state.

"You're not going to let him back into your life after this, are you?" Jane quizzed.

"Definitely not, but I can't believe he reacted the way he did. It was just as if I had flicked a switch when I said the word wheelchair."

Meg paused for a moment, thinking about her words carefully. The intense pain all over her body was marring her thoughts.

"I should have predicted something like this was going to happen;

he has been acting very strangely since I was diagnosed. I never knew what he would be like each day when he walked in from work. It all seems like a bad dream."

"How on earth could you have predicted he would react in that way?" Evie asked

"What on earth led you to believe differently?" Meg asked her neighbour.

Jane looked thoughtful.

"Maybe it's because I've had the same kind of bloke myself. You can see it in their eyes; well, I could anyway."

Evelyn didn't want her daughter any more upset than she already was, so interrupted the conversation.

"Let's not worry about it now. Let's just get you sorted. How are your legs, anyway - can you walk? Have you got the feeling back in your legs? Actually, forget that - we will get you a wheelchair; the last thing you want to be worrying about is getting into the hospital!"

Why was it that Evelyn understood and sympathized with her daughter, but Tim couldn't?

Evie checked her daughter into the emergency department and led her into the seated area, which was surprisingly quiet.

As soon as the nurses saw the state Meg was in, she was taken straight to a cubicle. They didn't give her a consultation in the triage.

Within half an hour, she was cleaned and stitched up. The nurse took great care in removing the last remaining pieces of glass.

"Do you know who did this to you?" asked the nurse attending to her.

"Yes, it was her boyfriend, or should I say ex-boyfriend," Evelyn said vehemently before Meg had the chance to admit or deny it.

"Mum!"

"Well, it needs to be said."

"Do you want us to phone the police? Do you think you are in any danger?"

"Yes!" Evelyn jumped in again.

"No, Mum, please, I really don't think he will do it again. I can't believe he's done it at all! He must have a lot on his mind - he has never done anything like this before," Meg said looking at the nurse. She was still trying to defend him.

"I understand," said the nurse sympathetically. Even though she didn't know Meg's particular situation, Meg knew she was used to seeing this kind of domestic violence.

Meg's mum looked at her in dismay.

"Don't do it, Meg. You didn't deserve this. I don't care what's on his mind or how upset he is. There is no excuse for this...cruel, evil behaviour towards my beautiful daughter." Evie was beginning to break down for the first time since seeing her daughter in this condition.

The nurse spoke, probably to calm the situation.

"Are you ok to go home?"

"I'm fine, really, it just needed tidying up." Despite the fact she was obviously still in a great deal of pain, Meg felt a little better knowing she was stitched up and no longer bleeding.

All the way home from hospital, Meg was in two minds about the whole ordeal. Part of her forgave him, as it was a huge shock to him, the thought of her in a wheelchair for the rest of her life. It had been a day neither of them was prepared for. A day they hadn't expected for months; years, in fact. Hell, not at all, not ever. Maybe it was her fault; maybe she'd broken the news to him in the wrong way, just coming out with it like that. After all, in a couple of days, she would probably be walking again.

But another part of her knew that he was already aware of that; they had discussed it many times. She could have weeks of suffering one symptom, it could go away, and she could never have that same problem again.

"The bastard!" Meg shouted out.

"Don't you know it," Jane said.

"Promise me something; never let him back in the house again. That should be it for you," she continued.

Although Evelyn could not believe Tim's actions, she had to

agree with Jane. No one deserved to be treated this way, particularly not her daughter.

Meg thought about it; she would be all alone. Who would want her with this awful disease? No one, but then again, she didn't deserve what he had subjected her to.

"Meg!" It was her mum who spoke bringing her back from her thoughts.

"Yes, I promise."

Just as they arrived at home, Tim was knocking on the door of Matt's house, after calling him on his mobile phone.

"Come in." Matt looked a little disappointed in his friend.

As soon as he walked through the door, Matt, looking at his friend in disgust, made him tell him everything; after all, he was a friend of Meg's too.

It wasn't as if he could tell it in his own words; he had just been a monster, even he knew that, but as he explained to Matt, how could he cope with a wife in a wheelchair?

"You're a son of a bitch, you know." Matt could see how selfish Tim was being.

"I thought you were my friend!" Tim still thought some of what he had done was justified.

"I am, but look, mate, can't you see what you've done wrong?"

"I suppose."

After they had chatted for a while. Tim felt an incredible pang of guilt.

"Did you hurt her badly?" Matt caught the look in Tim's eyes.

"I suppose I must have done."

"Well, the least you can do is ring her and see how she's doing."

"I don't think I can; that would be like admitting I was wrong."

"For Christ's sake, you were! Hasn't it gone through that thick skull of yours?"

Matt was exhausted with trying to reason with Tim and gave in.

"Can I stay here for a while?" Tim pleaded, almost ignoring Matt's grievances.

"Of course, but promise me you will try and make up with Meg for both your sakes. You are good together; that's if you haven't already screwed up."

Tim didn't reply. He didn't need to. The look on his face said it all.

It was almost a week now since the eruption. Tim had not phoned or called to see Meg. As far as she was aware, he was staying with his friend, Matt. She didn't care anymore. Actually, that was a lie. How could she not care about someone she had been with for over 6 years, even if she could still feel the result of his anger on her face?

As Meg sat on her bed, all she could do was weep. That one event had not only devastated and shocked her, but also it seemed to bring the whole diagnosis back to her. It hit her finally. She had Multiple Sclerosis. What if she did end up in a wheelchair? How on earth could she live with that?

She had been frightened when visiting her consultant, despite doing a very good job of hiding it. She had been alarmed at seeing all the patients in the waiting area. It had been a specialist clinic, just for MS patients. There were men and women limping around the room with sticks or being pushed in. Some had Motability scooters which they operated themselves. They all seemed to be much older than Meg, which had affected her in two ways: One, it was good because it may have meant it would be a long time before Meg herself was in that condition, but then again, two, she had not seen anyone her own age at the hospital to compare the severity of their illness with her own. From what she understood, she was one of the youngest people in the area to have Multiple Sclerosis. She was very frightened as to what her future had in store for her. Thinking back to this was making Meg realize why Tim had reacted in that way. There were also other possible symptoms that she could and already had experienced; failing eyesight, trouble with her bladder, fatigue that was apparently a very different type of fatigue, pins and needles, depression…the list was endless. Alone, they didn't seem like too much to cope with, not to other people anyway, but they were a lot to Meg. She wondered if, when she had shared her fears of the other symptoms with Tim, another reason for him to react the way he did, she wouldn't really want Tim to have to deal with it either. But he had taken care of that; he wasn't going to have to deal with it anymore. He had left her. Meg's mind kept going back to how he had left. She touched her face. All the good times they'd had were gone, wasted by one act of selfishness and vanity.

'Whatever happened to the man I fell in love with? Did I cause him to be like that? Was it something I did or said? Maybe I shouldn't have mentioned the wheelchair; after all, I may never need it.'

'Don't even think like that,' another part of her thought.

'You are better without him; what if you do need the wheelchair? What then? Will he react in the same way again?'

Meg was in total despair; she had no idea what to do, or where she should go from here.

The sound of a doorbell broke her thoughts.

She was now able to walk downstairs to the door. Wow, if Tim could see her now, how would he react to that?

She opened it to see the figure of a tall man in a dark blue suit, a huge bouquet of flowers shielding his face.

He moved them away to reveal that face.

"Can we talk?" It was him, the cause of all the pain and scars all over her body.

"Tim, I don't know, I...I..." Meg hadn't prepared herself for this encounter.

"I know you are angry with me and I am sorry." He paused.

"How is your face?" The scars were clearly visible.

"It hurts like hell, if you must know." Meg wasn't going to make it easy for him. She turned to show her worst profile. Her beautiful face was marred by the cuts, grazes and bruises that remained.

"I feel terrible."

"Good!" Meg looked agitated.

"I see you can walk again."

"What's that supposed to mean, that I could before? What are you trying to say?" Meg was distraught. Her voice was getting louder and more aggressive with every syllable that came out of her quivering mouth.

"Nothing! Calm down; I just mean it's good." Tim raised his hand in a stop position. He looked at her with clear remorse.

She didn't know whether she should let me in, after all the words of wisdom from Jane and her mother. She didn't seem to waiver until she looked into his eyes, his beautiful blue eyes. At that point, she realised why she had fallen in love with him. She seemed to forget the events from the week before.

"You'd better come in," she said, at which Tim smiled, either relieved or triumphantly. Meg didn't have the strength to decide which.

Tim walked into the house they had been sharing for the past few months.

"So," he began, feeling the uncomfortable silence, not to mention Meg's piercing eyes staring at him.

"How have you been?" he asked sheepishly.

"How do you think I've been?"

"I know, that's why I am here to try and apologise." Tim did look repentant.

"Apologise?" Meg said with sarcasm. "To say how sorry you are for being such an arsehole and putting me in hospital and to tell me…" Meg's voice was getting louder and shakier with every word.

"Yeah," Tim interrupted. "All of those things; you are right, I am sorry. I'm sorry I hurt you and you are right, I am an ar…well, you know!"

"Arsehole…" she felt good saying that, and took great pleasure in repeating the insult. "You know, even after all this had happened, I actually defended you, to my mum, to the hospital staff…"

"You did? Why?" Tim looked stunned.

"Why do you think? We've been through so much together. You are the first man I've been so serious about, the first man I have really let into my heart. I didn't want to believe that it was all happening. I was so in love with you and then you go and shatter everything by doing this!" Meg pointed to the scars on her pretty face, scars that could be there for a long time, reminding her, every time she looked in the mirror, of the events that had taken place.

"I don't know what to say." Tim's handsome face looked mournful.

"You could start by explaining why in the hell you did it!"

Tim looked at her helplessly.

"When you mentioned the word wheelchair and that you could barely walk, and well, I freaked out. I hoped it wouldn't come to that, and especially not at this early stage. I have heard so much about MS and the thought of you in a wheelchair, well, I couldn't take it."

"So you thought you would push me around and throw glasses at me, cutting me to shreds? You thought that would solve everything? You wouldn't even let me explain about the wheelchair, no, you just lashed out!" Meg's eyes were filling with tears.

"I thought, I thought… no, that's not true, I didn't think at all, I just panicked."

"And you think a few words of apology and a bunch of flowers will solve everything?" Meg took the flowers that Tim was still holding and threw them to the ground. Petals and foliage flew around.

Tim looked at the mess she had created and spoke.

"No, but I thought it was a good start. I thought it would help me to start to apologise; I thought we could talk."

"It's a little late for talking. If you were so worried about the illness and our future, then why didn't you bring it up BEFORE slicing me? And how worried could you have been if you've waited until now to come and see me?"

"I don't know, Meg. I was scared of how you'd react. All I know is that I love you and miss you. I can't stand not having you in my life. I've acted badly, totally out of character. I admit I have been acting terribly for the last few months and I really am so sorry."

"How long have you been practising that little speech then?" Meg quizzed.

"I haven't, I've just had a lot of time to think, and to realize how badly I've been behaving. I wanted to say everything I've been thinking.

I wanted to confess everything to you. I figured the only way I stood any chance of getting you back was to be honest with you."

"That's fresh, honesty - wouldn't have gone amiss before this exploded." If Meg wasn't confused before as to what she should do, she certainly was now. She couldn't deny she was pleased with his return, and she was particularly impressed with his speech. She thought it was heartfelt, that he really did mean every word. She did, after all, still love him; like she said, they had been through so much together. How could all that love disappear so quickly, even after those events?

The wind howled through the trees, whispering to Meg, as if to add to the tension, telling her what she should do. Snow started to fall, rapidly beating on the windows. It was a cold, bleak sight. Was this a sign? Is this what her future was going to be like? Cold and bleak? But was that with him or without? The wind howled again.

Meg caught sight of a wedding magazine, one of many she had bought when all the wedding preparations had started. He hadn't really been involved in that; he had left it all to her, saying that she liked that kind of thing and that he would be no good. Was that in itself a sign? No enthusiasm. 'The wedding,' she thought, 'everything is arranged…'

By now, Tim had made his way into the living room. Meg turned around to see him, sat on the sofa, looking at her, waiting for the reply that would decide his life. This was a reply that Meg was not ready yet to give.

As if reading her mind, he asked, "Have you called off the wedding plans?"

"No, I was hoping for a miracle, besides, what would I tell everyone? That I don't want to marry a bully who beats up on his wife?"

"You mean you haven't told anyone about this?"

Meg looked at him, stupefied.

"What would I tell them? The only people who know are Mum and Jane next door…"

"Why Jane?"

"She heard all the noise you were making when you were going hysterical, throwing the glasses at me." Meg just had to say it one more time, as if to etch everything into Tim's brain.

Tim hung his head.

"I am so ashamed."

"And so you should be, but I am sure your dad would be on your side. He would find some excuse to justify what you have done. In fact, I bet he would be proud of you, acting like a man…"

"That's not fair!" he protested.

"Maybe not, but I don't really feel like being fair; were you fair?"

Tim remained silent.

After a few moments, he spoke.

"How is work?" He was trying to change the subject and Meg could see he looked hurt at her words. 'Good,' she thought.

"I haven't been! Looking like this? Come on!"

"What did you tell them?"

"Why? Worried about what they might think? I've told you; no one knows.

I didn't tell them anything, just said I was ill and Anita just presumed it was the MS. I want to go back as soon as possible though; my promotion isn't going to be safe. With me taking all this time off, they are going to think that the MS is worse and that I am always taking time off because of it!"

"Screw that! Your health is more important!"

Meg was starting to see signs of the old Tim, the one she fell in love with. But what was she going to do?

"I guess you are right, but you know how much I like my job, especially now after getting the promotion. I am still in training for it. I just hope they keep it open for me."

"I'm sure they will. Besides, you will be back soon; don't worry about it." He put his arm around her to comfort her, and, to his surprise, Meg didn't push him away.

Before long, Meg realized she was talking to him almost like old times.

Tim looked at his watch.

"I'll go," he announced. "It's late."

"Stay if you like; have something to eat with me." Meg wished those words hadn't just come out of her mouth, now it sounded like she was the one desperately trying to apologise.

"No, that's ok," Tim replied. "I think you need time to think." Tim rose to his feet and gave Meg a kiss on the cheek.

"Don't get up - I know my way out," he said with a smile. Meg heard the door open and close. He was gone. For how long was totally up to her. Meg looked through the window of their beautiful house. The snow was falling heavily, settling on the ground. It covered Tim's footprints rapidly. Before long, all evidence of his visit was gone, as if he had never been there apologising and bearing his soul and giving her what seemed like genuine remorse. Was this another sign?

Chapter 12

Meg felt more alone than she had ever been. Tim had left her in despair. She was hoping she could wake up from what was obviously a terrible nightmare and everything would be all right.

But it was no nightmare. She felt sure that whoever she spoke to for advice, they would all say the same thing - ditch him! Forget him! Ah, everyone maybe except for his father. He would want them to separate, yes, but for very different reasons. She wondered if he had even told his parents.

Well," she said to herself, "I am going to have to take that chance."

She pushed herself up off the chair and walked towards the phone, but not before catching her image in the large, black, leather-effect mirror that hung above the old-fashioned fireplace. She gazed at the bruised and battered face which stared back at her blankly.

"What are you looking at?" She asked angrily.

She arrived at the tall oak table on which sat the telephone.

She picked up the phone and dialled.

A voice spoke.

"Hello?" The voice was soft and comforting.

"Hi, Jenny, it's me."

"Hello, you! I was just about to telephone you. How ya doin?"

"Not so good." Meg's voice was forlorn.

"The pain's come back, has it?" Jenny asked with concern. "You could say that; Tim came to see me."

As soon as Jenny asked if she would like her to go over to see her best friend, Meg sounded very grateful and replied that she would.

Jenny told Meg she was on her way to see her anyway and told her to get the kettle on.

Jenny was as good as her word and within ten minutes, she was knocking on Meg's door, dressed in her comfortable tracksuit but still managing to look beautiful, a delicious-looking chocolate cake in hand.

Meg's eyes lit up at what seemed to be the result of Jenny's baking. Her clothes gave her away as they were covered in flour and melted chocolate. Her face looked like she had been licking the spoon.

"You and your baking!" Meg greeted her friend with a big hug, taking care not to knock the cake out of Jenny's hand.

Meg couldn't express how happy she was to see her friend. "Right, let's get this eaten and start talking!" Meg nodded her approval to Jenny's suggestion and made the coffee whilst Jenny went to the cupboard to get the plates. They walked into the living room.

"So, what did the arsehole have to say this time? Are the flowers from him?"

Meg nodded and saw she had Jenny's undivided attention. She told her that Tim wanted to get back together with her. She had forgotten that she had left the scattered flowers on the floor. "What are you going to do?"

Meg just shrugged her shoulders looking very unsure.

"I don't know. I am very confused, that's why I called you over." "Ok, well, let's start with everything he said…" Jenny said methodically before taking a bite out of the cake.

Meg proceeded to tell her friend of Tim's arrival, not missing out any details.

"Ok," Jenny began thoughtfully. "Did he sound sincere? Did he seem remorseful?"

"Honestly? Yes, he did, he seemed really sorry." Jenny went on to ask her friend if she thought he would ever do anything like that again.

"No, I really don't think so. I have never seen him act like that before, no matter how pushed he may have been. I think he just lost it momentarily." Meg was sat, curled up on the sofa, resting her head on her petite hands, looking more vulnerable than Jenny had ever seen her.

Jenny was trying to be objective, saying that you could never tell and maybe there could be a repeat performance.

Meg looked at her, a little surprised. "You are supposed to be on my side!"

"I am, I thought you wanted me impartial." She just didn't want Tim to ever hurt her best friend again.

"I guess so," Meg admitted, apologetically. Jenny looked at her beautiful friend and asked, "So, are you willing to take the chance that it won't happen again, forgive and forget?" Meg removed her head from her hands and stared angrily at her friend.

"I can never forget what he did; how can I?" Meg pointed to her scarred face.

"Whose side are you on anyway?" she questioned her friend again.

"Yours, of course!" Jenny stood up and walked past Madison, who had been pestering her since she arrived.

Jenny sat down next to Meg and put her arm around her. Madison, who was still being ignored, jumped on Jenny's lap. "Look, Meg, I am sorry but these are questions that need to be asked. When something like this happens, you can't just decide lightly on the future, whether it be with or without Tim. Isn't this why you asked me to come here, to discuss it all with you? I am only trying to help you." Jenny put her hands on Meg's.

Meg broke down in floods of tears, apologising to her friend. Jenny shook her head, assuring her there was no apology necessary.

After a few moments of sobs, the emotions calmed down and the floods of tears had subsided to the occasional sniffle here and there. Neither woman said anything for another moment or two, but then it was Jenny who spoke; "Are you alright?"

"Yeah, I just don't know what to do. I thought we could get through all the shocks of my illness together. I never thought anything like this would happen."

"Of course you didn't, but I guess there are only two things you need to ask yourself."

"More questions!" Meg complained lamely.

Jenny just looked at her friend with slight desperation.

The questions were simple - could she forgive him and did she still love him?

Meg just returned the gaze; she had to admit her friend was very wise. She could answer one of those questions without hesitation; no matter what he had done to her, she couldn't stop loving him. She had loved him for far too long and they had been through far too much for her to just call it a day. As far as forgiving him was concerned, she wasn't sure if she could.

For a short while, the two women just looked at each other silently. Meg was thinking too much about what she should do. Jenny just looked helpless, not knowing what advice she could give to her friend. Meg could see Jenny's beautiful green eyes fixated on her own.

At the same time that Meg was discussing her situation with Jenny, Tim was just arriving at Matt's house, where he was still sleeping. He reversed the black sports car, his pride and joy, into Matt's drive. He let himself into the house using the spare key which Matt had given him.

'He must have gone out' Tim thought seeing no sign of Matt as he looked around the house which was so different to his own.

Much to Tim's dismay, Matt was walking out of the utility room. "Well?" Matt greeted Tim.

"Well, what?" was Tim's response. He then looked at his best friend's raised eyebrows.

"I think it went alright," was all Tim could offer in response. "I hope you got on your knees and begged for forgiveness." Matt was still upset at Tim's actions; Meg was his friend too, and regardless, what he had done was very wrong.

"Not quite, but I think I made some headway. It won't be long before she is calling me and asking me to go back to her!" The tone of Tim's voice was nonchalant, like she was in the wrong and not Tim himself. He nodded his head as if to seal the deal. "Honestly, Tim, I can't weigh you up sometimes. When you left here earlier, you seemed full of remorse and I thought you were really sorry about what happened…" Matt threw his arms up in the air in exasperation.

"I AM sorry but everyone deserves a second chance. I was provoked…" Tim said hoping Matt would agree.

"Provoked? I really don't have patience with you. I don't even know why I am letting you stay here!" Matt turned his back to walk away. There was clearly nothing more to be said.

"Because you are my best friend and I would do the same for you. AND I would be on your side. Look, I apologised to her; what else can I do? Nothing," Tim exclaimed arrogantly. "Whatever!" Matt replied, irate with his friend.

Tim walked out of the kitchen and up to the spare room.

He sat on the comfortable double bed, which had a simple grey bedding set, and looked at his surroundings. Matt was quite good at interior design and the room looked more to Tim's liking than his own bedroom. Pale grey fitted wardrobes and a grey bedside table. A tasteful, expensive-looking print hung on the wall. But then, why would it have a feminine touch when Matt lived alone?

Tim put his feet up on the bed and rested his back on the headboard.

He cast his mind back to the day before when he had been to see his parents but not before telephoning them to check that it was ok. His mother had answered the call.

"Of course it's ok. You know you don't need to ask." If truth be told, he had just wanted to hear a comforting, familiar voice. He walked through the door to find his mum in the kitchen, wearing her old apron, her long pleated skirt flowing underneath, baking, as usual, the aroma sweet and familiar. He walked over to her and smiled, kissing her on the cheek. She smiled at her only son. "No Meg?" she noted.

"No" was the succinct reply.

Tim's father walked in, smiling at his son. Tim felt sure the smile was wider because he was without Meg, or maybe he was just imagining it.

His father was dressed casually in his old jeans and a grey sweater which only just fit over his portly belly.

"Where is she?" Susan asked, disappointed not to see her young friend.

She washed her hands in the sink and grabbed a tea towel to dry them. She then took off the pink apron and motioned for her son to go into the lounge.

"Well…" he began. "I think it's over between us," he said getting straight to the point. He glanced over to see what his father's expression was like. He wasn't surprised to see a tiny smile emerging from his chubby face. His mother, however, did not look so pleased.

In fact, she looked horrified, the slight pink colour in her face disappearing to reveal an ashen appearance.

"Why? When? Whatever happened?" she asked frantically. "I can't believe it! You can't have split up, Tim!" Susan was panic-stricken.

"Take a breath, Mum, and I'll tell you all about it." Tim sat down on the sofa, followed by both his parents. Tim began to tell them of the argument they had gone through. However, after telling them of the harsh words spoken about the wheelchair, his story differed somewhat from the truth.

"I got annoyed with her and shouted. She stood up and walked over to me and slapped me. I just shouted at her and she went berserk, hitting and slapping me. Well, I had to get her off me so I pushed her away. There was glass on the floor. I don't know why; she must have dropped a glass or something and she fell on it, cutting herself."

"Oh, God, is she ok?" Susan asked anxiously.

"Yes, I think so, but I didn't know there was glass on the floor. How was I supposed to know she would cut herself?" Tim was desperately trying to justify his actions even though his interpretation of the story was a complete fabrication of the truth.

"Don't worry about it, son, you haven't done anything wrong." It was his father who spoke.

"But I think I've lost her." Tim lowered his head and slumped his shoulders.

His father didn't respond to this but he didn't have to. Tim knew what he was thinking.

Tim looked at his father. "You're glad, aren't you?"

His father thought for a second. "No, not at all, not like this…but I can't deny that it's a good thing. She was no good. You deserve much better than her. You don't realise how much you've changed since she came on the scene. And SHE has changed you.."

His mother looked in horror at her husband but chose not to respond. Instead, she looked at Tim.

"I am sure if you go and see her and say sorry, everything will be alright." Ever the optimist, Susan didn't see that this might not have a happy ending.

"It sounds like Meg should be the one apologising," Jeff commented.

Susan, ignoring her husband for once, continued.

"When did all this happen? Have you spoken to her since it all took place?"

"Last week and no, I haven't spoken to her. I can't bring myself to call her."

"I am ashamed of you, Timothy Dixon!" Tim had never seen his mum so enraged.

"The longer you leave it," she continued, "the harder it will be to speak to her!"

"I know."

"Well, call her then, or better still, go and see her!"

"I will; tomorrow maybe…"

"Just make sure you do."

"TIM!" the sound of his friend calling his name from downstairs brought Tim's thoughts to an abrupt end. He jogged down the stairs.

"Your mum is on the phone." Tim took the receiver from Matt. "Hello, Mum."

"Well? Did you speak to her?" No greeting, just straight to the point. Susan was acting very much out of character. She had always got on well with Meg and was still upset at the thought of the relationship being over.

Tim told her what had happened.

"Well, you go back to her and beg her for forgiveness until you are back home with the best thing that ever happened to you." "I was going to leave it for today and ring her tomorrow," was Tim's half-hearted response.

"Well, maybe that's not a bad idea," his mum paused. "Give her time to think about it, but as far as I can see, what you did isn't bad enough for her not to forgive you."

"Yes, well…" Tim knew that wasn't strictly true, but obviously he hadn't told his mum the full or even correct story.

"Well, what? You have told me everything, haven't you?" came his mothers' words, doubting her son. "Of course," Tim lied.

"Well then!" His mother seemed quite positive that everything had been resolved.

"Look, Mum, thanks for ringing but I need to go now." Tim didn't want to pursue the matter any further. "Ok, love, well, let me know how it goes."

"Sure, bye." And with that, Tim replaced the receiver. Almost immediately, it rang again.

"Ok if I answer it?" Tim called out to his friend.

When he received a nod from Matt, he picked up the telephone. "Hello?"

"Tim?" The voice seemed surprised that Tim had answered the call. "Yes?"

"It's me. I've made a decision."

Chapter 13

Meg had been thinking long and hard after Jenny had left her. She had a big decision to make. Even though she was glad of the company of her lifelong friend, she wasn't sure if their conversation and Jenny's advice had helped her reach a verdict. After much deliberation, however, she was there.

She had telephoned Tim at Matt's house and waited.

The knock on the door made her jump. She knew who was at the other side of the door though.

"Hey," he said with a lame smile, looking as stylish as ever in his designer shirt and jeans.

Meg managed to return the smile and gestured for Tim to enter the house.

Tim did as he was told, took off his shoes and walked into their beautiful kitchen.

He didn't look like his usual self at all. In fact, he looked dreadful. His complexion was terrible, like he hadn't slept in days. Not that Meg cared; in fact, she was pleased.

"Coffee?" she offered.

"No, just tell me what you want to do…please, Meg," he begged, a gesture he wasn't prone to at all.

"Ok," she replied and led him into the lounge. She sat down and took a deep breath.

"Before I start, I want you to let me speak and let me finish before you respond, no interrupting, saying 'but this' or 'but that'… ok?" Meg looked at Tim, focused and confident.

Tim just nodded. He seemed very apprehensive, naturally. He sat down and waited.

Meg took another deep breath, looked at Tim and then began. "OK, here it is. I WAS worried about how you would react to the wheelchair but I had it planned how I would explain it to you. So, since you didn't listen the first time, you are going to listen now."

"You are right," she continued, "I don't need the wheels. At least, not yet. But you are going to be my husband - for better or worse, in sickness and in health. The only reason I got the chair was as an energy aid. I hate to admit it but I can't do the same things I could. Like shopping, for example. It wears me out. But the doctor said if I got a wheelchair, that problem would be eliminated and I wouldn't suffer from so much fatigue. You see, it's the fatigue that affects me the most at the moment. I do the easiest of things and I am tired. With this chair, I don't have that problem as much. We all know I can walk." Meg paused for a second as if to see if Tim was really concentrating on what she was saying. She was pleased to note that he seemed to be all ears.

"Ok? I just wanted to get that out of the way."

"Ok," Tim responded, a very worried tone to his voice.

"Now, I have been thinking really seriously about it all and no matter how upset or annoyed you felt about everything, you had no right to act in that appalling manner. You went absolutely berserk. I probably could have coped with a shove and you shouting at me but that…there was no excuse for it and no amount of explaining on your behalf will EVER make up for what you did." Meg paused and shook her head.

"Even when the physical scars have healed, it's still in here!" Meg pointed to her head.

Everything went deathly quiet as they were both processing all the words that Meg had spoken.

Tim looked at her scarred but still beautiful face, the concentration in her eyes undeniable.

It was Tim who broke the silence.

"So, are you telling me it's over then?" Tim sounded almost annoyed that Meg was putting him through this prolonged ordeal especially if she was just going to break up with him anyway. Meg looked angrily at him.

"I told you not to interrupt me!" Meg scowled at Tim, spoiling her pretty face.

"I'm sorry, but you are making this very difficult for me. Why can't you just tell me if we are over?"

"And you made it easy for me?" Meg was furious at the comment Tim had made. She reminded him it was his fault they were in this position in the first place. Meg glared at Tim who just waited to hear his fate.

Meg lost her composure for a second and looked down, rubbing her hands on her legs. She was furious that he had made her lose her stride.

"The few people I have spoken to about this think I should kick you out for good."

Tim opened his mouth to speak but then decided against it.

"But I firmly believe that you will never do it again and I love you too much to let you go over this. I will never forget it all but I am willing to give you a second chance."

Tim rose to his feet and rushed over to Meg. He picked her up and held her tightly, not letting her go for a few moments. He was relieved to feel her arms around him.

He apologised more than once assuring her that nothing like this would ever happen again.

Meg believed him deep down in her heart as he had acted so out of sorts with his diabolical actions. She had never seen him like that and felt sure she would never witness that side of him again. "Do you still want to marry me?" he asked her gingerly.

"Of course I do… it's only a couple of months away, you know." Tim nodded; of course he knew.

"It will be the best day of our lives!" he assured her confidently. "I hope so." The couple stood in their lounge embracing for quite some time. Tim took Meg's face in his hands and kissed her passionately. It was the type of kiss she had missed so dearly. It lingered, neither one wanting to be the person to end it.

A few days later, Tim was back in the house with Meg. Just to say sorry one more time, he arranged to take her away for a romantic weekend. He knew how much she loved the country so he took her to where he had proposed.

Meg wasn't told where she was going but she knew, as they were on the roads she remembered from that beautiful evening which resulted in the proposal.

"And I thought you weren't romantic!" She looked at him, driving beside her.

He took one hand off the wheel and took her hand in his, lifted it to his face and lightly kissed it.

"With a gorgeous girl like you by my side, why wouldn't I be romantic?"

"Creep!" she replied, a huge beaming smile forming on her face.

This wasn't the only secret he was keeping. The honeymoon was also an undisclosed location.

"I am so excited about the wedding."

"Me too," he replied. "I am so sorry I didn't seem that way before." Meg cast her mind back to choosing her wedding dress. It had been such a perfect day…

Meg had already seen the boutique where she wanted to purchase the dress. It was only a small shop but Meg had passed it several times and seen so many beautiful dresses in the window. She did have an open mind, though. She knew there were plenty of shops but she just had a feeling that she would find the dress of her dreams there.

Meg did, however, have an exact idea of the dress she wanted and would settle for nothing less. She had already arranged to take Tim's mum along with her own. She knew it would make Susan's day to be invited.

They walked into the shop and it was a beautiful sight. Dresses, tiaras and veils, not to mention the flowers and men's attire. They were greeted at the door by Julie, the owner.

Julie was a very tall, slender lady with long brown hair. She was smartly dressed in a pale blue skirt suit. The jacket was tailored and accentuated her figure perfectly. The skirt showed off her slender legs.

She was very helpful and was naturally an expert in what kind of dress suited the future brides who walked in.

"Hello and welcome!" she greeted the three ladies. After a few pleasantries had been exchanged, Julie spoke;

"You are such a beautiful, petite little thing so you don't want too much fuss. Something with a little detail but not too much, hmm… off the shoulder, maybe…" Julie walked over to a rail where an assortment of beautiful bridal gowns was hanging. She proceeded to take four dresses but didn't seem quite happy enough. She hung the dresses on a chair and then spotted the one she must have been looking for.

"Ah, yes," she said to herself.

Meg, however, was still looking for the one she had pictured in her mind. She wasn't even looking at the dresses Julie had picked.

When Meg turned around, she was ecstatic to see it was the same kind of dress she had hoped for.

"Amazing!" Meg exclaimed.

Julie smiled and then led Meg into the changing room.

Outside the changing room, Evie and Susan just looked at each other, unable to hide the obvious elation they both felt.

Within a few moments, Meg stepped out of the changing room in a gown, followed by Julie arranging the train.

The look on Evie's face and that of Susan said it all.

Meg looked in the mirror and beamed at the image that beamed back at her. The off-white gown was stunning. It was off the shoulder and fitted to her tiny waist. The skirt flared slightly to the floor. The sequins caught the sunlight and glistened.

Tears welled in Meg's mother's eyes but she could only utter one word which Meg could barely make out. "Beautiful."

Meg looked at Susan who was fumbling about in her handbag for tissues. She looked up at her future daughter-in-law, mascara running down her face.

"I'll take that as a positive sign!" Meg laughed at both women.

Both ladies nodded, huge smiles on their faces.

"Goodness knows how they are going to react to the other dresses!" Julie said with a smile but since Meg had tried her favourite dress on first, she hoped their reactions wouldn't be as positive. She was correct.

There had been no point in going to any other boutique!

"Hello? Anybody there?"

It was Tim, bringing Meg from her lovely memory.

Meg apologised, explaining where her mind had been!

They arrived shortly after at the hotel. They spent three days at the hotel and they had been the best days Meg had experienced in quite some time.

The hotel was very stylish. Tim had booked the best room they had. After checking in at the reception and unpacking their bags, they both just flopped onto the king-sized bed and turned to face each other, gazing into each other's eyes.

They both showered and dressed for dinner. They enjoyed a beautiful meal followed by an odd glass of wine.

By the time they went to bed, Meg was absolutely exhausted and was sure she could feel pain in her legs. But she didn't say anything. She wasn't going to let one thing spoil this perfect weekend.

They arrived home on Monday evening. Meg had already arranged to take Tuesday off in case she had any jobs to do at home. She was wiser as to what she could and couldn't do within a certain space of time. She thought she had found a balance, figuring how much work she could do before she got tired. Or so she had hoped. The result of taking Tuesday off was her staying in bed as Tim left for work, rolling over and falling back to sleep until well into the afternoon. Even when she did get out of bed, she didn't have the strength to do much.

This hadn't been what she had planned to do with her extra day, but if this was going to be what it was all about, then so be it.

Chapter 14

Meg was really sinking her teeth into her new job. She was all trained up herself and ready to take on the new recruits who had joined the previous day. They had received their induction training on their first day. They had been given a tour of the huge building. Today was the day they started their training on the computer systems. Meg was dressed to kill in a new outfit she had bought that weekend. She thought she should make a good, professional impression. Meg had many suits for work but thought it was time for a new one. She knew Tim didn't approve.

"They are new people; they won't have seen any of your clothes."

He had said that to her when they were walking through the shops. She had decided against the wheelchair, mainly because she had not needed it. At the moment, she felt better than ever before. Besides, she knew how Tim still felt about it all. Even though he had shown no signs of a repeat of that fateful day, she still didn't dare test the waters.

She sat at the impeccably tidy desk, flicking through her training notes for at least the tenth time that morning. She took a sip of water to calm her nerves. She wasn't nervous about the training but today was really the first day she could put all her hard work into action. She would see how effective it all was.

"Don't worry," Anita reassured her, seeing the apprehensive look on Meg's face.

"I'm not really, I just want to do well."

"Meg, you are great at this; you've done it all before!"

"I know, I just want to make a good impression," Meg stated.

"You already have," responded Anita. Meg just smiled gratefully at this comment.

The training went as well as Meg had hoped, apart from the know-all, who appeared to think he knew more than she did, and obviously didn't like to be trained by a woman younger than himself. Meg didn't let him bother her. She just hoped that the next few days would be easier. Maybe he would realize, after a while, that she really did know what she was talking about. Or maybe not; either way, Meg knew she had done a good day's work. She went home that evening, happy with her achievements.

That was how things were to continue for the next few days at least.

The week passed quickly; Meg unlocked the door of the house. She looked in the window to the side of the door and tapped. The little face of Madison peered up and bounded to the door after seeing her. This had become the ritual every day since she had brought her home.

"Hello, Maddy!" Meg had just decided to shorten her name. "Good to see you too, my friend!"

The grey cat followed Meg up the stairs and waited patiently whilst her owner showered.

"I'm here, my little shadow," she said as she stepped out of the bathroom, seeing the little grey ball of fluff!

The following Monday at work, Meg got up to walk over to the drinks machine for a coffee, after asking everyone else around her if they wanted one.

She found it very difficult carrying the tray full of hot drinks. She was shaking and spilled most of it over her hands, without even noticing that she had scalded herself.

Anita, on seeing her struggle, walked over swiftly to offer assistance.

"Are you alright?" her concerned manager enquired.

"Yes, I think it's just a little heavy," Meg replied, somewhat embarrassed.

"You might want to put that hand under some cold water." Anita pointed to the already red hand.

"Oh, didn't see that!" Meg said.

"Didn't you feel it?" A puzzled look appeared on Anita's face.

"I guess not," Meg shrugged, apparently unperturbed.

Meg walked over to the ladies' room to cool down the scalded hand. She didn't think any more of it.

That evening, Meg got home from work, exhausted as usual. She thought it was due to the extra hours she was putting in, so she wasn't worried.

She prepared tea so it was ready for Tim when he walked through the door. Just as she was about to serve up, the telephone rang.

"Meg, hi, it's me." It was Tim.

"Oh, hi, where are you?"

"Look, a few of the guys are going to the gym and then going on for a drink, so I am going to join them, ok?"

"But what about your tea?" Meg felt exasperated.

Tim, who didn't really appear to be listening, simply replied, "Look, I've got to go; see you later."

He put down the phone. Meg was, to say the least, annoyed.

'Why couldn't he have phoned earlier?' she thought.

She sat down by herself to eat the dinner she had made. She decided to plate him some up; after all, there was no point wasting it, and he might be hungry when he got home. That was not to be for a few hours though.

Meg decided to run herself a hot bath. She locked the doors and, followed by Madison, went upstairs, turned on the taps and picked up her favourite CD.

The water was very hot, bubbles floating around, but that was the way she liked it.

"…Show her the way she makes you love her…" she sang the lyrics to her all-time favourite song. "…Show her the way she makes you feel…" Meg continued, singing at the top of her voice, undressing. When the bath was full enough for her, Meg stepped in.

After scrubbing herself all over and washing her hair, Meg got out of the bath only to find that her legs were useless. She fell straight back into the bath, causing the water to splash everywhere. She tried again, only to be met by the same fate.

"Oh, for God's sake, what the hell is wrong with me?" Then she remembered her uncle's words.

"Bloody hell, the water is too hot!" She let a little of the water out, allowing some room in the bath for cold water.

"I hope this works!" She allowed the water to cool down with the cold tap. She tried to get up after a few minutes. It took her longer than she had hoped and it was very difficult but, in the end, she managed to manoeuvre herself out of the bath. Using the sink as an aid, she dried herself off and carefully walked into their bedroom.

For quite a long time after that, Meg simply lay on the bed crying. She should have remembered about the bathwater. But there were too many things to remember like she was living her life by a set of rules which she didn't want. She hated it all, but most of all, she hated herself. There was a heavy clock at the side of her bed.

"Stupid legs!" she said, beating them repeatedly with the clock. She hardly felt the pain, not even when she saw the bruising, which had instantly formed on her leg. Somehow though, it made her feel better. Meg dried herself, dried her hair and decided the best thing she could do was to just go to bed. She was exhausted anyway.

It was after 12 when Tim walked through the door. Meg heard the door, but she really wasn't in the mood for a confrontation, so she just pretended to be asleep.

The next morning, Meg woke up, feeling none of the numbness that she had suffered the day before. She did, however, have several large bruises on each leg.

'What was I thinking?' she thought to herself.

Tim had already got up and was in the bathroom

"What happened in here? It's wet through," came his voice.

"Oh, I, erm…" Meg couldn't think of a plausible excuse "Did you have a good time last night?"

"Oh yeah, great, me and the lads got together and had a whale of a time!"

"That's great." Meg had managed to divert Tim's attention as he didn't ask again about the soaked bathroom floor. He appeared to be more concerned with his own reflection.

This gave Meg the perfect opportunity to quickly dress so that Tim would not notice the state her legs were in.

After sorting breakfast for the two of them and kissing Tim goodbye, Meg clambered upstairs to dry the bathroom. She drove over to Jenny's house about half an hour later. Meg decided not to share her ordeal with her.

The next few days were just as bad for Meg, her legs being the main problem. The fatigue was also much worse. On her way back to her desk the morning after the bathroom incident, Meg's legs gave way, causing her to tumble to the floor. After that, she blacked out and didn't remember any more until waking up at the hospital.

"Hey there!" Meg looked around to fit the voice to the person. It was Anita, with Jenny sitting beside her.

"What happened?" Meg asked.

"Well, you passed out, but I think you fell first, you clumsy clot!"

"Oh, yeah, I remember falling over. It felt like the floor wasn't there." Meg was frightened. At that point, the figure of a young slender man approached the bed. He looked at Meg and smiled warmly.

"Hello there! Decided to wake from your beauty sleep?"

"Hmm, think I needed more though!" Meg was still managing to maintain a certain air of joviality.

"Nah, I just have a few questions to ask you." The doctor seemed particularly nice.

"Ok." Meg's voice was very tentative.

"Do you remember what happened?"

"Vaguely; I fell over, couldn't feel the floor, and then I woke up here."

"Ok, well, let's have a look." The doctor walked closer to Meg asking the two visitors politely to move slightly out of the way so he could examine Meg. He lifted her right leg in the air and prompted her to try and keep it there while he moved his hand away. The very instant that the doctor did this, Meg's leg fell straight back on the bed. He tried it again with her left leg only to find that it did exactly the same thing. The look of horror on Meg's face was clear. She had absolutely no feeling whatsoever in her legs. The doctor produced a small pin-like object and instructed her to tell him if she felt its sharpness on her toes. There was nothing. He continued to press the object against various parts of her body, her cheek, her arm and chest, only to find little reaction anywhere.

Anita and Jenny looked at each other, equally startled.

"I can't feel anything! This is awful; it's like I don't have any legs!" Tears began to well up in Meg's eyes.

"Don't worry, we can help you. Has anything like this happened before?" The young doctor looked at Meg and gently touched her leg.

"Well, to be honest, I haven't really felt very well for a few days now. I fell down when trying to get out of the bath; I think the water was too hot though." Meg went on to explain the other little things that had occurred over the past few days. She mentioned how she had scalded her hand and didn't realise it, producing the hand to the doctor, showing the burn mark, which was still apparent. She mentioned how tired she had been. It wasn't until she recounted all the incidents that she realised how bad things had been.

"I am afraid to say I think you are having a relapse."

"What does that mean? How long will it last? Will I be able to walk again?" Suddenly, all the information that Meg had found out was useless. She knew nothing about it.

"It may only last a couple more days, maybe a week or so, and I can't say for definite if you will work, but I am sure you will be feeling better after we give you some steroids. Most people find it really helps when they are having difficulty with their walking. It usually helps. With any luck, you will be back on your feet in no time… sorry." The medic realised his mistake.

"But a lot of MS sufferers have this symptom once or twice in their life and then never have it again. Let's hope this is the case here." The doctor's voice was calm and very soothing, but it didn't help convince Meg enough that things were going to be all right.

She didn't know anything about the steroids; how would she take them? A tablet, maybe?

"I am getting married soon," she pleaded.

"Then I had better go and get the medication for you!"

The doctor disappeared down the maze of corridors, passing nurses bustling around the ward. Meg turned to her friends.

"We were so worried; you just kind of went!" This was all that Jenny could say.

Meg didn't need others to tell her about being worried. She only had to think about everything that had gone wrong over the past few days, weeks even, to be worried enough herself.

"Someone should call Tim and maybe your mum."

"No need for that, love, I am here!" Her mother greeted her with a warm smile. "Jenny already rang; I came as soon as I could."

"Hi, Mum." Meg held her arms up to hug her mum, who was only too happy to reciprocate.

"Hi, love, how are you feeling? Stupid question - you aren't well, that's why you are here!"

"Ok, confused I guess, really tired." Meg kept the leg incident from her mother, not wanting to worry her even more than she obviously was already.

At that moment, the doctor returned with a tray filled with various medications. He then proceeded to push the syringes full of medicine into a bag.

"This has been in the fridge so I am afraid it will be cold.

Tomorrow we will get it out early for you."

"What is this? And what do you mean tomorrow?"

"Oh, sorry, these are the steroids; we have to give you them intravenously."

"Great - a needle," Meg joked. To be honest, she wasn't in the least bit frightened of needles, when they were going into someone else!

"Right, I just need your hand; we need to put this cannula in. The needle just goes into your vein, with the cannula; the needle doesn't stay in, but the cannula has to be in for three days, ok?"

He needn't have explained. Meg had seen people with these things in them before; they just made it easier to give medication. The medicines all went in through the opening at the top so that needles didn't have to be injected every time.

"Oh dear," the doctor exclaimed as he took her hand.

"What?"

"Your veins aren't too good here; let me have your wrist." Meg turned her hand around to reveal the wrist, where the veins seemed no better.

"Hmmm," he pondered. He looked higher up on her arm, at the inside of her elbow.

"Ahh, that looks much better; we'll use that one."

"He placed the needle in Megs' vein, inserted the cannula, then held her arm to see if it bled.

"Yes, we have lift off!" he remarked, seeing the blood.

The tube at the end of the bag containing the steroids was placed in the cannula after the doctor removed the needle.

"Ok, I will have to leave you there with the steroids pumping through, so don't go anywhere," he joked, looking at the bag, which was clipped to the curtain rail. He disappeared down the corridor discussing the case with the nurse.

Meg watched as the medication dripped slowly through the tube and into her veins. After a few minutes, her arm felt how cold it was.

She sat, bewildered by the whole affair.

"We are going to have to go," Anita said to Meg after looking at Jenny.

"Are you alright now your mum is here?"

"Yeah, I'll be fine. Thanks for everything; I am sorry," Meg said mournfully.

"You have nothing to be sorry for," Anita said. "Don't worry about work; you just rest. Take all the time you need."

Meg just smiled as Jenny and Anita waved goodbye as they left the hospital.

As Meg watched the drip pumping the steroids into her arm, she let the tears flow.

"I don't like this," she said to her mother, who looked as distressed as she did.

"I know, love, but it will make you feel better."

"No, I mean I don't like being ill."

"Oh, sweetheart," her mum comforted Meg, sitting on the bed beside her daughter. Evie put her arm around Meg, who, by now, was in floods of tears.

"I can't cope with all this," she said between sobs. "Getting diagnosed, then feeling ok one minute and not the next, everything with Tim, and now this, just before the wedding, not even knowing if I am going to be able to walk down that aisle…"

Evie, not really knowing how to respond to this, just hugged her daughter even harder.

A few moments later, a nurse appeared around the corner of the ward and smiled warmly at Meg.

"How are we doing?" she asked.

"Ok, it's just a little cold."

"Yeah, we can't do anything about that, I am afraid, but tomorrow, we will get it out of the fridge in time for it to warm a little.

You look very flushed," she commented.

"Yeah, I am warm," Meg replied.

"The steroids, I am afraid. Did the doc tell you about the side effects?"

Meg looked a little concerned.

"No."

"The main one is that, the flushed cheeks; you may also have a metallic taste in your mouth for a few days, but this will wear off. The thing most people comment on after having steroids is restlessness. Not really knowing where you want to be, I guess."

"I see; that's great," Meg responded with a hint of sarcasm.

"You are not necessarily going to have any of these but we just have to tell you."

"What about long-term side effects?" Evie asked. "I have heard things about steroids and bone deterioration…?"

"Yes, if you are on steroids on a regular basis, it is possible that you may gain weight. As far as the bone situation is concerned, we do try to limit the doses of steroids to 2 every year, but only if absolutely necessary. This reduces the chances of your bones deteriorating, and we really do not like to give people steroids more often than that."

"Well, I am sure this is a minor setback and these are the only steroids I will ever need," Meg said confidently.

The nurse didn't respond. She asked Meg again how it felt.

"It's hurting a little," was the reply.

The nurse took her arm and gently rubbed it for her, easing the pain slightly. Meg noticed a beautiful tattoo on the nurse's arm. It was what Meg believed was called a tribal tattoo with a deep red rose entwined in it.

"How long have you had MS?" she asked her.

"Since just before Christmas," came the reply.

"Nice Christmas present."

"Hmmm, I've had better!"

"I'll bet. Did you know the hospital runs a support group for people with MS? Apparently, it is really good. They have guest speakers who come and talk about a wide range of issues, like disability, stress, fatigue - you know, that kind of thing, plus, of course, you can speak to other MS sufferers about their experiences."

Meg was horrified at that one word – disability.

"I don't know," she replied. "I have been ok apart from this. I just want to get on with my life and forget about it as much as I can. I have heard that I may only have one relapse every few years or so; maybe even less than that."

"That is true but there is no harm in preparing yourself." The nurse, with her long blonde hair tied neatly back in a ponytail, spoke very wisely, her slim face looking thoughtfully at Meg.

Meg thought her very attractive but really didn't want to talk about the group.

"I think I have taken enough in today. It has been a bad enough week without seeing people in a worse state than me, wondering if I am going to be like them."

"That is understandable," said the nurse, finally admitting defeat.

"Sorry, I know you are just being helpful, but I just can't take any more today. Sorry if that sounds a little dramatic."

"Not at all; it has been a tough time for you."

"Did that hurt a lot?" Meg asked, pointing to the tattoo.

"Not that much really," she replied.

"It is beautiful!" Meg looked at her mum for her opinion.

"Don't even think about it!" her mum responded.

The nurse smiled and walked off, with a beautiful posture that made her look like a model walking down a catwalk, but with not quite as much attitude.

"What a day!" Meg said wearily. "I really can't take ANY more!"

The nurse reappeared.

"I almost forgot," she said. "I need to take a urine sample after tomorrow's dose, to check that the steroids haven't given you diabetes."

The nurse disappeared a second time.

"And the hits just keep on coming!" Meg growled, not knowing whether to laugh or cry. She decided to laugh, making her mum do the same if only for Meg's choice of words.

After about three-quarters of an hour, the steroids had finished dripping through Meg's veins, so Evie looked up to get a nurse's attention. Within twenty minutes, the drip had been removed.

"How do you feel? If you feel up to it, you can go home now and come back tomorrow for your second dose."

"I don't feel too good, but I would prefer to go home," Meg pleaded.

"I'll make sure she is ok," Evie said.

"Ok then, I'll put a bandage on your arm to stop you catching it on something; you'll just have to be careful with it being where it is."

"Ok, I guess it's takeaway for tea then!" Meg forced a smile.

"Good idea," the nurse responded. "Although you don't actually have a needle in there, the less you move it, the better. Now, you take care of yourself. I won't be here tomorrow, so just in case no one tells you, you have to be careful for a couple of weeks, if not more. The steroids don't always work immediately and even if they do, don't go thinking you are bionic and that you can do anything. Don't go undoing all the good work that the steroids are doing for you, ok?"

"Ok, thanks."

Meg and Evie got her things together and went home. They were surprised to see Tim's car in the drive, but then it was after five. Maybe he had got home a little early, Meg thought. Evie walked Meg to the door; she still felt very uneasy and unsteady on her feet. As they walked through the door, they heard the shower running. The first thing Tim always did when he came home was to have a shower, so he had obviously not been in long.

"Hi!" Meg shouted. "I'm home!" She knew Tim wouldn't respond but at least he knew she was there.

Meg and Evie sat down.

"Do you want a coffee?" Meg asked her mum.

"You stay there; I'll make the coffee," she was instructed.

"Fine, whatever." Meg was already feeling restless. Part of her wanted to sit down but another part wanted to get up and do something, anything. She did as she was told and stayed put though.

A few minutes later, as Meg and Evie settled down to their coffees, Tim walked through the door.

"Hi, Evelyn," he said as Evie was the first person he saw.

"I wish you would call me Evie. Evelyn makes me sound so old."

"Sorry." He turned to Meg, and after seeing the bandage around her arm, he asked, "What on earth have you been doing to yourself? Did you fall over, you clumsy clot?"

He looked to Evie.

"She is so clumsy; has she always been like this?"

"Tim, I didn't fall. I haven't been well, and I collapsed at work, so I was rushed to hospital."

Meg went on to tell Tim about the other things which had led to the doctor prescribing the steroids.

"I have to go back tomorrow and the day after for 2 more courses." Meg hoped that Tim might take her to the hospital.

"She is not well at all, Tim. She really needs to rest if she wants to be well for the wedding," Evie said to her future son-in-law.

"Oh, I see. Sorry, Meg, I just thought you had been up to your usual tricks."

"Don't worry about it."

"How are you feeling?"

"In a word, rough!"

"I must admit, you don't look too good."

Meg went on to explain about the side effects and that it really was important that she rest.

Meg could see the look on Tim's face as she spoke. She knew the look; she had seen it all too many times. It was the 'you are so dramatic' look. She wasn't going to try and convince him anymore; she really didn't have the inclination. Instead, she changed the subject.

"I was thinking about us having a takeaway for tea," she offered hopelessly.

"Again? I thought we were saving up!"

"I know, but I have had the worst time and today has just been horrible. Besides anything else, I am a little handicapped today."

Meg lifted her arm to show Tim what she meant.

Tim, as if realising what he had said, not to mention the fact that Evie was there, lowered his tone.

"Sorry, would you like me to make something?"

"That would be nice."

"Pasta or something?"

"Yeah, with one of your lovely sauces. I think there is some chicken in the fridge," Meg offered.

"Right, then," Tim said, rubbing his hands. "Let's get cracking! Sit there and take it easy and I'll go and make some tea."

He looked at Evie as if for approval.

"Are you staying?" he asked.

"No, I just wanted to see that Meg was ok. I had best get off and make some tea myself."

"I am sure we will have enough if you would like to both come back, and Jack, of course," Tim offered.

"No, that's ok, love. I think Meg would be better if we didn't. You two just have a nice tea and I'll go." Evie got up and kissed her daughter. As she walked to the door to leave, she turned to Meg.

"Shall I pick you up in the morning?" Meg looked at Tim, hoping that he would offer to take the day off work to take her. She couldn't possibly drive herself there, not with her arm like this. Besides, the way she was feeling, she really didn't feel safe to drive herself there, not with her arm like this… No offer was forthcoming from Tim so Meg looked at her mum and nodded.

"Yes, please," she whispered.

"I'll be here around ten. Bye, love." Evie was gone but not before giving her daughter a kiss on the cheek.

Tim was in the room when Meg walked back in.

"Right then," she began, "I think I could manage to eat your special pasta." She looked at him, hinting for him to make the tea.

"Hmmm, I am watching this. Can't you manage to make something?"

"With this?" she retorted, waving her bandaged hand at him. She accidentally blocked his view of the television with her arm.

"Get your arm out of the way! I am watching that; this is why I came home from work early. I have already missed enough with your dramatic hospital story!" He knocked her arm out of the way causing her to wince with pain. She felt sure the cannula had shifted position. Her arm was throbbing.

"TIM!" Meg was boiling with rage.

"What? Oh, shut up whinging and get on with it. Honestly. Anyone would think you'd had a major operation. It was only an injection, for Christ's sake!"

"No, it wasn't, it was…"

128

"Will you just shut up and get some tea made…? I am hungry. You always overreact. What do you take me for?

You have only had something fed through in a drip; people have things like that done all the time. You see them in hospital and they are a lot sicker than you are and they never seem to moan." Meg thought of various responses but chose to just walk away.

"What time does this finish?" she asked him.

"I don't know, but if you don't shut up, I am going to miss it!"

"Sorry," Meg said scornfully.

"So you should be, now get out of my sight!"

"You really are evil, you know that?" Meg had pushed him too far. Tim got out of his chair and picked her up by her bad arm.

"How many times do I have to tell you to shut up? I can't believe you are answering me back like this!"

"Answering you back? Aren't I allowed to speak? You are not your Father, you know; I am not your little wife at your beck and call like your mother is, poor soul."

"What did you say? What did you say?" Tim repeated, shouting louder the second time. He slapped her hard across the face, leaving a red mark on her cheek. As she fell to the floor, the rage inside him did not improve, and he kicked her in the stomach. Not only did he cause her a great deal of pain but she had fallen on her arm.

She struggled upstairs, crying.

"Peace and quiet at last!" she heard Tim shout.

She carefully removed the bandage from her arm to see if the cannula was still in place. It was, but it didn't look too good.

The pain was intense; Meg didn't really know what to do.

She decided to leave it and replaced the bandage.

She walked downstairs quietly and past Tim into the kitchen. She helped herself to two painkillers to see if that would help. She decided to try and make the tea, finding it even more difficult now the foreign body in her arm had moved, but she knew if she didn't make anything he would probably get even more agitated. It really wasn't worth that.

"Do you want some tea?" Meg shouted to Tim.

"Of course I do!"

After a lot of wincing and trouble, Meg had finally prepared the tea. She carried it into the living room and held it in front of Tim. After a few moments, he took it from her.

She ate her own in the kitchen, at the breakfast bar; she had lost her appetite though. As she played with her food, chasing it around the plate before eventually forcing herself to eat it, she thought about how Tim had reacted to her.

'It's understandable,' she thought, 'I mean, how would I react? We both thought that I was ok and then weeks before our wedding, I go and get ill like this. It is MY fault, I have been overdoing it so much, and even after I have been warned. I asked for it really. I have spent time trying to convince Tim that everything was going to be all right and then I go and land myself in this… I am so lucky to have Tim, especially now. I could never find anyone else, not now, not with this thing hanging over me…'

Tim walked into the kitchen, interrupting her thoughts.

"That was delicious," he told her.

"Not as good as yours though."

"Oh, I don't know!" he smiled sweetly at her.

"I am sorry," she said to him as if the whole thing was her fault.

"I should be the one apologising. I just panicked, I…"

"I know; you don't need to explain, it's ok. Let's forget about it."

Tim pursued the point no more and agreed. He smiled at her.

"Now go and finish watching your program," she told him.

He didn't need much persuading and was gone within seconds. As far as he was concerned, everything had now been put right.

After a very restless night, Meg finally got off to sleep and awoke to Tim's alarm clock blaring out the latest number one single.

She got up with Tim, and after making his breakfast and getting dressed very carefully as she was still in a lot of pain, she was ready for her next dose of steroids. Her mum arrived, as promised, at ten o'clock. Meg didn't wait for her to get out of the car, she just left the house, locked the door and walked, or rather limped and swayed to the car door.

Luckily, the mark on Meg's face had almost disappeared and now looked more like she was simply flushed, which was ideal, given the previous day's events.

A different nurse greeted them at the hospital. This one was taller and slimmer with very dark brown hair and brown eyes.

Elizabeth was the name on her badge.

"Hi!" Meg spoke. "I am here for another dose of steroids."

"Meg Walker?" the nurse asked, looking at a file.

"Yep."

"Come this way!" They were shown to the day-care section of the hospital ward, where another patient was sat, apparently having the same treatment as Meg.

"Hello," she greeted her.

"Hi!"

The nurse took off Meg's bandage carefully, ready to insert the tube.

"Goodness me, what on earth have you done to this?" the nurse asked, seeing that the cannula was somewhat out of alignment.

"I think I must have done it in my sleep," Meg lied.

"I am not sure we will get this flowing," said the nurse, looking at the cannula dubiously. She inserted a syringe into the top of the cannula.

"I am just flushing this out to get rid of the blood," she told Meg.

"If it works, then we are ok." The nurse plunged the syringe down successfully.

"Well, there you go, wrong again." She placed the tube into the cannula and, as it had the previous day, the steroids slowly began to drip through.

"Would you like a drink?" the nurse asked.

"Yeah, a coffee, please; milk, two sugars."

"And you?"

"Coffee, no sugar thanks," Evie replied.

A few moments later, the nurse appeared with two cups of coffee.

"Now if you need anything, just press the buzzer over there."

Elizabeth pointed to a red buzzer, which was on the wall.

"Ok, thanks."

The steroids seem to drip much slower today and cause Meg even more pain.

"MS?" a voice asked. It was the lady sitting opposite them who appeared to be having the same treatment.

"Yes; you?" Meg replied.

"Yep, 'fraid so. What's your name?" The woman had red hair not dissimilar to Meg's but considerably shorter.

"Meg, and yours?"

"Vanessa."

"Hello, Vanessa. Nice to meet you," Meg replied. "Can I ask you something?"

"Sure!"

"Have you had steroids before?"

"Yeah, I am afraid I seem to need them every 5 or 6 months, why?"

"Is it me or is it really not nice?"

"It is really not nice," Vanessa replied, "but it feels worse for at least a week after for me."

"Oh great, thanks!"

"Sorry!"

The two of them chatted for quite some time and Meg found out that Vanessa was a dentist and had had MS for over 6 years. At times, she had felt so bad she wanted to quit working, but at twenty-eight years old she was not going to; she had worked too hard to become a dentist. It was surprising how many symptoms they seemed to have in common. They swapped phone numbers and promised to ring each other.

"Don't take this the wrong way, but it has been nice speaking to someone else with MS!" Meg said.

"Yeah, I know what you mean. I have to admit, not many people I have spoken to seem as similar as you are to me, if you know what I mean."

"Sure do!" Meg looked up at Vanessa's drip. "I think you are done."

"Thank goodness for that! That was my last one- always the worst. That took nearly an hour and a half; you know, it is almost as if my body doesn't want the last few drops, it always takes so long!"

Evie, who had been listening to their conversation with great interest, stood up to get the nurse.

"Why don't you press the button?" Meg asked her.

"No bother, I'll go get her." Evie disappeared.

"Is that your mum?"

"Yep."

"She's great!"

"Yeah, she is. How are your family? You married?" Meg asked.

"Yes, my husband is great but I don't get on so well with his sister. It's like I am not good enough for her brother because of my MS. She has no idea how I feel, but because I look ok most of the time, I am sure she thinks I am putting it on or being over-dramatic…" Vanessa paused. "Does that make sense?"

"Perfect sense!" Meg replied. "I think I will definitely be talking more to you!"

Vanessa was slightly puzzled but thought she knew what Meg meant. "You married?"

"No. I get married in a few weeks; I just hope I am ok for it."

"You will be if you rest and don't overdo it; easier said than done, I know, but you really need to rest."

"Ok!" They smiled at one another.

The nurse, Elizabeth, reappeared to see which lady was finished. She unhooked Vanessa and carefully took out the cannula.

"Right, I hope we don't see you for a while; you take care now," she said, pointing her painted finger at Vanessa.

"Thanks; likewise," came the response.

"See you, Meg. Maybe we could meet up sometime? I'll call you!"

"Ok, take care!"

"You too."

Meg watched as Vanessa left the day-care room.

"Nice girl," Evie said.

"Yes, she was; sorry I ignored you though."

"Don't worry about it. I think it was good for you to talk to someone who knows where you are coming from. I am always here for you, you know that, but I can't begin to know how this all feels for you."

"You are great, Mum." Meg smiled, hugging her mum with her one good hand.

When the treatment had finished dripping through, Meg needed the toilet. She told the nurse what had been said the previous day but was happy when the nurse came back after testing her urine and told her that everything was normal.

"Same time again tomorrow?"

"Fine!" The nurse confirmed she would be there for Meg and would be ready with her final treatment.

When Meg got home, there was a message on her answerphone. It was Vanessa, enquiring how she was.

She rang her straight back and after talking in-depth about the illness and family's attitudes, they agreed to meet up later.

Tim had arrived home early that day with a huge bouquet of flowers, just to apologise one more time.

"There was no need to do that," Meg said with delight at the look of the flowers.

"Well, aren't you supposed to buy people flowers when they are unwell anyway?"

"I guess so. Thanks."

"You are very welcome," he said, winking, and producing a takeaway with the other arm.

"I guess we should have had this yesterday, but you are still a bit 'armless so I thought I would bring one home."

"Oh, ha, ha!" Meg got out the plates whilst Tim opened up the cartons. The smell of Chinese food filled the room and immediately made Meg hungry. Despite still not feeling well, she felt much better in herself. Meeting Vanessa and making up with Tim had really made her feel good.

A couple of days later, whilst Meg was resting on the sofa watching one of her favourite films, the telephone rang.

"Hi Meg, it's Susan. How are you?"

"Oh, ok, recovering, I guess."

"What do you mean?"

Meg was annoyed that Tim obviously hadn't telephoned his mum to tell her what was going on, so she explained it all herself. Susan was very distressed at hearing all this and at once shouted to Jeff to take her to see Meg. Meg could hear Jeff's grunts but he agreed and later that evening, Tim and Meg were joined by Jeff and Susan.

Jeff spoke to his son for a moment but walked quickly through to the living room where Meg was sitting with her feet up. He stormed over to her, standing right over the chair.

"Hi, Jeff."

What's up with you?" he asked abruptly.

'I've got MS, Jeff, you ignorant bastard,' she wanted to say, but instead, she opted for, "I've just not been too good recently."

"You look alright."

"Yeah, well, looks can be deceiving." He had just uttered the three words Meg was beginning to hate these days.

"You never said anything before."

"Well, what do you want me to do, ring you up and tell you every time I feel ill? Maybe I don't want to moan to you all the time!"

Jeff just shrugged his shoulders.

"You know," Meg continued, "I really can't win - if I talk about it, say at work, I get criticised and people think I do nothing but moan about it and if I keep quiet, just trying to get on with things, I am accused of making things up when something like this happens, and it is all a surprise to you all that I am not well. You know, they wouldn't just give these steroids out unless they really thought I needed them. They are not just like taking a couple of painkillers, you know." Although Meg was trying to talk calmly, her voice was getting more shaky and rapid. She took a deep breath and was struggling to remain calm. Fortunately, Susan came in at that point. She walked over to Meg and gave her a big hug, calming Meg down a little.

"Thanks for coming, Susan, it was really nice of you."

"Not at all! I would have been here sooner had I known. Is there anything I can do to help? Cooking? Ironing? Cleaning?" Jeff grunted at the suggestion.

"No, really, I will manage, but thanks."

After a short while, Jeff announced they were leaving and a few moments later, they were gone.

Neither Meg nor Tim said anything about the visit; they hardly spoke at all for the rest of the night.

A few weeks later, Meg was feeling a little better. The side effects had calmed down and she was once again able to sleep. A few days later, everything was back to normal.

"Looking forward to the hen night?" she was asked.

"Oh yes! it's soon, isn't it?"

"You would forget your head if it wasn't attached!" Jenny teased.

"Yeah, well, I've been busy. No surprises up your sleeve, I hope!"

"Of course not!" Meg had told Jenny in no uncertain terms that she just wanted to have a nice night out with none of the usual hen night antics.

Jenny was as good as her word and there were no surprises at the hen night. Meg just enjoyed her last big night out as a single woman.

She was so excited about the wedding. Everything had been ready for months. It had seemed to take forever to get to the day, but they were nearly there. Only a few more days before she would be going home to her parents' house to spend the last night before the wedding.

Meg knew that her mum was particularly pleased, as the weather had been perfect for the flowers and plants in the garden. They all bloomed, and Meg knew that Evie's wish would come true – the garden would look perfect for the photographs.

The day before the wedding had been rather exciting for Meg, the build-up. Meg had been very busy going to the bridal wear shop to pick up the dresses. They had been altered for the final time and were ready and clean for the big day. She dropped them off at her mum's house, where she was naturally staying, and then had gone back out again for her manicure and pedicure. It was just what she needed after the tension and stress of the previous few days. She sat back and relaxed whilst the bubbles popped around her toes. The beautician carefully lifted one foot from the foot spa and dried it. Meg sighed with contentment as her foot was massaged before her feet were pedicured and painted. This had to be one of the most relaxing activities possible. The manicure had completed her relaxation and Meg was now ready and excited for the day that lay ahead.

Katherine, the beautician, wished her well for the wedding before saying goodbye and watching Meg leave.

Later that evening, Meg's dad picked her up from her house to stay with her family for her final night of being a single woman. Her mum had prepared her favourite meal, which the whole family enjoyed. She was pampered by both her parents for the entire evening before she retired to bed for the night. The excitement wasn't too much for her, as she was asleep in less than 10 minutes.

Chapter 15

The wedding day arrived and Meg was upstairs in the shower. Her mum and dad were downstairs making breakfast.

"I checked on her last night and I can't believe she was asleep," Evie said.

"You too? I couldn't sleep so I checked on her at about 1 am and she was sound asleep. She needs to rest though. I am a little worried that the whole day is going to be too much for her, and I'm sure that dress will only make her very warm all day."

"Stop worrying, David; she will be fine. I am sure everything will be ok."

It was at that point that Meg walked downstairs.

"Morning, Mum, Dad. What's for breakfast?"

"I wasn't sure if you would be hungry."

"Of course I am; have you ever known me not to be?"

"Good point," her dad chipped in!

As they were sitting having breakfast, there was a knock on the door. It was the hairdresser, closely followed by the chief bridesmaid, Jenny, of course!

The two girls were very chatty whilst they were having their hair done. Meg's lovely long locks were perfect for most styles, but Meg had chosen to wear it pinned up with just a few tendrils down over her shoulders.

Her mum and dad went upstairs to get ready. Coming downstairs first was Meg's dad who was rather nervous, then his wife was not too far behind him.

"You look beautiful, love," he said to his wife.

"You don't look so bad yourself," she replied, walking over to give her husband a peck on the cheek.

After all the preparations were complete and the make-up was applied, the two girls went upstairs to put on their gowns.

Naturally, Jenny was ready first.

But when Meg was finally ready, helped by the hairdresser so as not to spoil her work, she took a deep breath and walked down the stairs.

"Mum, are you ready? Here I come!" Meg beamed with pride. She had insisted on just having the professionals with her whilst she had her make-up done and put on the dress so that her parents could see the full effect of the transformation.

"Wow, you look beautiful!"

"Thanks, Mum. I do love the dress; I've never seen one like it and I can't believe it suits me!" The ivory gown hung off her right shoulder. Small diamantes were sewn around the sweetheart neckline. The dress was fitted perfectly to her slim waist. The lower half flowed beautifully. The back of the gown was gathered in, leading to a small bow at the base of her spine.

"I wasn't just talking about the dress! I just mean you; you are so beautiful!"

"What do you think. Dad?"

"I'm speechless, Meg!" was all her father was able to say.

"I will take that as a compliment."

"Good! Tim won't know what's hit him; he is a very lucky young man."

"You are biased!"

"Well, of course I am; you are my daughter, but it's true."

Hearing all the noise, Jenny came from downstairs all ready.

"What's all the commotion?" she asked. Peering her head around the living room door, she stood there smiling.

"You look great!" Meg said, beaming at her Chief Bridesmaid.

"You don't brush up too badly yourself!"

At that point, Sarah arrived dressed beautifully in her bridesmaid gown. Upon hearing the noise, she entered the room.

"Let me look at you! Where is she? Oh, there you are …stunning; simply stunning!"

"You look great too, Sarah. I knew you would make a great bridesmaid - that colour really suits you."

"I feel good but you, you just look unbelievable! Look at the way that dress sparkles in the light!" Sarah was Meg's cousin; they had always joked that they would have each other as bridesmaids on their wedding day.

All three girls looked and felt great. Sarah, along with Meg's parents, left the two girls in the living room whilst they were putting the finishing touches to their outfits.

Meg decided to ask Jenny a question that had been on her mind for a while.

"Jenny…? "

"Yes?"

"Have you noticed anything unusual about Tim recently?"

"In what respect?"

"I don't know; you've seen him in the past couple of days - does he strike you as different?"

"I don't know - maybe a little - I'm sure it's just nerves."

"Yeah, probably." Nothing more was spoken on the subject.

There was a knock at the door.

Meg's mum went to the door to find the florist.

"Good morning, Madame; your flowers…"

"Thank you!"

"Thank you, Madame, and have a good day!"

"The flowers have arrived, oh, and they are so gorgeous! Look, Meg, Sarah, Jenny, your flowers have arrived!" Evie was so excited.

"Wonderful! Everything is falling into place; this is going to be the best day of my life!" Meg announced.

"It certainly is, love. You enjoy every minute; this is your day!"

Knock, knock… The door went again.

It was Meg's father who answered the door this time.

It was the photographer.

He was invited inside and was delighted to see that the wedding party was ready and waiting. They were all led into the garden, and, as Meg had hoped, the garden was beautiful; the flowers were blooming everywhere and the sun was shining. Meg had absolutely no problem keeping the smile going for all the photos. It was already the happiest day of her life and nothing was going to spoil it. The weather had been abysmal for the past few weeks but as if by magic, today was an exception. Just as the photographer had finished and disappeared to take photos of the groom waiting at the church, there was another knock on the door.

"Busy day! Anyone would think there was something going on today!" Meg joked. It was the chauffeur.

"Good morning! I believe we have a special day today and I am here to take you all to the church. Could I have the bridesmaids and the bride's mum, please? Are you all ready? Oh yes, you are, and you all look stunning. Let's go then!" The chauffeur led the way to the old-fashioned Rolls Royce which was decorated beautifully for the occasion. He walked Evie outside, her arm in his.

A small gathering of neighbours had appeared from the houses to watch the wedding party depart. They all smiled and waved at the bridesmaids and Evie, wishing them well and complimenting them on how gorgeous they all looked.

After the car had taken its first trip, there seemed to be total silence, leaving Meg and her father alone together to await the return of the chauffeur.

"Well, Dad, it's just me and you!"

"Yeah, look, have a fantastic day, won't you, and be careful; don't tire yourself out. I know what you are like, mingling and dancing, and running around to see if everyone is ok, but there will be no need for that today. Everyone will be looking after you!"

"Don't fret, Dad! Everything is going to be just perfect - today will just be the best!"

"I only worry about you. I want you to enjoy every minute today and I don't want anything to spoil it."

"Thanks, Dad. I love you!" Meg glided over to her father, carefully giving him a hug.

"I love you too, now how about a little tipple before we go?"

"Why not?"

"Brandy?"

"Lovely!"

As much as Meg didn't really want to admit that she was nervous, she had to confess that she felt a little better after a little Dutch courage! She was glad of this quiet moment with her father to gather all her thoughts and emotions. She didn't want to rush one second of the day she had dreamed of ever since she was a little girl. She wanted to enjoy every second of the day.

Knock, knock!

The chauffeur had returned.

"Are you ready?" he asked the two.

"Yes, definitely!" said Meg enthusiastically.

"Off we go then!" Meg's dad said as they got into the car.

"Can we go the long way round? It's such a short distance away." It had been the only downfall according to Meg, the fact that her mum and dad lived so close to the church, she could have walked it, but hardly appropriate in a wedding dress!

"Certainly! This is your day and you might as well enjoy this car while you can." The chauffeur had predicted this and had allowed plenty of time.

"Isn't it a beautiful day? Look at all the flowers!"

"It's perfect," her father responded. It was true, the weather hadn't been that great for weeks and had just perked up at the right time.

"I hope everyone turns up," Meg worried.

"No one is going to miss the wedding of the year, but I believe Hello magazine had to attend another wedding today so I'm afraid you won't be in there!"

"Ha, ha, very funny, Dad! I hope Matt didn't get Tim too drunk last night; I want him to enjoy the day as much as me."

"Have faith; he wouldn't do that to you."

"You know, I am a little worried about him; he hasn't really been himself lately."

"Probably just nerves," was the same response Meg received from her father.

"Probably. It's just that he has not been his usual self around me. We have hardly talked for the last week. He has seemed really cold and distant, not to mention the fact that I have hardly seen him; he's spent all his time with Matt."

"Don't worry, you are fretting about nothing. It's your wedding day, for goodness' sake; stop it!"

"I'm sorry. I guess I am just nervous."

"I can tell."

"How?"

"You're babbling!"

"Sorry," Meg replied, smiling a cheeky smile!

"Don't worry. Well, here we are and here is Matt to greet us."

"He should be in church."

Matt walked up to the car looking very sheepish and nervous.

David opened the door.

"What's happening?"

"Erm, erm, we have a bit of a hold-up, I'm afraid. Tim isn't here. Could you drive around for a minute?"

"What do you mean he isn't here? He was with you last night, wasn't he, he stayed over…?" Meg was very confused.

"No, where did you get that idea from?"

"He told me a couple of days ago, he was to spend the evening at his Mums and he was to stay over at your place."

"Nope, sorry, but don't worry. I am sure there is a logical explanation."

"Ok then, close the door and let's drive around again."

"Don't worry, miss, he'll be there when we return. At least it's a nice day and you are in this beautiful car." The chauffeur was doing his best to reassure the bride.

Meg wondered if he was used to this kind of thing.

"I don't want to be in the car! I want to be in the church, getting married! What on earth has happened to him, for goodness' sake?"

"Meg, dear, don't worry - everything will be ok. He's just been held up. Relax, will you?"

Her dad joined in the efforts to calm his daughter down, gently touching his daughter's hand.

After driving around in a circle for a few minutes, they were back at the church.

"Here we are again; talk about déjà vu!" This was the chauffeur's attempt at humour, a bad one at that.

"Matt's still here, that means he's not here."

"Erm, I don't know what to say, Meg, …" Matt was very apologetic but could offer no reassurance.

But then, a familiar face appeared at the church entrance, sharply spotted by Meg.

"He's there, he's there. Let's go!" she said, eager to get into the church.

"Easy, tiger, what is your rush?" her father asked, looking more than a little relieved to see his future son-in-law.

"Right, go on, you go into the church."

Matt followed her instructions and walked up to Tim.

"Where the hell have you been, Tim? You had us all worried. You look a mess; what on earth…? Oh, never mind; come in. We'd best get in or the bride will beat us to the altar." Matt did his best to tidy up his best friend.

Tim looked very worried but followed Matt into the church to huge sighs of relief from the waiting guests.

"Told you it was going to be alright, didn't I? Listen to your old dad!"

"You should trust your dad - he obviously knows what he is talking about. Now, don't move; I'll get the door," said the chauffeur, whose name was Alex.

David stepped out of the car as the chauffeur assisted Meg, her dress trailing far behind her.

Her dad took his position around the side of his daughter proudly, ready to walk her into the church to become Mrs Tim Dixon.

"Right, love, are you ready?"

"Certainly am!"

They smiled at each other.

"Let's go! Look, here are the bridesmaids," her dad said as the two girls walked to Meg to help rearrange her dress.

The wedding march played and everyone stood to await the arrival of Meg and her father. She took a deep breath and stopped her father from racing down the aisle. Her composure was perfect. She looked around at all her friends and family, and at the new family to her right. She even felt herself saying "Hi" to one of Tim's relatives, standing out due to the great height he carried!

As Meg's father stopped to present his daughter, he moved her veil back.

She smiled broadly at her future husband who looked visibly nervous.

They both looked at the vicar who instructed everyone to be seated.

"Good afternoon to everyone on this beautiful day! We will begin by singing the chosen hymn, a very popular choice, All Things Bright and Beautiful."

"He sounds like a DJ!" commented one of the guests

The organist began the hymn and everyone stood to sing.

"All things bright and beautiful, all creatures…" Again, they were all instructed to be seated once the hymn was complete.

"We have come together in the presence of God to witness the marriage of Timothy Dixon to Meg Alice Walker, to ask for his blessing on them, and to share in their joy…" the vicar continued with Meg still holding onto Tim's hand and beaming broadly. She could feel many pairs of eyes looking at the two of them, and at one point, heard…

"Doesn't she look beautiful?"

"Of course, she…"

"Shhh!" The women were instructed to be quiet.

"But first, I am required to ask anyone present who knows any reason why these persons may not lawfully marry to declare it now."

"Phew!" It was Meg; she always dreaded someone speaking up at this part!

"The vows you are about to take are to be made in the name of God, who is judge of all and who knows all the secrets of our heart: therefore, if either of you knows a reason why you may not lawfully marry, you must declare it now." The vicar paused for a second.

"Tim, will you take Meg…"

"Wait a minute, Meg, I'm sorry; I can't do this!" came the startling announcement from Tim.

Tim ran out of the church much to the shock of Meg and everyone else in the church.

Chapter 16

It was the day after the wedding that never took place and Meg was sitting, her tear-stained face down in the pillows. She looked at the two cases, ready and packed at the end of the bed, ready for the honeymoon which wasn't going to take place.

'I wonder where it was?' she thought. Meg was so annoyed and so upset. She knew she had to do something to release all her anger, but what good would it do, talking to Tim? Granted, it would definitely make her feel better, but would it achieve anything? Not really. She would have spoken to her mum, but thought it best not to upset her.

"I know!" she said to herself and retrieved her diary from beneath the mattress. Pen in hand, she began to write.

Well, here I am again; I knew I would be writing in this diary again. But not for this.

He couldn't go through with it, I got to the altar, so excited, I felt good, better than I have in a long time, to be honest, but then, it was my wedding day, so I suppose everyone feels good on their wedding day. All that and he couldn't do it. I suppose I should tell you the story properly.

I arrived at the church on time and he wasn't there. I should have known something was wrong, but being the naïve person that I am, I didn't. Actually, that's a lie - when he wasn't there, I did think, in the back of my mind, that he wasn't going to show. My fears were put to rest though; he did turn up and was whisked into the church to await my arrival!

147

That sounds a little OTT, doesn't it? Well, it's true, the biggest day of my life!

Anyway, I walked down the aisle with Dad, we sang the hymn but when the actual service started, Tim said he couldn't do it and raced out of the church, leaving me there, stunned, speechless and without a clue as to what had happened - another lie - actually, I knew his reasons, but never thought he would back out. I thought he would get used to it! Matt wasn't far behind him though, chased him outside he did!

Well, Dad apologized to everyone not really knowing what to say, but it was the strangest thing, not that I have ever been to a wedding where this sort of thing happens, but no one moved.

It was the longest time I have ever known, stood waiting for him, staring at Mum and Dad, who tried their best to console me, telling me that Matt would find him and everything would work out, there would be an explanation, and we would be married. My mum even said that Tim may be playing a joke on me and that he would return looking as handsome as ever with that mischievous smile... Ha, ha, very funny prank, I said to her, why would he do that to me...?

Eventually, Matt returned with Tim firmly in his grasp.

Here he was, being dragged back into the church, but for what? To continue with the service? To explain? I was soon to find out.

"Look, everyone," he said, "I'm really sorry to spoil everyone's day but I need to talk to Meg. The wedding is not going ahead, so if you would all be so kind as to leave us..."

Can you believe it? They all left! I wonder what they were all thinking? Did they have any clue why he did it? I think so, at least the ones who knew about the MS anyway; why would he marry a woman with such an unpredictable future? Ok one day, cripple the next, who knows what the day after that?

Would anyone blame him for leaving me? I doubt it; maybe his timing was a little off but I bet they are all talking about it in his defence.

Anyway, after all the guests had left the church, the beautiful flowers looking very lost at the end of the rows, the vicar, stunned, did leave us together alone. I don't think he was as forgiving; how does the line go? In sickness and in health? No, I don't think he will have been on Tim's side.

But who gives a flying… well, you know, who gives a damn what anyone thought of him? What matters is how I feel, isn't it? He couldn't marry me; what about my feelings? The man I have been in love with for almost 5 years going and leaving me because I'm not as healthy as he thought; but is that so bad? Who knows what could happen to him; get struck down with a deadly disease, or get hit by a car…with any luck. No, I don't mean that, or do I? Yeah, why not? He could have at least had the decency to tell me before the wedding day, to sit me down and tell me he couldn't go through with it, but no!

I can't remember his exact words, his reasons, excuses. He didn't mention the illness for a while actually! He said all the wedding preparations made him realize how much of a big step he was taking and that he didn't think he was ready. He realized that he didn't love me enough to stay with me for the rest of our lives, that he was too young to be stuck with (as he put it) one woman; was he trying to tell me that he had someone else? Rose from work, maybe? She'd had her eye on him ever since I can remember… No, let's not go down that path; we both know the truth. Well, anyway, he was too young for such a responsibility and then it came like a bolt of lightning striking, confirming exactly what I thought, I mean as if he hadn't upset me enough, telling me he didn't love me enough… That's a point - why the hell did he propose then? Didn't he think that through? But anyway, he had to make it worse.

"Sit down," he said, and after I followed his instructions, he continued, "I can't do it. It's not just the responsibility of the marriage itself, it's you, it's the… the… well, you know…"

"MULTIPLE SCLEROSIS, I think, are the words you are looking for! Can't you even say the bloody words? Do they scare you so much? Go on, say it!" God, I was so livid, I should have known after he struck out at me that this should have gone no further, but like I said at the time, I didn't ever think I would find anyone else, anyone who could take on the excess baggage. People with kids think they have a hard time finding someone, so what chance would I have?

"Ok, Meg!" he said "If it makes you happy, I will say it. The MS is the problem; you are the problem; I can't live with a cripple."

"But I might not be!" I protested.

"But you might be, it's likely, and nothing you can say can make me change my mind. I can't help the way I feel."

Well, I couldn't believe it!

"Should I be grateful for your honesty?" I asked him sarcastically.

"Well, I guess so."

"For Christ's sake, Tim, you are serious, aren't you? You expect me to be grateful that you told me you can't marry me, on my wedding day…?"

"It's better than living a lie," he had said.

Well, what else can I tell you? That's how it ended; oh, except for one thing…

As he left the church, leaving me heartbroken and shattered, he turned round and shouted my name. He smiled and said that he hoped we could still be friends.

"Yeah, right Tim, do me a favour?"

"What's that?" he asked.

"Drop dead!"

I still don't know for sure what everyone else thinks, but I

have my suspicions. His family and friends will be proud of
him for breaking it off. They agreed all along, if I am honest.
Ever since they found out that I had MS they have been
panicking, desperate for him to end the relationship, but I
thought he wasn't going to listen to them. I thought he loved
me enough to see past it, to care for me like any husband
should. The question is, if the roles were reversed, would I
have left him? The answer is simple -
Of course not…

Meg was about to write on but there was a knock at the door.

It was Matt.

"Oh, what do you want?" she said, Matt wasn't exactly her favourite person at the moment. He had, after all, seemed to be on Tim's side throughout all of this. Surely, he must have known about Tim's doubts…

"Just to give you these." Matt handed an envelope to Meg.

"What is it?" Meg was puzzled.

"Open it." Meg did as instructed, only to find 2 tickets to Mexico. She looked even more puzzled.

"It was your honeymoon. I sneaked the tickets out of Tim's pockets. I have spoken to Jenny and the travel agent…"

"What has Jenny got to do with it?"

"She is going with you, as you can see, the ticket is still in Tim's name but the travel agent said the tickets would be ready for you at the airport. I explained everything to her. She was very understanding. I guess this kind of thing happens…and well, you are going on holiday. I know this isn't how it was planned, but I thought with everything that has happened…well, you could do with a holiday!"

"Matt, I don't know what to say!" All kinds of thoughts were going through her mind…about Tim, about why, where was he…?

As if Matt could sense this, he spoke;

"Now, I don't even want you to think about Tim, ok? We can talk about all this when you get back, but according to these tickets, your flight leaves tomorrow lunchtime; the taxi is booked, thanks to Tim! So, get yourself ready. I presume you are already packed?"

"Well, yes, I was just thinking about the case actually, how it wasn't going to get used…"

Meg started to get upset about everything.

"Now, now, all this can wait until you get back. Jenny knows I am here; she is going to ring you any…"

As if on cue, the phone rang.

"That will be her now. I'm off!"

"But Matt, I…"

"Bye!" and with that, he was gone. Meg went to answer the phone. As Matt had expected, it was Jenny.

"Hi, Meg, has Matt been?"

"Yes, but I don't understand."

"There is nothing to understand; we are going on your honeymoon."

"But Jenny, I don't think I can."

"Of course you can! It's just what you need."

"That's what Matt said."

"Well, he talks a lot of sense; you know he really cares about you?"

"Yeah, I know, he's a great guy."

"Yeah, he is. Now. I am packed, so I thought I would stay over at your house tonight, and then we are ready, ok?"

"Well…"

"That's settled then; see you later!"

Within an hour or two, Jenny had arrived at Meg's house, suitcase and bottle of wine in hand.

"I don't know what I am supposed to think about all of this…" Meg looked at her friend, puzzled. She let Jenny into the house and helped her with her case.

"That's your trouble, you think too much. Don't think at all, just look forward to your holiday… I mean, our holiday!"

Meg had to admit that this was probably true so she just shrugged her shoulders and got a couple of wine glasses.

The following morning, the two friends were out of their beds and dressed in plenty of time. The taxi arrived for them promptly and took them to the airport. As promised, the altered tickets were ready for them. They checked in and went to the departure lounge.

The flight seemed a particularly long one, but Tim's final wedding surprise had been first-class tickets. The seats were very spacious and comfortable. Even the food was delicious and Meg was not prone to enjoying aeroplane food. They had all been well looked after. Fruit and chocolate, not to mention all drinks, were being handed round all the time. Meg thought it a little strange that Tim seemed to have gone to all this time and effort to organize such a perfect honeymoon, only to have backed out of the wedding. As if Jenny had read her mind, she spoke.

"His loss!"

"Yeah, I know, but…" Meg's face appeared sad, but before she had the time to get upset or say anything, Jenny again spoke, raising her hand in the air.

"Hey, don't do that," she ordered. "We are here, we are going to have a great time…"

"But…"

"But nothing! Let's see a smile on that pretty face. It looks to have taken you hours to get ready! We are going to have a fantastic time."

Meg did as she was ordered and smiled. Her eyes sparkled. Then she realized what her friend had said.

"Hey, cheeky, what do you mean it must have taken hours?"

Jenny just smiled at her. The comment had the desired effect. Her mind had changed direction instantly. Meg did have to admit that she did look good. She was wearing one of her favourite dresses with a bolero jacket. The outfit suited her perfectly. Her make-up was lovely. Meg had always prided herself on her appearance and knew exactly how to enhance her striking features.

"Are we nearly there yet?" Jenny groaned a short while later, sounding just like Meg herself as a child going on a day trip with her parents.

"I don't think so; we only set off a couple of hours ago!" But as they stepped off the plane a few hours later, to have the beautiful warm sun on their faces was simply wonderful. They arrived at their hotel after a short bus ride. The scenery was breathtaking. The sea looked more than inviting. Meg stood for a second to take it all in.

"Jenny, you have got to see this!" she shouted to her friend.

The view was magnificent. The sea started as a pale turquoise, and then there was a sharp change of colour to a deep blue, with the sun shining and sparkling on it.

"Wow!" Jenny exclaimed.

Meg looked at Jenny, not the companion who should have accompanied Meg on this, her honeymoon, but nevertheless, a great friend. Meg knew, deep down, that she would have a great time; well, she would certainly do her best.

"I knew the beach would be too far away to walk!" Meg joked, looking the short distance they were from the sea.

"I know; miles away, isn't it?"

Naturally, as this was meant to be a honeymoon, the bed was a four-poster king-size one. Meg, catching sight of this, said to Jenny, "I hope you don't snore!"

"Ha! Likewise! This is going to be like when I used to sleep over at your house."

"Only we'll have a little more room!" Meg laughed looking at the size of the bed.

Meg wandered around the room to see what there was.

"Meg, come on, let's go for a walk around this dump!"

"Coming!" The two got changed into something more suitable and were off.

Meg and Jenny took a stroll around the resort. Everything they could have possibly wished for was there. The water sports were fantastic. They sat on the beach and watched the scuba diving lesson that was taking place. There were also people playing volleyball and windsurfing.

"This would be so perfect for…" Jenny, realizing what she was about to say, stopped herself short.

Meg obviously knew what she was going to say.

"Yeah, it would have been."

"Oh, Meg, I am sorry. I didn't mean to upset you."

"You didn't; I plan on having a really good time here. It's like everybody said, and I need this."

"Yes, you do!" Jenny patted her friend gently on her leg. "We will have a great time. I believe we get a scuba lesson too!"

"Great!" Meg really did want to try and have a good time, but nothing could take away the fact that this was supposed to be the happiest time of her life, spent with her husband.

Meg and Jenny discovered a buffet restaurant, a Chinese one, a steak house and naturally, a Mexican restaurant.

The complex was huge, with tourist-type shops, several beautiful boutiques, four swimming pools and a golf course, not to mention a few bars dotted around.

After about an hour of wandering around and getting acquainted with the hotel, Meg and Jenny were ready to eat. They went to their room, showered and dressed for dinner. They opted for the Mexican. The staff at the restaurant were incredibly friendly, particularly liking the fact that Jenny spoke fluent Spanish.

"Show off!" Meg said enviously; she couldn't speak a word!

Jenny, pretending to look hurt, defended herself.

"No, I'm not, I learned how to speak Spanish so what is the point of not using it here?"

"I am only jealous." Meg smiled.

After they had chosen from the huge range the buffet had to offer, they ate their meals and were delighted at how delicious it all tasted. The restaurant was tastefully decorated in authentic Mexican style. The tablecloths looked like Mexican rugs. There was a large sombrero adorning the central buffet display of main courses, and there were displays of sweets and starters to the left and right of that.

After finishing a small pastry, Meg said, "Well, I think we need to walk off all that food!"

"Hmm, I just might have to have another one of those delicious desserts!" Jenny said. Seeing Meg's eyebrows rise at the comment, she continued, "Besides, after all the food you have eaten, I think you should let it settle a bit before you do any walking. I'll be surprised if you can stand up!"

Meg chose to ignore the comment.

After Jenny had eaten more pastries, they left the restaurant holding their stomachs!

Jenny turned to Meg, grinning.

"What are you looking at?"

"I just think you look really well."

"Considering everything, you mean?"

"No, sorry, I didn't mean it to sound like that; I meant you look good in that outfit."

"Oh, thanks, you think so?"

"Stop searching for compliments! You know you do; you look good in everything. You'd probably look good in a bin bag!"

"Well, thanks, you don't scrub up too bad yourself!"

They walked along the path towards the sound of the live music. The path led them to a large theatre-style room with a stage and dance floor to the front and a bar to the rear. They looked around for two available seats and were surprised to find some near the stage. A young man was singing a Billy Joel number, accompanied by a small band. Meg thought he was very good. As soon as they sat down, a waitress came over to take their order. They sat happily chatting, listening to the songs and sipping their drinks. However, before long, they were both exhausted. They walked back to their hotel room and were asleep within a quarter of an hour.

The next morning, they both awoke surprisingly early and, after dressing for the beach, they went for breakfast. The welcome meeting followed, where they were told about the various excursions available. Meg and Jenny both agreed that they had everything they needed right here in the complex. The only thing that really appealed to either of them was the dolphin discovery. They booked it immediately. Before too much longer, though long enough, Meg thought, the meeting was over. She didn't want to waste this beautiful day listening to the rep raving on and on! They were relaxed on the beach.

Meg was surprised at how much she enjoyed herself considering the arduous time she had endured beforehand. The dolphin trip had been towards the end of the holiday and was a perfect finish. The dolphins seemed to be so happy, swimming around in the enclosure. They spent over an hour playing with them and being pushed through the water, holding up poles for them to jump over. But the highlight had been the kiss she was given by one of them! Both the girls had bought all the photographs possible; they knew they would never forget the experience but the photographs just captured the magic of their experience.

All too soon it was time for them to return home. The flight had seemed even longer than before, presumably because they didn't have it all to look forward to.

Meg sat back in the luxurious leather seats and drifted away, remembering the great time they had spent, but then thinking with the greatest of respect to her friend, how much better it would have been if it had been spent with the man she was supposed to be married to. As she was beginning to get upset about it all, Jenny brought her from her reverie.

"Nearly home, unfortunately!" she said.

"Are we?"

"Hmmm."

They were greeted by the taxi driver at the airport after waiting around for their cases, seeing the same green case go by over and over again before noticing a burly man racing towards it!

"Good time?" he asked, seeing their brown smiling faces.

"Definitely!"

"Best honeymoon I ever had!" Meg found the strength to jest.

"Great!"

The taxi driver was very friendly with the two of them and seemed very interested to hear about everything they had done on their holiday.

Within the hour, they were home and after the taxi driver had helped them with their luggage, he was gone.

Meg was alone in the house. Even though she had enjoyed her time with Jenny in Mexico, she felt alone. The house was empty and Tim wasn't going to appear through the door after work. He wasn't going to throw his coat over the sofa and leave his shoes in the middle of the kitchen floor. He wasn't going to climb the stairs and go in the shower, expecting his tea to be ready when he had finished. No, it was safe to say she was on her own in the house. She didn't even have Madison for company. The cat had spent the two weeks at Evie's house and was going to remain there until Meg collected her the following day.

Chapter 17

After Meg had unpacked and made a start on the washing, she telephoned her mum to say she was home.

"Hi, Mum, it's me!"

"Hi, how was Mexico? Did you have a good time?"

"Great, thanks. How has everything been here?"

Meg's mum was reluctant to respond so Meg didn't press the issue. Instead, she told her about the holiday and decided to phone Sarah to ask her what had been going on.

"Ah well, now, there is a story…" Sarah began. She went on to tell her that the party had gone ahead, whilst Meg went home with her mum.

"I offered to come home with you but your mum said it was probably best if you were left alone."

"She was probably right. I don't think I could have coped with anyone else there. I was humiliated enough without having someone else watch over me whilst I cry about an arsehole who wasn't worth it!"

"Anyway," Sarah continued, "Tim's father said there was no point in all the money and food going to waste so everyone might as well go and enjoy themselves!"

"What? I don't believe it! I wonder what would have happened if my father had paid for the lot, as tradition would dictate? Well, he didn't, it was a joint effort but I still think he had a cheek! Well, like father, like son! I don't think he had the right to say that; how could everyone enjoy themselves knowing the whole occasion was just a farce?"

Sarah let Meg get all of the pent-up anger out and then continued to tell her that everything was going as well as was possible until Tim turned up.

"Can you believe it? The nerve! Well, after everything else that he's done, no, I don't suppose it's so much of a surprise. Anyway, he walks into the reception area as bold as brass, closely followed by the faithful puppy himself, Matt…"

Meg still didn't know what to think of him. He was supposed to be Tim's best friend but Meg thought he was a good friend of hers too.

'But how could he be, after sticking by Tim after all he's done to me,' Meg thought. However, Sarah continued to say he had gone under protest and was trying to convince Tim that going to the do was not a good idea. Sarah told Meg that there was a lot of whispering going on and that naturally, Tim was oblivious to all the dirty looks from Meg's side of the family.

'But hey,' Meg thought, 'who are they to criticize? If they had so much sympathy for me and hated him as much as their looks suggested, what were they doing at the party?' But apparently, Tim even attempted to defend himself asking people what they would do, and then saying they have no idea how he feels. Matt turned round and said, "What about Meg's feelings, eh? How do you think she feels?"

"Who gives a damn? I've done her a favour, really."

Sarah told Meg that must have been the straw that broke the camel's back, as Matt punched him!

"Ha! I should think so too! Good on you, Matt, thanks, mate!" Meg said, starting to enjoy herself.

"That was the end of the party," Sarah concluded.

"What a shame!" Meg added.

Matt came round to apologize the following day for not being there for Meg, and not trying to warn her that something was wrong.

"How is he?" Meg had to ask.

"Absolutely terrible. He is feeling so guilty - he knows what he's done to you is inconceivable. I think he has finally realized what a tosser he really is! I don't think he dared go back to the house in case you were waiting for him to give him a piece of your mind. He rang me to see if I knew where you were."

"And?"

"I asked him, where should you be now?"

"What did he say?"

"Not a lot - he said he did wonder what had happened to the tickets. I don't suppose he could blame you. I think everyone and their mother has rung him to tell him what they think of him, and get this, even his father had a right go at him."

"Never!" Meg couldn't believe that.

"Oh, yes. He wasn't livid about the wedding being called off but he said his timing reeked worse than his socks."

"Why was that? Because he'd shelled out on a couple of suits, that didn't seem to amuse him?"

"Meg, I'm serious. He was furious with him. He came to see me to tell me."

"And I suppose you put him up for a few days?"

"Well, no, actually, I sent him away with his tail firmly between his legs; remember, I was the one who flattened him. I don't think he expected me to be sympathetic, I think he was just very hopeful."

The following day, Meg went to visit her mum and when she returned, she was amazed at what was waiting for her.

Flowers - they absolutely filled the room and smelled beautiful; there was every variety, but mainly lilies, as he always knew they were her favourites!

There was a card. It simply read "Sorry".

There was a box next to the card, and when Meg opened it, she found it contained the most stunning diamond bracelet that she had ever seen.

Then the phone rang and it was him. He sounded so lost and sorrowful, telling her how much he regretted what he had done to her. He said he was sorry and that he wanted to take Meg out to dinner to at least go some way towards making up for his terrible deed.

"Now? But I have nothing to wear - I've just got back from OUR honeymoon!"

He'd even thought of that, by telling Meg if she went upstairs there was something suitable to wear.

It was a dress Meg had seen in a shop window some months ago but thought it was way too expensive. She couldn't believe he had remembered; "Is he back to his old self?" she wondered.

Meg took her time to get ready; she wanted to look really good, to make him see what he was missing out on if nothing else. He picked her up a short while later.

Although he looked a little tired and weary, he still had that gorgeous look about him, his eyes twinkling.

The two hardly said a word to each other on the way to the restaurant. Incidentally, it was the same one where he had proposed. They both sat down and ordered the meal.

Tim made a very emotional speech to Meg at dinner, saying how he could never forgive himself for what he had done to Meg, so he hardly expected Meg to forgive him. He went on to say he really wanted to try. He said he would do anything for Meg. Seeing the look in her eyes, he looked as if he thought he had worked his charm and that Meg might forgive him. He noticed the faltering in Meg's voice when she thanked the waiter who brought the meal. Tim smiled at Meg with those beautiful eyes she had fallen in love with all that time ago.

He apologized once more, telling Meg how terrible he felt, and that he couldn't live without Meg.

She was melting at the look in his eyes.

He knelt down on one knee and, after apologizing one more time, he asked Meg again to marry him. He begged and pleaded with her telling her that although he had been so terrible, he knew that she still loved him deep down. He looked like a little lost boy and Meg was overwhelmed.

She smiled at him and stood up.

"Tim…" she began.

"Yes, baby?"

"Fuck off! I could never forgive you, let alone be stupid enough to be jilted at the altar again!"

She realized she had spoken a little too loudly when other restaurant guests all became quiet and looked at her.

"Goodbye, Tim." Meg walked out of the room.

Chapter 18

Although Meg was very proud of her reactions towards Tim and his proposal of marriage, yet again, she was still incredibly upset with the separation. That evening, Meg struggled to sleep, voices in her head going through the days' events, wondering if she could or should have arrived at a different decision. When she eventually did get to sleep, she was awoken a few short hours later by a storm that was brewing outside. The rain was tapping at the window like some angry neighbour trying to get into her room… The wind was battling against it as if trying to stop this from happening. The wind and rain seemed to be engaging in a boxing match, coming to blows with each other. The rain was tapping furiously on the window, followed by the wind howling through the trees and around the house. Suddenly, the storm stopped and there was an eerie silence. Meg shuffled back feeling unnerved. She was hoping to find Tim's perfect torso to touch and hold. She wanted to reach out and place his arm around her for comfort, to protect her from the storm. She needed reassurance, but of course, Tim's body was not there. Instead, a big empty space filled his side of the bed. Meg lay there and cried.

It had now been several weeks since their meal at the restaurant and her outburst; in fact, it was 3 weeks and 5 days. She knew perfectly well exactly how long it had been. She couldn't believe that after 5 years of them being together, it had ended so bitterly and within a matter of weeks.

Speaking about it to Jenny on numerous occasions seemed to help. At one point, she even apologized as she felt she spoke of nothing else.

"Don't be silly; that's what friends are for," her friend had reassured her.

She decided that no matter how distressed she was, she would start all over again, go back to work a new person and forget the past and the flashbacks. Autumn was here and the weather was beautiful. The colours around her were stunning. Browns and golds, reds and yellows filled the scenery like a warm, patchwork blanket. The leaves were falling from the trees. Yes, now was the perfect time. She would start with her hair. Since long before she had met Tim, she had wanted to cut her hair, but after he had told her how much he loved her long red locks, she had reluctantly agreed to grow it further. Now, with all that behind her, she could do exactly what she wanted. Maybe even a tattoo, something like the one that nurse had.

"What do you think, Madison?" she asked the cat, who just purred around her ankles.

"Fat lot of use you are!" She was a little unsure so she called Jenny for her opinion.

"Hi, Jenny, it's Meg. How are you doing?"

"Ok, but more to the point, how are you? Feeling better now after getting rid of that, well, you know…?"

"I'm getting there. I can't deny that I am upset about the whole thing though."

"You've got to be; you've been together for a while. It takes time to get over something like that, but you did the right thing and I am really proud of you. I sound like my mum, but you know what I mean?"

"Yeah, of course. Thanks, Jen, but I didn't actually call to talk about that prat; I am trying not to think about him."

"In that case, what can I do you for?"

"I want your advice…"

"I'm listening," came the inquisitive response.

"I want a new image - a whole new image, and I thought I would start with my hair. I have been wanting to go short for a while now so I thought now was my perfect opportunity. What do you think?"

"You mean, should you get all that beautiful, thick, shiny long hair all cut off…?"

Meg was at work, everything seemingly back to normal. The job was going well and she was feeling better than she had felt in a long time. The office was buzzing with activity and everyone was very busy. Meg hadn't really talked much about her recent misfortunes with the wedding and none of the new staff really knew a lot about her. That was how she liked it to be. There was nothing worse than people knowing what was wrong with her and not knowing how to react towards her, either because of Tim or the MS. Thoughts of Tim were not really in her mind though; she had recovered surprisingly well from the whole ordeal. She knew that people would be talking about her but she didn't really care.

She had discussed her illness with Anita who had decided to find out more about it for herself. Meg had leaflets, some of which were recommended to be shown to employers, but Meg would rather leave that up to Anita. She didn't want to ram the whole thing down her throat but she was prepared to answer any questions she might have about it all. The last thing she wanted to do was to make excuses for herself, should anything be going wrong with her job.

It would be easy to blame the MS and take it easy, taking a few days off here and there, but Meg was not that sort of person.

Anita seemed to respect that about her. It was fair to say that her working relationship couldn't have been any better.

What Meg didn't know was that people who didn't really understand about the illness seemed to talk more about it.

That lunchtime, a group of young girls who had recently joined the company were sitting in the works' refectory, chatting. It was a large room situated on the top floor of the building. Tables and chairs were scattered around the room with a drinks machine at the far left and a snack machine right next to it.

The girls had all been to the local sandwich shop to buy their salads and wraps. After chatting in detail about what a terrible morning they'd had, the conversation seemed to change. Sallie brought the discussion around to Meg.

"She was off again yesterday," she commented with her large mouth almost full of her sandwich. She was a rather large, obnoxious girl. When she ate, her cheeks mimicked that of a hamster storing food.

"So, what's wrong with her then?" Rebecca asked indignantly.

"She has ME or something," Sallie replied with no empathy whatsoever.

"I think it's MS," Grace, the newest of the recruits, commented with a timid voice. She pushed her thick, black glasses over her freckled nose.

"But what does that mean? She looks fine," Sallie questioned.

"I think she is fine most of the time, she just has 'off' days." Grace was trying to defend the training coordinator.

"Well, we all have our 'off' days." Rebecca's voice appeared irritated.

"That's what I think. I think it's just a technical term for hypochondriac." Sallie was equally exasperated with where the conversation was going.

Grace, not knowing anything about Meg and the illness, spoke up; "I've never heard her complaining… maybe she is sick."

"Does she look sick to you?" Rebecca asked the attractive new recruit.

"No, but I don't think you are being very fair; has anyone ever asked her about it? Do any of you even care?" Grace was totally offended by all the girls talking about Meg in this manner.

"Who rattled your cage, new girl? Who asked for your opinion?" Sallie spat her words at Grace.

Grace walked away, leaving the rest of the girls discussing poor Meg's condition.

She decided to do something about it, taking the whole affair very personally. She went to see Anita to ask her opinion.

"You could always talk to Meg yourself, you know," Anita offered.

"I don't know if I could. She may think I am being nosey."

"I doubt it. She finds it difficult talking to people when she doesn't know if they are interested. She wants to carry on as normal but knows it is not always possible, so she needs for people to understand. Talk to her!"

Grace decided that it was probably a good idea and went home thinking about how she should approach Meg.

The following day, whilst Meg was sitting at her desk, sorting out her training sheets, the young woman approached her.

"Meg?"

"Hi, Grace, what can it do for you?"

"Could I have a word with you?"

Anita, sitting opposite Meg, smiled.

"Sure! Here, or in private?" Meg was puzzled but more than happy to help Grace.

Anita chirped in, obviously knowing what the conversation would be about.

"Go into meeting room 3, if you like; it's free."

"Ok, thanks, Anita." Meg led the new recruit into the meeting room.

"Right, how can I help?" Meg asked warmly.

"It's about you, actually," Grace replied sheepishly.

"Oh?"

"Yes. A few of the girls were talking about you at lunch, about, you know, your…"

"The MS or the wedding?" Meg was annoyed at having been talked about.

"Wedding?" Grace was very confused. Fortunately, that was one piece of news that hadn't been the idle gossip of everyone.

"Oh, the MS then, what about it?"

"Well, I didn't really like what everyone was saying about you so I thought it would be better to ask you about it. Well, Anita suggested it, actually."

"I see."

Meg went on to explain the illness to Grace, how hopefully, a lot of the time she would be fine but then sometimes, she would get very tired.

"Is that all it is, being tired?"

"No, not really, it is fatigue. It's a different thing entirely. I get tired after doing the smallest of things and can't always do what I want, like walk in a straight line. There are many sides to the MS but I am hoping that it won't flare up much."

The two discussed everything in detail and both were very glad of the other one's attitude.

"I think people just get scared because it sounds so bad, they just would rather not know about it; ignore it."

"More fool them!" said Grace.

"Yeah, I guess so, but I can't get everyone to understand it. People have their own problems and trying to get them to understand all about my illness is like flogging a dead horse. I just don't have the energy to do that."

"Well, I think I understand. I am glad you talked to me, and the next time I see you wandering around the office, I won't think you have been drinking!"

"Oh good! That means I can probably get away with drinking a bit!"

Grace and Meg smiled at each other and left the room.

"If you want, I can talk to the others about you."

"No, don't worry about it; it's their problem if they don't understand. I have more important things to worry about."

"Ok, then!" Grace smiled at Meg. "Thanks again!"

"No problem."

Meg went back to her desk and continued with her work, glad that she had just had the talk with Grace.

"Everything ok?" Anita asked.

"Yeah, fine; thanks, Anita."

Anita just smiled and returned to her computer.

The next few days went without incident. The only thing Meg noticed was how tired she was after getting home from work, even falling asleep in Jenny's car and having to be woken to be told she was home.

A few days later, Matt called to see how she was feeling.

"Never better!"

"What about Tim?"

"Who?"

"Ahh, I see. Well, that's good. I wondered if you would like to go out sometime, maybe tomorrow, for a bite to eat? I don't seem to see you these days."

"Ok, fine, what time and where?"

"8 pm at the old Halfway House?"

"Fine!"

"I'll pick you up."

"Ok, bye, Matt."

Throughout the next day, Meg couldn't help but wonder if there might be more to this than met the eye. It wouldn't be such a bad thing; Matt was a great bloke and they did get on well with each other. He was on her side throughout most of her troubles with Tim. Taking all this into account, she took extra special care when getting ready.

"I hope he likes my new haircut," she wondered.

Matt was true to his word and arrived on her doorstep at 7.30, with a bouquet of flowers.

"Oh, they are beautiful!"

"So are you! I like the hair."

Meg blushed. "Are you sure?" she asked, toying with her short locks. "I know it's a bit drastic!"

"You look fantastic!"

"Well, thanks; are we ready?"

"Certainly are!"

Matt was his usual chatty self with Meg on the way to the pub, but Meg felt strangely nervous, wondering what might happen between them and whether it would be the right thing to do... would he make a move? If so, when? She felt like a teenager on her first date.

Maybe she should make the first move, let him know that she was interested.

"Hello, where are you?"

"Sorry, miles away. Are we here already?"

"Yep!"

They got out of the car and walked into the pub, where Matt bought the drinks and led Meg to the table.

The meal was delicious and the two seemed to chat quite happily about this and that and nothing in particular. Once again, Tim's name never came up.

When Matt drove Meg home, she was deciding whether or not to kiss him when she got to her door.

The moment arrived when Matt pulled up and got out of the car to walk Meg to the door.

'To hell with it,' she thought and leaned over to kiss Matt.

He looked horrified and stepped back.

"What is it? Have I done something wrong?" Meg was rather embarrassed.

"Oh, God, Meg, I am so sorry. I thought you knew."

"Knew what…?"

"I think we had better go inside," Matt responded furtively. Meg had an idea what Matt was about to tell her but just walked into the house and led him into the lounge. After a few moments of uncomfortable silence, Matt spoke.

"I am really sorry; I thought you knew."

"Matt, are you trying to tell me that you are… that you are…?"

"Gay? Yes, that is exactly what I am trying to tell you."

Meg was amazed.

"All this time we have known each other, and you never told me!"

"Yeah, well, I guess I assumed you knew. Stupid, I guess."

"Yeah, very; how the hell am I supposed to know unless you tell me?"

"I am sorry; maybe I thought Tim would tell you."

"Tim? So, he knows? Oh God, you and Tim, you aren't t…?"

"No! No! No! Calm down; Tim is, or should I say was, a very close friend. He has always known."

Meg was looking more confused than ever.

"Maybe I should start from the beginning; are you really shocked? Have I put myself in your bad books?"

Meg just laughed.

"Of course not; I am just surprised. I can't believe I didn't know."

Matt took a deep breath.

"Well, like most people who are gay, I always knew I was different. I guess the best time was when I realised what it was that made me different; the day I realized I was gay."

"Do your parents know?"

"Sure, they are great about it. In fact, it wouldn't surprise me if they knew about it before I did!"

"Well, I don't know what to say!"

"I am sorry."

"You have no reason to be sorry, but like I said, I am just surprised," Meg walked over to sit with Matt and put her arm around him.

"I am really glad you told me, I just wish you had done it earlier," she said, gently pushing him, smiling.

"You really don't mind?"

"Why should I mind?"

"I am so glad you have taken it like this. I guess I have held it back because I didn't want to lose you as my friend."

Meg just laughed.

"What are you laughing at?"

"I just spent forever getting ready. I thought I was in there!"

"You look great! You would have certainly been in with a great chance, but you are not my type!"

The two sat, arm in arm, laughing. They talked for hours, and it was the early hours of the morning before Matt left.

"Fancy going shopping at the weekend?" Meg said with a wry smile as Matt walked out of the door.

"Was that an anti-gay, stereotypical comment?" Matt asked.

"Me? Never!" Meg said with a wink.

"Ok, well, I am off," Matt said. Meg followed him as he walked to his car. As the engine started, the window was wound down.

"So, shall I pick you up at 11 then?"

Meg looked puzzled. "What for?"

"Shopping, of course!" And with that, Matt sped off leaving Meg laughing.

Meg didn't tell her recent revelation to anyone, not even her best friend. She didn't think it was her place to do so. If Matt had wanted anyone else to know, surely, he would have told him or her himself...

Chapter 19

The following morning, the sun was shining brilliantly through Meg's curtains. Meg awoke dazed and confused after the previous day's events, wondering why Matt hadn't shared his secrets with her. Did he really think so little of her that she would think any less of him after telling her? Ah well, there were much more important things to worry about at the moment, like how to sort out the details of the house. How would they sort it all out? Would she be able to afford to pay the mortgage on her own? What about giving Tim his half of the deposit? Maybe he would be generous, bearing in mind what had happened. She would certainly have to take measures to get a solicitor, or at the very least, arrange a meeting with Tim. Meg got dressed quickly and walked downstairs to the kitchen, which she had loved so much. Upon looking in the cupboards and bread bin, she realized that she couldn't have done any shopping for a while. Meg opened the fridge and took out a carton of milk. She took off the lid and stuck her nose into the carton.

"Yuk!" she exclaimed, and she decided to go out for breakfast. She grabbed the car keys and drove to the café that was situated a few miles away. She was quite happy to be dining alone and greeted the cafe owner with a smile. The aroma of bread and coffee hit her senses.

"Do you have freshly baked bread?"

"Of course, madam; croissant or bagel?"

"One of each, I think," Meg replied hungrily.

The café owner smiled and wrote down her order.

"Coffee with that?"

"Yes, a large one, please."

The owner disappeared around the corner to the kitchen.

Meg looked at her surroundings. Someone had once recommended the café to her and she could see why. It was nicely furnished with lemon walls and beautiful crockery along the shelves. Meg spotted the magazine rack. She grabbed the magazine that looked the most interesting. Meg sat with the magazine admiring her atmosphere.

The café was quite busy with many of the tables full of young people; friends meeting up for breakfast, chatting away about their week. A few moments later, the owner approached with the breakfast. Steaming hot coffee, accompanied by a bagel and croissants with homemade raspberry jam and cream.

"Thank you," Meg said. "This looks delicious!"

"You are very welcome; just shout if you want anything!" The owner smiled and disappeared around the counter.

A short while later, Meg was tucking into the homemade baking and sipped her coffee.

She decided that now would be as good a time as any to write down a few ideas. She got out her notepad and pen and began to write.

TIM: Need to talk to him and sort something out. See if he will come to a reasonable agreement - have some money set aside, think I can buy him out, just a case of how much he would want.

Meg turned over the page and made a note of all her outgoings and incomings. Her rise for the promotion had been good enough. Meg was sure that somehow, she would be able to manage. She was certain she would rather do without a few things if it meant holding onto this house that she had so loved from the minute she set eyes on it. She had worked far too much on making the house into a home.

When Meg was clear of everything in her mind, she took a sip of coffee and picked up her mobile phone and called Tim.

"Hello?"

"Tim, it's me, Meg."

"Oh, hello."

"We need to talk."

"About what? Decided to give us another go?" Meg laughed out loud.

"No, I didn't think so, so what do you want to talk about?"

"The house."

"Oh?"

"I don't want to talk about it over the phone."

"Ok, well, I am free now; shall I come over?"

"Well, I am just at that café on Madison Street, but I am nearly finished. I'll meet you at the house in about an hour, is that ok?"

"Sure, whatever." Tim was rather despondent. Meg knew he wouldn't be looking forward to the conversation which would follow, but nevertheless, she didn't really care. It had to be done. They had hardly spoken since the outburst. Tim had been reluctant, so anything he had to say he sent in the form of a message through Matt. Matt, seemingly not wanting to cause any friction, had just agreed to be the messenger. She finished her meal, paid her bill and thanked the owner. Meg seemed to stumble to her car and drove home. On the way, she passed a tattoo studio and something seemed to make her stop.

"Hmm," Meg said to herself. She wondered to herself about having one.

"Maybe not," she said and carried on driving.

Within a few moments, she was on her way home, feeling a little nervous but sure that the words would come to her when she needed them. She pulled up outside the house, admiring the garden once again. It had taken some time to plan it all and pick all the plants and flowers, but one look at the results proved beyond reasonable doubt that it had been well worth it. However, this had been something else that Tim hadn't been particularly interested in. He had, though, let her have her fun and design it all herself.

She walked into their kitchen and tidied around. The house wasn't in the best possible state; she had had far too much on her mind to be bothered about the housework. She picked up the cups from the worktop and ran the taps into the sink, washing everything up and wiping all the worktops. She walked through the dining room, which hadn't really been used all that much, so it looked tidy enough. The living room just needed a few cushions straightening out. Meg walked up the stairs and washed her face, walked into the bedroom and brushed her new short hairstyle.

A few moments later, there was a knock on the door. Meg looked out of her window and saw Tim's sports car parked outside.

She slowly walked down the stairs composing herself, letting him wait, looking awkward at the door.

"He is cheeky enough," Meg thought. "He won't wait, he'll just let himself in!" but when Meg arrived in the kitchen, she was surprised to find he was still waiting outside the door. Taking another look at her reflection in the mirror, she opened the door.

'Not bad,' she thought.

She went to answer the door to see a very surprised look on Tim's face.

"Wow!" he said.

"What?"

"Your hair; it's gone!"

"Yeah, well, I decided I wanted a change, and besides, I don't need to keep it the way YOU want it anymore," Meg said with a little sarcasm.

"Do you have to be like that?" he asked.

"No, I guess not; come in," Meg conceded.

Tim followed her into the living room and sat down.

"Do you want a drink?"

"No thanks," Tim replied.

"Right, then, I guess we'll get down to business."

Meg took a deep breath and began.

"Right, then, I want the house so I am prepared to give you my half of the deposit to buy it from you and…"

"Hold on! What if I don't want to sell? And what about everything else that's in the house?"

"What about everything you have done to me? Don't you think you owe me?"

"£10,000."

"What?"

"£10,000; you pay me £10,000 and we'll call it square."

"But the deposit was only £6,000, so that makes £3,000."

"I have put a lot of hard work and money into this house; it is just as much mine as it is yours."

"I don't believe you! After everything you have done to me, you still can't be reasonable."

"Reasonable? Were you being reasonable when you conned me into believing that everything was going to be ok with your illness? I have read up about it - you will be in a wheelchair by the time you are 30 and I would have no life. I would have spent my days looking after you."

Meg couldn't believe what she was hearing.

"Well, at least you got out of it; I am going to have to live with it for the rest of my life, not knowing if I will be in that wheelchair by the time I am 30."

"Still being dramatic as usual; nothing changes."

Meg was furious; she was more than furious. How could she have ever loved this man?

"Look, just get out!" she screamed. Thousands of emotions ran through her mind. She didn't expect him to be understanding about the house but this was really taking the biscuit. It wasn't enough that he had to humiliate her by hitting her and then leaving her at the altar. She had to be mad to have been at that church. But this, this…

Tim stood up, seemingly oblivious to what he had said to her. He seemed only too happy to oblige and go.

He looked at her and walked out of the door nonchalantly.

Meg watched him leave, his tall body walking awkwardly out of their house.

Should she call Jenny, or her mum, or neither? She had no idea what she should do at this point.

As if on cue, the phone rang.

"Hello?"

"Hi, Meg, it's me." The 'me' was Jenny.

"Hi."

"Are you ok? You don't sound too good."

"No, not really; I saw Tim."

"Oh, about the house?"

"Yes, it didn't go quite as expected, and I think that is an understatement really" Meg's voice was breaking as she was speaking.

"Give me 10; I will be there."

"Are you sure? I am sorry to be such a pain."

"Shut up and get the kettle on!"

Meg was already feeling a little better at having spoken to Jenny. It just seemed that all she had been doing lately was offloading all her problems onto her.

Within 15 minutes, Jenny was walking into Meg's house.

"Oh, Jenny, I am glad to see you. I am so sorry that you had to come here."

"Like I have loads better to do! Now, don't be stupid and just tell me what is going on."

They sat down in the room and Meg told Jenny the whole story. Meg watched the astounded look appearing on Jenny's face.

"Did I overreact?" she asked.

"Don't be stupid - he's the one who is overreacting! After everything you have been through, he dumps this on you. You know, you really don't need this crap; you know what stress does to you."

"Well, yeah, but..."

"But nothing; stress is one of the main attributes to bringing on an attack, you do know that don't you? What have all the doctors said about it? You really have to avoid stress!"

"How can anyone avoid stress? It is impossible!"

"You are avoiding the issue - what are you going to do about that arsehole?"

"I don't know, find the money. I guess..."

"Like hell, you will! You sit down and think about everything logically, and you work out a fair amount and offer him it, or tell him where to stick his offer."

Meg and Jenny sat talking for quite some time about plans of action, and about what exact words to use when telling Tim what Meg really thought about his plan.

Tim had left Meg earlier that evening, going straight to Matt's house.

Upon seeing Matt's inquisitive face, he just shook his head and walked upstairs.

'This wasn't supposed to happen like this,' he thought.

'I knew this conversation would be coming up soon, and I had it all planned out. I was going to be reasonable. I can't believe I acted so badly…'

A knock on the bedroom door broke Tim's train of thought.

"Well?" asked Matt, walking in the door.

"Well, I screwed up."

Tim explained everything to Matt, who sat amazed at how his so-called friend had acted.

"I really can't believe you! You are such a…"

"Don't tell me, I know."

"Well, if you know, why aren't you on the phone to her sorting this out?"

"I have blown it. I can't face her now."

"Yes, you can! Ring her up and apologize; meet up with her; sort it out, for Christ's sake, man!"

Tim knew Matt was right, he had to call her and sort out this mess, but not now.

Jenny left Meg a few hours later. Meg was at an all-time low. The only thing she could think to do was to ask her parents for the money. Although Jenny had spent the past few hours trying to convince her that Tim was being unreasonable, Meg really didn't have the energy to put up an argument. The easiest thing to do would be to just get hold of the money, and pay Tim out, be done with it.

She picked up the phone and dialled her parents' number.

"Hi, Mum, it's me. Can I come over tomorrow?"

"What sort of a question is that? You know you can come anytime!"

"I know, sorry, I meant are you in tomorrow?"

"Are you ok, honey? You don't sound too good."

"Yeah, I just need to speak to you."

"Ok, then."

"Well, I am tired so I'll see you tomorrow."

And with that, both women put down the phone.

Meg went up to bed wondering whether she would be able to sleep or not, with everything running through her mind.

The next morning, Meg was awoken bright and early yet again by the beautiful sunlight creeping through the curtains. She got out of bed, washing and dressing like a robot, not really thinking about anything she was doing.

By 10 am, Meg was pulling into her parents' drive and was surprised to see her father's car sitting there.

She walked into the house and was greeted immediately by her father.

"Hi, sweetheart, how are you feeling? Not overdoing things at work, are you? Are you coping alright in the house on your own? You are taking it easy, aren't you, I…"

"Slow down; I am fine, you don't need to worry."

"But you know you have to take it easy and help yourself as much as you can by not getting too stressed…"

"Dad, I am ok! My health is fine; don't fret!"

At that point, Evie walked into the room.

"Hi, love! How are you feeling?"

"Ok, really."

"Good! Are you taking good care of yourself?"

Meg's dad looked at his wife, smiling.

"I have been told off for nagging her so don't start or you will be in for it too!"

"Dad, I didn't mean to nag. It's just I can take care of myself, you know…"

Meg's father winked at her, making her realize he was only pulling her leg.

"We just worry about you, that's all."

Meg walked over to her father and gave him a big squeeze. She held onto him as tightly as she could and it was quite some time before she let go.

"Hey, don't squeeze all the life out of this poor old man!" he said to her.

"Sorry, Dad!"

"That's ok. Is there something troubling you, other than the obvious?"

Meg took the obvious as being her illness, which wasn't really bothering her at all.

"Someone, more like." Meg sat herself down on the suite and looked up at her parents, noting the intrigued look on both their faces.

"This someone wouldn't be a tall, nice-looking man who we don't really talk about anymore, would it?" It was her father who spoke.

The tone of his voice was evidence to Meg that he was still bitterly disappointed in what that particular young man had done to his daughter but then why would he be any other way?

"Could be," she said with a wry smile.

Evie and David sat down to listen to their daughter.

Meg began to explain that she wanted to buy Tim out of the house and stay on. She saw the nods and heard the occasional noises coming from her parents, knowing she had their full attention. Meg decided to skip out the details, which she knew would make them both despise him even more than they already did. Instead, she just got to the crucial point.

"The truth is, I can't afford to pay him what he is asking, so I wondered if I could borrow some money from you. I would get a loan to do it but it's just…"

"No need for you to explain; of course you can borrow some money. How much would you like?" Again, it was her father who uttered the words.

"£5,000 should easily cover what I need." Meg had saved a fair amount herself and, at that exact moment, was suddenly relieved that Tim and she hadn't opened a joint account. This was another one of her ideas which Tim had hastily rejected.

"No problem!" Evie joined in with her husband.

Meg was relieved that they didn't ask her exactly how much money was involved. She was only thankful that they were willing to help her.

"Where's Jack today?" she asked cheerfully to change the subject.

"Ah, now, there is a story," Evie said with a grin.

"Hmm?"

"He is out with Claire."

"And Claire would be...?"

"His girlfriend," Evie replied.

This news brought a smile to Meg's face; she was always worried that because Jack was so dedicated to his studies, he would have no time for a romantic interest, especially after the short romance with his last girlfriend had gone sour, presumably because of that dedication.

"Is she nice?" she asked her mum.

"She is very nice indeed!" replied Evie, grinning.

"Good enough for your little son?" Meg joked.

"No one will be good enough for my baby, just like no one is good enough for you, but she will do for now!"

Meg looked at her father bemused by her mum's attitude. Jack had always been spoiled by Evie; some would go so far as to say smothered, but there was always a special bond between mother and son. Just like there had always been a special bond between Meg and her father. These special connections raised a question in Meg's mind.

"Mum?"

"Yes, dear?"

"If I ask you something, will you be really honest with me?"

"Always - what is it?"

"If Jack was with someone who was really ill, you know, who had something really wrong with her..."

"I think I see where this is going!"

"Both of you, how would you be with her? Would you think that she was ruining Jack's life?"

Meg knew by the silence that she had probably asked a very difficult question, the answer to which was irrelevant considering the relationship with Tim was over.

"Never mind; don't answer that."

"You are a wonderful person, Meg. You will find someone who treats you the way you should be treated and his family will love you because you deserve to be loved just as much as anyone." Her father beamed at Meg.

"Sorry; guess I was just curious. I am not really looking for anyone anyway. I am happy just plodding along like this."

Meg could see the unconvinced look on her parents' faces.

She said no more about it and, having been invited, stayed for lunch with her parents.

Over the next few weeks, Meg's life seemed to be very much on the up. Work was in full swing, and Meg had been very busy. In fact, it was fair to say she had hardly noticed that there was anything wrong with her. The recent check-up at the doctors had confirmed that she was in remission. The course of steroids she'd had previously, although painful and uncomfortable, seemed to have done the trick. The doctor who had administered them had mentioned that it was no cure, but it should keep Meg's batteries charged for quite some time. She was glad this was the case and that they had done some good because it was not wise, she was told, to administer them at less than 6-monthly intervals. She had been very pleased to see that the various examinations she had been given had been easy. The doctor was very pleased with her condition at present. He had made no secret, though, of telling her she needed to slow down and take things a little easier. She had not seen the point though; there was nothing wrong with her so why should she take it easy?

The doctor himself, along with many of Meg's relations, had expressed concern with her that maybe she hadn't taken everything on board. She couldn't believe that the doctor had hinted, in a roundabout way, that maybe she was in denial.

"It's a very difficult thing to take on board. It's understandable that you are acting like this. Maybe you could come along to the support group that we have here at the hospital?"

"Why? I feel fine!" had been Meg's response. She didn't want to be with other people who would probably just moan on about how much of a bad day they had been having. She just wanted to get on with her life and didn't need to listen to other people telling her what her life was going to be like 10 years down the line. If the truth were known, she was frightened that she would see people in a really bad way, a way that she herself may be like in a while. No, she would stay away from the support group.

It was a Saturday morning and the alarm clock had just gone off.

"Am I sane?" she said to herself as she hit the clock to turn it off.

"Going to work on Saturday?"

It seemed to be a regular thing these days. Overtime. But the money was good and running the house on her own, she needed it. But Insurefirst was booming. What with the takeover and the new staff, the office had never been better.

She drove to work alone. Jenny enjoyed the job but she drew the line at weekends. However, Meg really didn't mind. There was nothing else going on in her life; her social life was really nonexistent. Her work was her life at the moment. She was one step away from being a workaholic.

"Anyway, I will be home by 2," said Meg in the midst of her thoughts, as if trying to justify to herself why she was working so much.

Meg was at work by 8 am and walked slowly to her desk, or at least, that's what she tried to do. Her desk was situated on the left of the large office, but Meg seemed to be veering to the right. The only things to the right of the office, besides a lot of filing cabinets and the stationery supply, was Rob. There were a few other desks scattered around that area of the office but only Rob was working at one of them. So, her only course of action as she wobbled even further to the right, was to talk to Rob.

"Morning," he said to her, and then in a somewhat quieter voice,

"Are you ok?"

"Yes, why?" Meg tried to act surprised at the question.

"Because you came to my desk and not your own. Was that by accident or design?"

"I just thought I'd say hi."

Rob raised his eyebrows at Meg.

"You know you can talk to me?"

Rob had always been a good friend to Meg. He was the comedian of the office, standing at 6 feet 4, towering above the majority of the rest of the staff. Meg had always liked him. He always had the ability to make her smile, however she felt.

"I don't know, Rob, I just didn't seem to be able to walk in a straight line."

"Try sitting down here with me for a second, and when you get up, don't stand up too quickly. Maybe you turned your head too quickly or something."

"How do you know so much?"

"I had a look in the local library."

Meg couldn't believe that he had taken the trouble to do something like that.

"We're not all like Trudy, you know."

Meg looked up at him.

"I know how she talks about you; it's not fair, but like I said, we are not all the same."

"I don't know what to say."

"You don't have to say anything but Anita is looking over here so you'd better get back to your desk. Do you think you can manage?"

"Yeah, I'll be ok. Thanks, Rob, you're a star."

"I know!"

Meg walked back to her workstation and was surprised to see that she did it with ease.

As she sat down, she felt warmed by Rob's comforting words. She knew that Trudy was not the only one to have been badmouthing her. She couldn't understand this though, but not to worry. As she thought time and again, she had more important things to worry about than what other people thought. What mattered was that the people who mattered to Meg did care. And that was that. Meg sat down to her work and before she knew it, it was 1 pm. She walked up to Rob and spoke.

"Thanks again."

"No problem; what are you up to now?"

"Just going home, I guess."

"Fancy a quick drink across the road before you go?"

"Sure, why not?"

The two walked across the road to the large country-looking public house that stood there.

Rob opened the large wooden doors to allow Meg to go through.

Meg walked in and straight to the bar.

"What are you drinking?" she immediately asked.

"If you are buying, I'll have a double whisky!"

"Yeah, right, and the police will be happy to see you on your way home!"

"I'll just have a Coke, in that case."

Meg bought the drinks and they walked to the large oak table which was situated near the window of the pub. They overlooked the beautifully maintained garden.

"Nice place this; I like it," Meg said. It was the place most of Insurefirst went at lunchtimes for a quick drink or lunch. The large room contained a huge fireplace, which, naturally, was lit at this cold time, and all the tables were a beautiful oak with huge high-backed chairs and buffets. The pub was decorated with the usual brass ornaments, which furnished most pubs of this genre.

"So, how come you never talk about it then…the MS?"

"I just don't see the point. I'm not a moaner, I just like to get on with my life."

"Well, I think maybe people would be a little more understanding with you if you talked about it."

"I don't really care what people think of me," she lied.

"I see, well, I guess there is no point in trying to change your mind then?"

"No, not really. I think it will only make it worse if I started moaning every time something went wrong or whining like half the rest of them do at the petty little things. Then they would really have something to talk about.

I am determined not to let this get to me, so, if I keep it all to myself, then I can carry on and lead a normal life; well. as normal as possible. As far as my walking towards you this morning, maybe I was just drawn to you!"

"I could see how that would happen," he said with a wink, running his fingers through what hair he had!

The two spent quite some time chatting and Meg was delighted that they had spent this time together. Meg looked at her watch.

"Wow, time flies when you're having fun - it's after 3!"

"Well, when you're with me! What's the rush anyway? Going somewhere?"

"No, actually, nowhere to go and no one to go anywhere with!"

"Do you want to come home with me, stay for tea?"

"What will Sue think of that? Come to think of it, what will she think of this?"

"What? We are not doing anything wrong, are we? We are just a couple of friends having a drink together."

"I know that, but will she?"

"You obviously don't know Sue that well."

"I guess not!"

Sue had been Rob's girlfriend for over 4 years. Meg had met her on a couple of occasions, staff parties, Christmas parties, but she hadn't spoken that much to her.

"Ok then!" Meg felt good; she was free, she had no one to call to tell them she was going to be late, no one to be home for to put the tea on. There was a lot to be said for being single.

Meg followed Rob out of the pub. Walking back to their cars, Rob turned to Meg.

"Do you know where I live?"

"Not exactly, but I am a big girl; I think I will manage to follow you."

"Ok, smarty pants!" And with that, Rob stepped into his car and waited for Meg to do the same.

Within twenty minutes, the two were pulling up in front of Rob and Sue's house. Rob waited patiently outside for Meg's arrival. Meg turned off the engine and got out of her car. They both walked into the house and were greeted by Sue in the hallway. She had just got in herself and was hanging her coat up. The floor was full of shopping bags.

"Hi, baby," Rob said as he walked through the door. "No need to ask if you had a good shopping trip!"

"Hi, yes, it was pretty fruitful!" Sue walked up to her boyfriend and gave him a long kiss. Rob, a little embarrassed at this, stopped the kiss short.

"Sue, remember Meg?"

"Yes; isn't she the one with MS? I…"

"Erm, yes, she's here." Meg had been standing awkwardly outside as if waiting to see if it was ok for her to come in. Hearing those words from Sue's mouth, she wondered if that was how everyone remembered her.

"Come in, Meg," said Rob.

"Oh, hi! Sue greeted her furtively. "Sorry!"

"Hi! No need."

"I have invited Meg for tea; thought we could all get a takeaway and go out for a drink."

"Oh, erm, yes, sure." Meg could see from Sue's response that she didn't seem too happy at the arrangement.

"If it's a problem, I can go," she offered.

"Don't be silly, there is no problem, is there, hon?"

"No, not at all!" Sue perked up her voice.

"Ok, well, thanks!"

"Sorry, where are my manners? Come in! Let me take your coat."
Sue took Meg's coat from her and hung it up next to her own. They

walked through the extensive hallway into the kitchen. It was not dissimilar to her own with the fittings and breakfast bar.

"Would you like a drink?" Rob asked the two ladies.

"Coffee for me," Sue answered.

"The same, thanks." Meg felt very nervous about being in Sue's company as she felt like she was really not welcome.

"Do you need to sit down or something?" Sue asked.

Meg wanted to respond differently but simply said, "No, thanks, I am fine."

Sue disappeared for a few seconds and reappeared with the stacks of bags that cluttered the hall only a few minutes earlier.

She placed them on the breakfast bar, getting each item out in turn to show to Rob. She really had gone mad, with dresses, shorts, shoes and three bikinis.

"We are going on holiday, you see; to Mexico!" she said, boasting about their destination.

"Oh, whereabouts?" Meg asked with interest.

"Playacar; it's…"

"Yes, quite close to Cancun, but a little quieter," Meg responded.

"Oh, how do you know? Have you been?" Sue's voice seemed somewhat sarcastic.

"Yes, I went for my hon… well, with my friend this year. You will love it!"

"Oh, I see; good." This flattened Sue, which really wasn't what Meg intended. She had been simply offering praise of the country. She decided against telling her about interesting things she had done on the holiday.

"Right then! It's a nice day, so I suggest we get the drinks and go outside. Anyone hungry?"

Both girls uttered in the positive, so Rob got to making the coffees and opening the drawer to find a list of takeaway menus.

Sue just stood and watched him, occasionally looking at Meg. Meg felt it was to see if she was still all right.

As the afternoon went on and the three sat drinking their coffees,

Meg felt more and more uncomfortable. She wanted to say something but decided not to. As if Rob had read her mind, he said, "Sue, don't worry. Meg is fine now; she is in remission. She only gets the odd few symptoms here and there."

Meg was horrified at him speaking for her so decided what the hell, she would speak for herself!

"Yes, I am fine thanks. Sue, why do you keep looking at me like that?"

"I'm sorry, I just thought you looked really well. I didn't mean to stare, I was just, I don't know, looking to see what was wrong with you. I am sorry."

"It's ok, really. Some people do seem uncomfortable around me but don't worry; I am not going to do anything stupid or suddenly be ill!"

"Look, I am really sorry; I guess I just don't know how to act."

"Don't act any differently really. Rob, how about another coffee?" Meg didn't really want another drink but felt sure the other two felt as uncomfortable as she did, so thought the best thing to do was to change the subject.

The rest of the evening didn't go along much better. Rob had suggested to Meg that she should stay the night so that they could go to the local pub for a few drinks.

"No, really, I'm not that bothered about drinking."

"Oh, go on!" It was Sue who insisted. Meg finally gave in and they all went out for a drink. Meg felt a little drunk earlier than she had anticipated, wobbling around the room after going to the ladies' room for the fifth time that night.

"She is so drunk!" Meg heard Sue whisper to Rob, watching her sway around the room.

"I'm not sure that she is," Rob said, remembering the incident earlier in the day at the office.

"She is! Look at the state of her! I knew it was a bad idea, her being here." Sue seemed totally oblivious to the fact that there was nothing wrong with Meg's hearing.

"Well, I wanted to invite her. I felt sorry for her; she has had a tough time of it lately."

"So? It's not up to you to nursemaid her; she is embarrassing - everyone is looking at her!"

Meg found her way back to the seat and was silent.

"Are you ok?" Rob asked.

"Fine," Meg replied with slight anger in her tone.

"Shall we go?" Rob asked.

Sue, not giving Meg time to reply, said, "I am not ready to go yet."

Rob just looked at Meg, who answered

"I am fine, but I don't think I'll have any more!" Meg tried to make a joke out of a situation that was just not funny.

She sat for the remainder of the evening studying Sue. She was attractive but not striking or beautiful in any way. She was a good 3 inches taller than Meg and was a good 10 pounds heavier.

She wasn't big; it was more that Meg was small. Sitting there sipping her drink, she had enough attitude to fill the room. Meg knew she had made a mistake spending the evening with her.

The evening dragged on from then on, and Meg was only too pleased when Sue announced that she was, at last, ready to leave.

Meg used the bathroom and was shown to the spare bedroom.

She was the first to waken the next morning and got washed and dressed quickly. She tidied her room and went downstairs. She was closely followed by Rob, who had heard her moving about.

He was dressed in his pyjamas.

"Morning," she said as he walked through the door.

"Morning; listen, I am so sorry about last night. I don't know what's wrong with Sue; she acted terribly."

"That's ok. You were the one who felt sorry for me."

"Oh! You heard that? Look, I am sorry, it was the first thing that came into my head. I didn't mean to say I felt sorry for you. Look, I am sorry for me and Sue."

"Don't worry about it. Look, if it's all the same to you, I think I will go home now. Thanks for yesterday; I'd like to say I had a nice time but…"

"Yeah, I know, but stay and have some breakfast with us."

"No, I'd rather not, thanks anyway." Meg was a little curt with Rob, as she was still upset by the actions of both of them the previous night. She walked out of the house leaving Rob wondering if he had ruined the good friendship they had.

Meg stepped into her car, her pretty head hanging down in shame.

She had lost all her self-respect in those few hours. She ran her fingers through her hair, forgetting that there was not much hair for her fingers to run through. She suddenly wished she had left it in its entirety. The colour and the length were beautiful, and now, she was regretting the whim that had led her to such a drastic change. She placed the oversized black handbag on the passenger seat and straightened her lilac blouse to drive home. She was alone in the car and was grateful for the solitude. But this time, she would not phone her mother or Jenny; no, it was time she dealt with things on her own.

She remembered a time when she was a happy soul, with no worries, not a care in the world, long before Tim, long before the MS; she was a child again…

She was out in her parents' garden, playing with her friends.

Jenny was there, as usual. Her mum was watering the plants in the garden where they were playing. Her dad was mowing the lawn at the front. It was an Indian summer, late in the year, everyone was in shorts and Meg's parents were having a barbeque party that evening. The children were all invited; all seemed to be already there. The garden was filled with children. Meg was a very popular girl at school. Jack was toddling around, getting quite a lot of attention from all the girls, and the occasional look from his mum to check that he was all right. She could trust Meg, though, to watch out for him. Meg suddenly felt water on her head; she looked up to see no rain. She carried on playing but shortly afterwards, felt the water again, this time soaking her through. She turned round to see her mum spraying the hose onto her, much to the delight and surprise of the other children.

"Mum!" Meg said with exasperation.

"What?" her mum replied innocently.

Everyone was hysterical. The sound of giggling schoolchildren echoed around the garden.

"Mum, what's that?" Meg quizzed, pointing at nothing in particular. Evie fell for it hook, line and sinker, turning to see what was being pointed at, as Meg swiped the hose from her mum, spraying it directly at her.

Pretty soon, everyone was drenched and laughing. Poor little Jack seemed quite bemused by the whole antic. David, hearing all the commotion, walked around to the back garden, only to be caught in mid-jet by Jenny who had now commandeered the hose.

"Oh, oops! I am sorry!" Jenny was most embarrassed.

"Jenny Smithson, what are your parents going to say about this?" David boomed.

"I, I, I…"

David quickly snatched the hose from Jenny, pointed it towards her and fired! The whole scene must have been quite a sight for any onlookers passing by the house.

"I think we may need to get changed for this evening, don't you, dear?" David said to his wife, laughing at the frivolities.

"Hmmm, maybe!"

The guests, mainly parents of the children already there, began arriving shortly after, many of them armed with food, wine or both. Meg's aunt and uncle, Jackie and Peter, stopped by to talk to their favourite niece before inquiring as to the whereabouts of her parents.

"They were a little wet, so Mummy and Daddy have gone to get changed," Meg said, pointing mischievously at the hosepipe, which was now lying on the grass.

"I see; that explains why you are a little damp!" Peter said, smiling at the wet crew.

The barbeque party was a complete success with the adults on one lawn enjoying themselves, and the children on the other having equally as much fun. It had been quite a year of parties and barbeques. Evie and David were in a circle of friends who took it in turn to have the others over for dinner. But today was special - they were celebrating a big promotion David had just received. It seemed all of the village was at the party…and then some!

There was a knock on the car door window. Meg was abruptly torn from her memories.

"Are you ok?" Meg adjusted to her surroundings. She was still at Rob's house.

She wound down the car window.

"Yeah fine, why?" She had no idea how long she had been sitting there.

"Because you seem to have been sitting there for over an hour. I never noticed - Sue's just got out of bed and was confused when she saw you out of the bedroom window."

"I am fine; bye!" Meg quickly started the engine and was gone.

Chapter 20

Work had not been its usual happy place to be for Meg since then.

She became very aware of people talking about her… uncomfortably aware. One particular day, some people were smirking as she walked past them or into the same room as she was. She couldn't really understand it though until it was pointed out to her.

"Meg, I think maybe you should go home and get changed," Anita said.

"What do you mean?" Meg was puzzled.

"How can I put this delicately? I think you have suffered a small accident."

Meg could feel the heat in her face rising. She turned a brilliant shade of crimson. She ran to the toilets and felt her behind. It was very soiled. Meg at once realized what all the sniggering was about. She had been wondering. She had simply thought it was because she stumbled around the office occasionally. She did look like she had been drinking. Or maybe she thought it was nothing to do with the MS, but maybe Tim. She knew people had been talking about it. Once word had got out as to what had happened, it had taken no time at all for the whispering and rumours to circulate around the office. She could have probably handled any of these, but this, how would she handle this? She ran out of the office and to the nearest bus stop as Jenny had driven to work that day; she didn't care if it took her to the right place. As it turned out, it wasn't too far away, so she was easily able to find her way home after that. The very second she got home, she stripped off and threw the clothes into the laundry basket. She turned on the shower, which was far too hot, and stepped in. She stood there for a long time, washing away all the hurt and anger that was inside her. She scrubbed hard, taking out all her frustration on her poor body.

'Why does this have to happen to me?' she thought as she stood, the water steaming up the room.

'What did I do wrong? What did I do to piss someone off so much to give me this horrid disease? I can't seem to do anything right - why can't people just forget about what's wrong with me? Why do they have to be so awful?' She heard the telephone ring and ignored it.

"Go away!" she said. The phone, paying no attention to her, continued to ring until the answerphone picked it up. After hearing her own voice singing the message, she heard the voice of the caller.

"Hi, Meg, it's me. Just ringing to see if you are alright. Erm, I am really sorry about what happened. I was about to tell you but Anita did it. I was going to run you home. Oh, I'll ring you back - I hate answerphones." The line went dead.

Meg let the tears flow freely as she showered.

'Why did people have to be so cruel?' She had plenty of friends before this started; now, they all seemed frightened to be near her. There had been the odd few like Grace, who had taken the trouble to ask her about it, but most of her friends seem to have defected. She could maybe understand it if she had done nothing but talk about it to everyone. She could see how that would put people off. But she had tried to keep herself to herself and she had asked for no special treatment - quite the opposite, in fact. She had been happy to let it go unnoticed. The only problem with that being when some symptom flared up, half the staff wondered what on earth was wrong. And, on the odd occasion that she had been off work, tongues would have wagged no doubt as to why she was off work. This was too much to take; she was in total despair. The phone rang again. Once again, Meg let the answerphone take the call. No message this time; the caller obviously didn't want to leave a message.

Later in the evening, Meg took out the bottle of vodka, which was situated in the cabinet, the same cabinet that had once contained many sets of beautiful glasses, glasses that had broken her relationship. It now contained just a few glasses that Meg had bought over the months to replace those from which she still had the scars. She helped herself to one and poured it full to the top with the vodka. She sat and drank and drank and drank until the glass was empty. Before the evening was out, the bottle, which, granted, had not been full right to the top, was also pretty much empty. The phone rang once again.

"Why can't they leave me alone?" Meg screamed for the third time. Meg ignored the call but was sick of hearing her stupid song which she had composed for the machine.

"Meg, I am sure you are there. Pick up the phone. It's Jenny… please, Meg, I am worried about you."

Meg decided that she should really pick up the phone.

"Hello," she said drowsily.

"Hello, Meg. How are you feeling? No, don't answer that, shall I come over?" Jenny's voice was full of concern.

"No, don't. I'm not in the mood for company." Meg sounded very stand-offish.

"This is me you are talking to, your best friend, the one who went on holiday with you, the one who soaked your dad with the hose!"

Ironic that she should be thinking of the incident not long after Meg herself.

Upon hearing no response from Meg, Jenny spoke again.

"Meg, please talk to me. I feel terrible for what happened to you."

"Jenny, really, I will be ok. I am just a little embarrassed."

"Of course you are, but Anita pulled the ones who were smirking into the office and they came back with their tails firmly between their legs. Between you and me, they came out with faces like smacked arses!" Jenny tried in vain to lighten the mood, but it would take more than a little humour to cheer Meg up.

"They still know about it though; it still hurts!"

"I know, but you have to try and forget about it."

"It's not as easy as that!"

"I know, honey, but you have to try. You really can't let this upset you. You are bigger than that; at least, the Meg I know is.

You are brave - laugh it off and come into work with your head held high."

"But I am ashamed…"

"You have nothing to be ashamed of!

Is there anything I can do to help?" Jenny pleaded helplessly.

"No, just let me deal with it in my own way." Meg put down the phone on Jenny and immediately regretted it.

Meg knew exactly what she needed to do.

She walked into the kitchen to the cupboard which contained all the medicines. There were two boxes of painkillers, all in blister packs. One by one, she popped the pills out of one pack, and then another. She had 15 tablets as one of the packs was half empty.

'This isn't going to be enough,' she thought. 'But I have had so much to drink, maybe, oh, what the hell, why am I even thinking about this?'" She took all the tablets and went to lie down on the sofa. Now she would be free, free of all the pain, physical and mental, free at last…

"Meg, oh God, Meg, can you hear me?" Meg didn't know if she was hearing things or not but she was sure the voice belonged to Tim. After that, she remembered nothing…

She awoke in a hospital bed feeling very groggy. It took her eyes a few moments to adjust. Someone was holding her hand. It was Tim.

"Tim…? Is that you?"

"Yeah, baby, it's me; how are you feeling?"

"Hmmm," Meg was very confused, "I don't know."

"Well, you just rest. You had us worried there for a second." Meg could hear the faint sounds of his voice but was not quite clear on everything he said. She had no idea where she was or what was going on. ' 'Am I dead?' she thought.

"No, you are not, thank the Lord!" Ok, so she had said it, not thought it. She fell asleep.

She awoke later with a terrible headache. She sat up slowly in her bed.

"Careful, sweetheart, take it easy!" She recognized that voice straight away.

It was her father. She looked over to see him sitting beside her mother who was sobbing into a handkerchief at one side of the bed, then, as she looked to the other side, she saw Jack looking anxious.

"What on earth were you thinking about?" Jack asked her, almost in tears.

Meg didn't respond, she just began to weep.

"I don't know. I don't know that I meant to... I don't know."

"Well, we are just glad you are all right," her father assured her, touching her hand softly.

"Why couldn't you talk to us if things were so bad? Why didn't you tell us?" Evie seemed inconsolable. But Meg couldn't take it all in. She just sat, dazed, looking from her mum to her dad to her little brother.

Over the next couple of days, Meg underwent various examinations and various nurses and psychiatrists visited Meg's bedside. After Meg had been in hospital for three days, it was decided that she could go home. Her father came to pick her up and the nurses wished her well.

As they walked to the car, Meg posed a question to her father.

"Did I see Tim a couple of days ago? I didn't know if I had dreamt it."

"Yes, you did. Tim actually saved your life. I hate to admit it, but we have a lot to thank him for. He was the one who found you."

Meg didn't really know what to say.

Over the next few days, Meg's head was in a spin. She really didn't know what she had been thinking when she took those tablets, but she remembered being humiliated by the incident, which had been the final straw towards her doing it.

As she sat brushing her hair in the bedroom, the telephone rang. It was Tim announcing that he was coming over to see her. He didn't give Meg the chance to argue, hanging up after he had finished speaking.

Shortly after, Tim arrived at the house and didn't wait for Meg to come to the door. He walked into the house, straight up to Meg and threw his arms around her.

"My God, I thought we'd lost you," he said, holding onto her and not letting go.

"What happened?" she asked since she was still hazy about the events.

"I came to see you, to talk to you and found you in a state of, well, you were as good as unconscious. I rang the ambulance, and they came and took you to hospital. I went in the ambulance with you and stayed with you for a while."

"Did you speak to me?"

"Yes, I did, but you weren't really very responsive, so I left you to sleep, I didn't want to come back to the hospital. I thought I would wait until you got home and now, here we are."

Everything cleared up in Meg's mind.

"Why on earth did you do it? It didn't have anything to do with me, did it? It's not my fault?" Tim's voice was very worried.

"No, it's not you; well, I'm sure it didn't help; well, I…" Meg hesitated for a moment to think about what she was saying.

"I think it was a combination of everything. I am sick to death of being ill and not knowing from one day to the next if I am going to be ok. Never knowing which bit of me isn't going to be working each day, and people at work, I mean, people can be so cruel; why do they have to be like that? And I have been working like a dog, trying to sort out the money for you…"

"People are scared of the unknown; I don't know, they don't think. And I am sorry for contributing to all this." Tim didn't seem to know what else to say. For the rest of the evening, he was very sweet to her, having her sit down while he made her a drink and something to eat.

Meg did as instructed and sat down, putting on the TV beforehand.

She suddenly wondered what Tim had come over to talk to her about.

When he had made her supper and sat down with her, she asked him.

"Oh, I was coming to apologize for my behaviour earlier in the week, over the money. I was terrible so I came to agree to what you offered me for the house. You are right, you did all the work, and after the way I treated you, you deserve better. In fact, what the hell! Take it; don't give me anything for it," he offered.

"Don't feel sorry for me just because of what happened. I can give you the £5,000."

"No, you won't! I can't believe what a bastard I have been to you! You deserve to be happy; I am just a total, well, and anyway, I am sorry. I know I will never be able to make up for what I have done but I truly am sorry. As soon as I left here after we argued about the money, I knew I had acted badly. I don't know what's wrong with me; I've been like Jekyll and Hyde."

"Funny you should use that comparison. I thought that too," Meg said with a slight smile.

"I don't know what to say. My only excuse is that I was frightened of the unpredictability; I don't know…"

Tim looked mournfully at Meg.

"Can we at least be friends? Please?"

"I guess so. I suppose I owe you my life."

"I wouldn't go that far," Tim said humbly. "From what I could see, you didn't take enough to do any serious damage, just maybe give yourself a hell of a headache."

"I thought painkillers were supposed to get rid of headaches," Meg said, trying to be lighter.

"Come here, you fool!" Tim opened his arms out to Meg who reluctantly walked over and accepted the hug.

They spoke for a few moments longer and then Tim announced that he should go home and let Meg rest.

Meg went to bed that night not knowing how to feel. She just wished that Tim had been more like this earlier, but she knew there was no chance of reconciliation. Too much had gone on for that.

At least he had realized his mistakes. She felt a little better knowing that. For better for worse, the vows went.

The following morning, Meg woke up feeling surprisingly refreshed. After speaking on the phone to her mum and dad, she decided to go out for a ride. She got in the car and set off. She wasn't sure why but it was as if the car had decided where she was going. She was heading in the same direction as the little café she had visited with the fresh bread. She suddenly knew exactly where she wanted to be. Within a few more moments, she was outside the tattoo studio. She walked in and was greeted by a very attractive lady.

"Hi, my name is Tracie. What can I do for you?"

Meg smiled at Tracie and replied with a slight giggle, "I'm after a tattoo!"

"Well, you've come to the right place! Do you have any ideas as to where and what?"

"I think maybe a rose somewhere and then maybe, another time, a butterfly!"

Tracie sat down with Meg and talked through some ideas. She advised her to just think about one for the time being and live with it for a while before deciding on another one.

Meg decided to opt for a rose twisted around some tribal design. Strangely, she seemed to know exactly what she wanted.

"Well, leave it with me for an hour or so and I'll draw something up for you." Tracie went on to say that Meg had come on the perfect day as she wasn't very busy at all.

Meg left Tracie to draw and decided the best place to go was the café. In about an hour, as promised, Meg returned to the studio to a very smiley Tracie. The design was ready and Meg loved it. She was advised to lie down on her right side as she had decided to have the tattoo on her left leg.

"Are you ready?" she was asked.

"Yeah, go for it!"

Meg lay down and watched Tracie at work. She was surprised to find that it didn't hurt anywhere near as much as she thought it would. She even managed to have a nice chat with Tracie, who turned out to be the same age as Meg herself. Meg thought, as she was chatting to her, that Tracie seemed like the kind of person she could go out and have a few drinks with. She looked around the studio carefully as the tattoo was being drawn onto her skin. There were drawings all over.

"Did you draw all these?" Meg asked, impressed at the creative artwork.

"Yes, I did. I've always loved drawing, so this is the perfect job. I get to design pictures for people and then draw it on their skin with permanent marker," Tracie said with a smile.

Meg almost found the process therapeutic. Yes, it did hurt a little, but the pain would go away and at the end of it, she would have a lovely piece of artwork on her skin, rather than the horrible scars inside her skin. Maybe this was going to be a new hobby for her!

After another hour or so, the process was complete.

"What do you think?" Tracie asked Meg.

"Wow, it's gorgeous! Exactly what I was after," came the excited reply.

"I am so glad!"

Tracie placed some dressing over the tattoo and gave Meg explicit instructions not to pick at it once it started to scab. She was also advised to put cream on it every day.

The two young women went into the reception and Meg paid for the tattoo. She left the studio a much happier human being, wondering where she could have a butterfly on her body as she was sure she would be back for more work.

Chapter 21

Other than going out for her tattoo, Meg refused to go anywhere or see anyone; she had been too embarrassed and humiliated. How could she have been so stupid as to try and take her own life? Not face up to her problems and take the coward's way out? To let other people get to her so much? She had been coping with the illness so well, considering the severity. So why did she go and let some small-minded people who really didn't matter reduce her to doing what she did? Well, there was a little more to it than that, but maybe now people would understand; maybe people would have a little more compassion; maybe…

"Hold on, what am I doing? Still caring about what other people think… who gives a damn what they think? I am supposed to be sorting my head out and thinking about myself. The only people who matter are the people who I know care. Why should I really give a damn about anything or anybody else…?" Meg's thoughts drifted off the subject. In a few days, she was going back to work. She couldn't keep taking time off like this; what would people think? They would certainly be gossiping about her… 'Stop!' Meg thought to herself. She was still worrying about other people instead of thinking about herself.

The day finally came. She was going to work for the first time since her little embarrassment, soiling herself. She wondered if people had been laughing at her and even if they knew what had followed, what those people had driven her to.

"Stop it!" she shouted at the angry face who glared at her as she washed her face. She took her time getting ready, composing herself. She picked out her favourite outfit - a dark green trouser suit that fitted

205

her small frame perfectly. Being dressed in smart clothes, which she loved, gave her a little more confidence. She at least knew she looked reasonably good even if she didn't feel it. Once again, she drifted into self-pity.

'I need to look and feel good after that humiliating incident,' she thought.

"I don't know if I can do it." Just as Meg was about to break down, the sound of a car pulling up, raucous music playing out, stopped her in her tracks! If nothing else, it made Meg smile.

"Honestly!" she said as she stepped into the car.

"What?" Jenny replied innocently.

"I have to live in this neighbourhood!"

"Whatever! Hello, it's good to see you so cheerful anyway!"

"Hi, well, yeah, you've got to shake yourself down and get on with life."

"Hear, hear!" Jenny smiled at her friend warmly. She had certainly given her cause for alarm lately.

"Are you ok?" Meg asked her friend. "I feel like I haven't seen you for ages!"

"Yeah, well…no, it doesn't matter."

"What?"

"It just seems so trivial with everything you are going through."

"Oh Jenny, don't be like that. Tell me if there is something wrong. I would never undermine your problems." Meg was concerned about her friend. She wanted to talk to her and maybe help with Jenny's problems, rather than whining about her own.

"I know, but…well, ok, I am just fed up! I am sick of Mum and Dad fighting with Sam over his school grades. Every time I come home from work, they are at each other's throats!"

"Is your brother that bad? I thought he was doing ok."

"Well, yeah, he is doing ok, but if it wasn't for that girlfriend of his, he would be doing even better!"

"Ah, the old girlfriend trouble!"

"Hmmm!"

"I'm sure things will improve," was all that Meg could think to say.

"Yeah, I guess so."

Nothing much was said on the subject, although Meg tried to think of what she could do to help. About 15 minutes later, they arrived at work. However, as their favourite song was playing, they weren't getting out of the car until they had finished singing at the tops of their voices, much to the amusement of fellow workers walking past!

As the song finished, they both looked at each other and laughed!

"Good to have you back," Jenny said. "I have missed our little sing-songs!"

"Yeah, me too! I guess we'd better get in there!"

They walked into the office and got in the lift to go to their floor. Notices were stuck on all the walls; some were work-related and some were about upcoming social events for the entire company. Meg never bothered reading such things anymore. She had no intentions of going to any social gathering with work colleagues these days.

All of Meg's confidence drained through every inch of her body as she walked through the large office doors and saw all the faces of those who had sniggered at her only weeks before.

"Come on, kiddo, you'll be fine!" Jenny said, encouraging her friend who had frozen at the door. She gave Meg a gentle pat on the back.

"Yeah!" Meg sounded somewhat unconvinced.

"You know they are not all like those few, don't you? Most people have been really concerned, asking about you almost every day!" Meg panicked. "What do you say?"

"That you were having another relapse."

"Oh, I was a little worried about what you had told them, you know…"

"Give me a bit of credit!" Jenny raised her eyebrows at Meg.

"Everyone was really worried; I think even the Witches of Eastwick felt bad!" Meg smiled at the familiar name the two of them had come up with for the nasty trio.

"I doubt it but I should think so!"

"You know, even they aren't really that spiteful; they are just confused with everything. One minute you look great, and the next you are really ill, but you don't really look any different. People are just ignorant, I guess. You know what it's like in these offices - people are bored with their own lives, so they thrive on gossip, no matter how wrong they are or how much they may be hurting people's feelings."

"Yeah, I guess so. You know, you are not as dumb as you look; what you just said made a lot of sense!"

"Thanks…I think!" Jenny and Meg both laughed as they parted company to go to their desks. The day passed relatively quickly and was somewhat better than Meg had expected. Even the guilty group had looked very ashamed.

After a few days, everything seemed to be back to normal; no one seemed to be talking or whispering behind her back. She was surprised to find that some people even came up to her to ask her more about the illness and how it affected her. Meg had become open to discussing everything with people, glad that people would know the truth, instead of drawing up their own conclusions and being spiteful towards her. There had still been the odd few who had resented this openness, thinking it was a ploy to gain sympathy, but Meg had gone past caring.

And so, that was how it continued for some weeks. The only problem Meg noticed was how increasingly tired she was becoming. That wasn't too much of a problem to Meg though - the weekend overtime had drawn to a halt, so she simply slept throughout most of it, recharged her batteries, as it were, and she was ready to face another week. She did, however, dismiss the problem, putting it down to working too hard and for such long hours. Most people slept through a lot of the weekend, didn't they? Other people close to her weren't quite so unconcerned at her fatigue, in particular, her neurologist at her next appointment.

"You really should be taking things a little easier, you know, Meg?"

"Why? I am too young to be taking things easy." Meg shrugged her shoulders despondently.

"Meg, don't you realise what you are doing to yourself? Your body is saying no! Yet, you continue to push yourself."

"But I work best under pressure," Meg protested, ignoring the issue brought up by the anxious consultant.

"Meg, listen to yourself. You can't do this; slow down." The neurologist was becoming somewhat annoyed at her patient.

As far as Meg was concerned, there was no need to slow down. She was a young woman, and she thought the doctor was seriously overreacting. What was the point in taking things easy when she felt fine…? Well, maybe if she was honest with herself, she didn't exactly feel fine but then again, she didn't feel ill either! Meg was determined not to let the doctor get his own way. The meeting was left at that. Meg wasn't going to let the neurologist win that battle; no, she had won!

Soon after that, Meg started to appreciate his point. Everything seemed to be crumbling around her. She was making silly mistakes at work, forgetting what she was talking about mid-sentence. Every day, she was finding it more and more difficult to get up in the morning, but the worst of that problem was that no one seemed to understand, saying things like, "Oh, everyone forgets what they are talking about sometimes, you have just got lots of things running round your mind."

OR

"Well, who does like getting up in the morning?"

No, no one understood. Work was getting more and more stressful. Work colleagues continued to talk about her, saying how she used the MS as an excuse for everything that went wrong and that she did nothing but talk about it.

Most evenings, when she got home from work, she was too tired to put a fork to her mouth, let alone make herself something. Every time this happened, she vowed to go shopping for easy-to-cook food! This in itself was a battle to overcome as Meg loved to cook and hated the idea of buying microwave meals. The telephone would ring and she would just be too tired to get up to answer it. She was slipping fast…again.

One particular morning, she awoke to the alarm and simply decided she couldn't face work. She telephoned in and took the day off. One day turned into two and then eventually, a week. Mid-week, she decided to telephone Vanessa. She hadn't spoken to her for quite some time but felt she needed to talk to her. She knew, or hoped, that Vanessa would know what she was going through. Although Meg felt quite guilty for only phoning because she needed someone to talk to, Vanessa seemed quite happy to meet up with her. She gave Meg the directions to her house and the following day, Meg drove over to see her. The drive was a beautiful, peaceful one, through extensive countryside and although it was the wrong time of year for the foliage, Meg could imagine how picturesque it would have been that summer.

Meg was greeted at the door by a happy, smiling Vanessa, looking very attractive with her slight build and beautiful locks of hair. She looked in particularly good shape, no stick beside her and no wobble.

"Hi, you've cut your hair!"

"Oh yes! I am surprised you remembered what it was like before."

"It suits you!"

"Thanks!"

"Come in!" Vanessa invited her into her beautiful house. Meg took a look at her surroundings. The house was small but very cosy. The living room was very tastefully decorated and reminded Meg of the colour scheme in her own home. There was a beautiful fire with a large cross-stitch design above it of a house not dissimilar to Vanessa's. They walked through into the kitchen, which again was attractive and very old-fashioned-looking with a stone floor and old-style oven. There was an aroma of beautiful food being cooked. The bread maker was also operating giving out another beautiful smell.

"I have been waiting for this for some time," she said as she invited Meg in.

"What do you mean?" Meg was puzzled.

"Well, I know how I feel; no one seems to understand how it feels, and the problems we encounter. I was fortunate enough to have met someone with MS a couple of years ago. We seemed to hit it off straight away and talked for hours, and it really helped me!"

"I don't really know anyone else with it."

"I know, that's why I am surprised it has taken you so long to call me!"

"I don't know why, I guess we get busy and forget, and I know this sounds awful, but I have never needed to call you; never felt as bad as I do now. Oh, sorry, that sounds terrible!"

"No, it doesn't, I am glad we met. I am sure we can have a really good chat that may put both our minds at rest. I bet you don't really talk about it in detail to other people, do you?"

"No, not really, I try not to."

"And my guess is that's because a lot of the problems are just little ones that hit you every day and you don't want people to think you talk about nothing but MS and that they make think you are using it as an excuse for everything."

"Exactly! I guess you have been through it all."

"Of course, no one understands other than someone else with MS, but they should understand that MS is you - it is a big part of your life. I know you might not want to admit it, but it is true. I am sure you know people who go on about the same things all the time and you sit and listen to them… Am I right?"

"Yeah, but this is different."

"No, it isn't, I used to know someone who did nothing but talk about her irritable bowel syndrome and every time she had something wrong with her, it was 'the irritable bowel syndrome', you know."

Meg giggled; she could relate to that. She wasn't the only person who talked about an illness and she didn't talk about it anywhere near as much as others did. No, she couldn't deny what Vanessa was saying was true.

They sat down to a coffee and the biggest biscuit barrel Meg had ever seen! Vanessa had also made a coffee cake which looked mouth-wateringly delicious!

"I'll tell you what, it's a nice day, let's sit outside." A nice day it was, which was highly surprising since winter was looming.

Meg followed Vanessa to the patio-style garden and sat down at the table.

"You have a beautiful house," Meg commented. "And the area is gorgeous."

"Thanks! I like it here; it is very peaceful."

They talked in detail about the various symptoms they suffered from; some were the same, some different. Meg was surprised to learn that they shared so many, especially since she had been told that no two MS sufferers were the same. It was still true but not as much as Meg had previously thought. Meg talked openly about her illness without feeling like she was doing nothing but complain.

"Do you get pins and needles in your legs and arms?" Vanessa asked her.

"Constantly." This was the first time that Meg had been so open in admitting all the problems she suffered from. The fatigue, the depression, the limbs feeling numb occasionally, not to mention not being able to remember things.

"You see, you are not a hypochondriac, you have a chronic illness. People should know that."

"Why do you mention other people like that?"

"Because I am betting that you are coping reasonably well with all the symptoms but your biggest problem is other people and what they think of you…"

"How did you know that?"

"Stupid question - I have MS."

"Yeah of course, sorry."

The conversations carried on for hours. Meg would start to say something, and Vanessa would know exactly what she was going to say next.

"People know exactly how my MS affects me," Vanessa said. "I have grown weary of having to explain myself so if they know how it is affecting me, they know what is going on when I am not well."

"I admire that. I wish I could do that, but I think it is too late. People see me around and I am fine but they don't see me at home and how difficult it is to cope.

I mean, I know how lucky I am in comparison to other MS sufferers and people keep telling me I am, but …"

"But it is still bad…? Of course it is!"

"It bugs me how it stops me from doing things I used to love doing," Meg said sadly.

"Tell me about it! I am thinking of giving up work," Vanessa said, suddenly changing the mood from them both being angry at the world to saddened.

"Oh no! I am so sorry!"

"Yeah, well, I do love my job but it is getting to be too difficult, too many sick days, too many mornings waking up not knowing if it is going to be a good day or a bad one." Vanessa sighed.

"Speaking of which, doesn't it bug you when that happens? People just say they are like that and then they say 'We all have mornings like that'!"

"Yeah, but my all-time favourite is 'But you look so good!' Yes?"

"Without a doubt! You know, I know this sounds awful, but sometimes I wish there was something visibly wrong with me then it wouldn't be so difficult trying to explain ourselves." Meg was enjoying releasing all her thoughts, knowing that she didn't have to worry about what Vanessa would think of her.

"I know what you mean, but have you noticed how all we seem to have talked about is other people? Never mind all that we are going through, all we seem bothered about is others!"

"Hmmm," Meg agreed.

"Well, I think today ought to be the day that we changed that. Think about number one because all the stress of worrying about other people is not helping us at all. You know, stress is one of the worst things we can come across in our situation?"

"Yeah, that and blokes called Tim!"

"Sorry?"

"Long story!"

They both chuckled.

"Going back to the work thing, do you think it is for the best?" Meg asked.

Vanessa looked at Meg thoughtfully.

"I don't know. I really do love my job and everyone there is great and, to be quite honest, I really don't know what I am going to do with myself with all the time, but I know that I am making myself worse by going to work. My days are so long. I leave the house at seven every morning and don't get home until after six. Then I have to start on cooking and looking after the house. I work six days a week. I can't keep up. I have to face facts that I am not the person I used to be. I may still be young, but I am certainly not fit and healthy. I can't cope with it anymore."

Meg feared she recognised this whole speech, but she really wasn't ready to give up work yet, so she refrained from responding.

Meg left a few hours later and promised to keep in touch with Vanessa. Part of her didn't want to though; she was concerned that Vanessa had got to a stage that Meg herself wasn't ready for yet. If she spent too much time with her, she may find out things about her future, things that may happen to her. She certainly was not ready for that.

For the rest of the week, Meg thought of nothing but her meeting with Vanessa. It had done her a lot of good visiting her, as it made her realise that she really did need to slow down and take things a little easier. Who knows? Maybe doing that would prevent her from getting into the same situation as Vanessa was in now. If she took things a little steadier, maybe she wouldn't need to give up work. She figured if she just took a little more time from work to recharge her batteries, she would be ready to face the world again.

A couple of weeks later, Meg did feel a lot better and more refreshed. She went back to work. She was back to her usual routine of going to work early and the car-sharing with Jenny was less frequent as Meg found herself staying late most evenings. She would go home every evening to be greeted by Madison and usually a kitchen to clear up from the night before, as she was often too tired to do it in the evenings.

"I don't know," she said to Madison, bending down to stroke her. "Never seem to quite catch up, do I?"

Madison just purred, delighted at the affection she was getting.

"Ah well, we'll manage."

However, it wasn't long before she was back to square one again, feeling exhausted and needing more time off work. This time, it was her balance that was affected, and more than once, she overheard people talking about her, saying that she must have been drinking. Her fatigue was now at an all-time high. It had still been very difficult discussing it with anyone; even those close to her at work couldn't really comprehend that fatigue and tiredness were totally different. Tongues were starting to wag again about how she was exaggerating her illness to get time off work. But she knew if she let that bother her, she would be even more ill.

"At least you are listening to your body and taking time off when you have had enough and you are not pushing yourself even more," her mum commented. Both her parents were concerned, naturally, but glad she was resting.

"But I feel like I am giving in," Meg protested, not seeing any good side of her being off work. She was now starting to worry about whether she would still have a job, given the amount of time she had taken off.

"So what if you are giving up? You just have to give in sometimes," her father had insisted…

One evening, not too long after, Meg sat and studied her options. It really couldn't be good for her career taking so much time off work. What would all the managers be thinking of her? Was her job in jeopardy? She decided that there was only one option.

"I have been thinking about it for quite some time now," Meg announced one evening after driving over to her parents' house after work.

"What's that, sweetheart?" her father said with an air of concern.

"I don't like to admit it, but I don't feel like I am coping very well. I am trying to forget about the MS and get on with things, thinking I can still do all the things I could before, but the truth is I can't. Work is getting more and more difficult for me, and then I have everything at home to deal with. If it wasn't for the fact that you make my meals for me, I wouldn't even have the energy to cook for myself."

What are you saying, honey?" her mum asked. "That you need help with the housework? You know you only need to ask and I am there! The trouble is you are too independent."

"Yeah, I know, but I don't want you doing any more for me; you do enough already."

"I am your mum; that's my job," Evie insisted, keen to help her daughter.

"Well, maybe, but that isn't what I meant." Meg paused as if to give herself one last think about her decision.

"I've been thinking of working part-time, if they will let me."

"I think that is a good idea!" her father said with a certain relief in his voice. If the truth were known, Evie and he had secretly wanted that for their daughter for quite some time now.

"It is a great idea!" Evie agreed.

"The only trouble is, I will probably take quite a pay cut."

"Don't worry about that. We are always here to help, and besides, your health is more important."

"Yeah, I guess so, and anyway, it is just the early mornings that bother me. I may just go in an hour later; I am sure we can work something out that won't hurt my pocket too much."

"Of course, you'll sort something out. They are very lucky to have such a dedicated worker as you, my love. I think they would rather have you for fewer hours on a more regular basis than not knowing whether you will be there at all."

"I guess so!"

Her father left the conversation at that and changed the subject. He could see how difficult it all was for Meg, having to make all the decisions, by the teary look in her eyes. He was very proud of her bravery.

When Meg left a couple of hours later, she felt totally drained. She was so delighted that her mum had insisted on her staying for tea. She didn't realise that even conversations wore her out so much. At the same time, though, she felt relieved, like a great pressure had been lifted from her shoulders. She had hated to admit it all but it was true, the early mornings and long hours were simply too much for her. She knew that of everyone, her mum and dad would understand; she didn't need to explain herself or her plans to them. They didn't criticise her or think she was overreacting. In fact, they had reacted in the exact way she was hoping. They were very encouraging. She knew what she had to do.

The following day was Saturday, and, even if there was overtime at work (which there wasn't), she didn't do it; instead, she stayed in bed most of the morning watching children's television and laughing at the presenters and their antics. After debating for a while, she got out of bed and was feeling up to cooking. She made a few lasagnes to put into the freezer for when she was not up to cooking, and even baked a few cakes and biscuits. She was amazed at how much lighter she felt after making such a tough decision; a decision that she hoped would solve all her problems. She would set off from home on a morning a little later and maybe leave work a little earlier. She may only cut her day by an hour or so, but she really thought it would make all the difference.

After pottering around the kitchen for most of the afternoon, she sat down with a cappuccino, made from the coffee maker, which had been one of the many beautiful engagement presents. Hmmm! That was another bone of contention. Tim had thought it was a total waste of time and money!

"It is too expensive," he had said. "No one will buy us one so there is no point in mentioning it."

As it happened, a few of Meg's relatives, knowing how much she wanted one, had all put together to buy it for them!

She was sat in the living room with the cappuccino and one of her home-made cookies, still warm. She was surprised that she didn't feel too tired. She turned on the large wide-screen television and was surprised to see the evening news.

"Five-thirty already! It's no wonder I am hungry!"

She stood up and walked into the kitchen, without her five minutes relaxation, and looked in the fridge. She decided to cook Chinese food.

She put the rice in boiling water and on the stove to cook. It would only take ten minutes. She would then make it into egg fried rice.

"Oh damn, with all this cooking, I forgot to clean upstairs!"

Meg went up the stairs with the vacuum cleaner and set to tidying round. If there was one thing she hated, it was coming home to an untidy house, but what could she do? She had been too tired to do anything. This whole thing annoyed her so much, not being able to do the simplest of tasks, but what was even more annoying, was that some days, she could do all these things. She just couldn't balance everything out, not knowing from one day to the next if she was able to do things, things that she had no problem doing before. Just as she was reminiscing on the days not too long ago when she could do it all, the sound of the smoke alarm interrupted her.

'What on earth?' she thought. She ran downstairs into the kitchen to find a black mess that slightly resembled rice in a water-free, black pan.

"Arghhhh!" she yelled and picked up the pan, burning her hands in the process. She threw it on the work surface burning that too!

"The bloody thing!" Meg just screamed and burst into tears. Sheer frustration came over her. When she had calmed down, she had lost all interest in cooking and telephoned the Chinese takeaway.

"Be with you in fifteen minutes, Miss Walker."

"How did you know it was me?"

"Are you kidding? You are our best customer! I guess cooking is not your forte! Bye!"

"Cheeky bastard!" Meg shrieked at the phone as she replaced the receiver. She had always loved cooking. She sat down in front of the TV waiting for her meal to arrive. She had worked herself up into a frenzy. There was too much to take in. She had the feeling she would never get used to it all. Every day was different, not knowing how she was going to feel or how much she could do before feeling ill - was this the way it was going to be from now on? At that point, there was a knock on the door. Her food had arrived. She thanked the driver and plated up her food, not really knowing if she still wanted it. Fortunately, the glorious aroma soon made her mind up for her! She tucked into the beautiful-smelling noodles, chicken and mushrooms, trying to forget not just about the days' events, but also about dwelling on her future life. Pondering over it, feeling sorry for herself could only make her feel worse. She put on her favourite film, losing herself and forgetting her problems...for now.

Chapter 22

Meg decided not to tell anyone of the recent events. After all, there was really nothing to tell. As usual, she was thinking of other peoples' opinions. Maybe telling people about it would just confirm their thoughts that she did nothing but moan about it. The only people who wouldn't think that were the people who would worry if she did tell them. Meg came to the conclusion that there would be no benefit from it. The whole incident should have made her think more about working part-time. Unfortunately, it was all too much to cope with.

Meg was at her mother's house for probably the fourth time that week. The three of them were sitting in front of the television when her dad finally spoke.

"Meg, your mum and I were talking about you after you left."

"Oh, yes?"

"Hmm, it's not that we don't want you to come and see us but we think you should be going out a bit more, you know, with your friends."

"I see, well, you know, I seem to be getting tired so easily these days. I know it seems like I am using you, but if I didn't come here for my tea, I probably wouldn't eat!"

"We understand that and I am more than happy to cook for you, you know that. It is nice to have you around again, but maybe you should go out more, come here for your tea and then go out or something," Evie suggested.

"Right, and have you been discussing anything else about me?" Meg was a little agitated.

"No, there's no need to be like that, sweetheart, we are just concerned that you don't seem to be socialising anymore."

"I don't have the time or energy to socialise!"

"You work too hard; have you thought about working part time again?"

"Yes, I have."

"Well, we think that would be the solution, if you worked part time or even just slightly fewer hours, you would have more energy to do other things. It can't be doing you any good, working all those hours and then sleeping the rest of the time - you need a life other than that."

"Are you saying I have no life?" Meg was even more upset that her parents had been discussing her life in such detail; her eyes were beginning to well up.

"Sweetie, you know we just worry about you and we think it is time you moved on."

"Ah, I see where this is going; you are talking about Tim, aren't you?"

"I guess we are. Get yourself out and have a good time - you never know, you might meet somebody." Evie was so concerned for her daughter's happiness, as was her father.

"Maybe I don't want to meet somebody! Besides the fact that I am worried it may end up like Tim and me, I don't want to burden anyone with, well, with me."

"Honey, that really shouldn't stop you from going out and enjoying yourself."

"I guess not." Meg was calming down a little; she knew what her parents were trying to say.

"I guess I need to have a good long think about my life, but I have been feeling so tired and I keep feeling like the MS is flaring up."

Her father started to get a little sterner with her; his eyes were almost looking angry at his frail daughter.

"That's because you are doing too much! You know what the doctor says - you should learn to listen to your body. Everyone admires how you are trying to get on with your life and how hard you have worked in trying to forget there is something wrong with you, but I hate to be the one to break it to you, there IS something wrong with you; you have a critical illness and you shouldn't be working the ridiculous hours that you do."

"You think I don't know there is something wrong with me? I wake up every morning not knowing if I am going to feel alright. Do you know what it is like waking up wondering if my legs are going to let me get out of bed? Or if my arms are going to work, or not knowing if I am going to be able to remember what I am doing at work?" Meg was sobbing between words now.

Evie stood up and walked over to where Meg was sitting. She sat down beside her and put her arm around her.

"We can't begin to imagine how it feels for you but we are trying to, and that is why we are talking to you like this. We have been hoping for some time now that you would give up work or cut down your hours at the very least. You don't seem to be getting much enjoyment out of anything these days."

"I do enjoy my job, but it is too much for me," Meg admitted.

Evie smiled with relief.

"What's funny?"

"Nothing, I have just been wanting you to admit that it is too much for so long!"

Her dad spoke:

"It is no shame to admit that, you know. Most people would have given up a long time before you. We really think you are brave, but it is time to think about yourself. You are more important than your job; look at what it is doing to your poor body!"

"Why do I get the impression you want me to slow down as far as work is concerned?" Meg joked. If nothing else, she had certainly understood that point!

Neither parent responded, they just smiled.

"We just love you so much," her father finally said. "We worry - it's part of the parenting thing!" David looked as if a great weight had been lifted from his shoulders.

"You guys are great, you know that? I guess I needed someone to reassure me that I wasn't a hypochondriac and that I wasn't giving in too easily."

"Never!" her mum said, looking offended that her daughter could even think such a thing.

That was pretty much how the conversation ended. The following day at work, Meg spoke to Anita who agreed that it was probably a good idea to reduce her hours. A suitable timetable was sorted out for Meg and, much to her relief, the wage packet wasn't too drastically reduced. The knock-on effect was that Meg was taking less time off sick, which worked well for all parties concerned.

A few weeks after her new hours started, Meg began to pick up in herself. She slept longer hours, her workload was reduced and thus, the stress also reduced. She decided to take up a new hobby. She had always enjoyed swimming so made a point of going every week. Jenny was more than happy to go with her.

"Yeah, well," Jenny had said, "I need to shape up and trim down!"

"Me too!" Meg had agreed.

"Yeah, right! Look at you - I wish I had a figure like that!"

"Whatever; I'd rather be fit and healthy." Meg looked insulted at the compliment.

"Oh Meg, I am so sorry, I didn't mean to offend you!" Jenny's smile disappeared from her face in an instant.

Meg tapped her friend gently on the arm.

"Ignore me; I am just a grouch! You didn't offend me at all, but you know what I mean."

"Of course; I am still sorry!" Meg tried to smile at her friend, but it was not easy for her.

So, every Thursday was swimming night. She left work, had a small bite to eat and an hour or two later, she and Jenny would go swimming at the large sports centre.

As much as Meg enjoyed her weekly visits to the Sports Centre, she was disappointed at how tired she felt after only a few lengths of the pool. A few years ago, she would have had no problem. In fact, it hadn't been that long since she had done a five-mile swim to raise money for charity. The only problem she had encountered was that of sheer boredom! Length after length after length! However, it had been her poor mum who had endured the most boredom, sat in the balcony counting the laps! She had even shown Meg the chart she had come up with, working out an average speed per 10 lengths and so on! Not to mention the doodling all around the paper.

However, rather than brooding over a previous life, she must get on with the new one.

One Thursday, Jenny had mentioned a basketball team who practised at the centre. She had suggested that they go and watch after their swim. Meg had protested, saying she preferred to go to the bar for a drink! Jenny had managed to get her way, however, persuading Meg with the news that some of the teams were rather 'dishy'.

"Honestly!" Meg had said, rolling her eyes at her friend.

Jenny and Meg watched the basketball team after every swim and Meg had to admit, Jenny had been right! One in particular had stood out to Meg as being particularly good-looking!

Weeks passed and Meg was coping well with everything. She had decided to adjust her hours, slightly reducing them. She found it helped her a great deal. She had even explained to other work friends why she was working part-time. Most understood; they knew more about the illness now and some even praised her for even working at all. Obviously, there had to be the odd one who said, "I wish I could work part-time!"

"And I wish I could work full time!" Meg had replied with spite, putting Lindsay very much in her place. Meg regretted it as soon as she had spoken. She should have known better by now just to ignore such remarks.

It was Thursday evening and Meg arrived outside Jenny's house to take her swimming.

Jenny ran out to the car but Meg noticed she wasn't holding the usual sports bag.

"Where's your stuff?" Meg asked as Jenny opened the car door.

"I am full of the cold," Jenny responded with the odd sniffle here and there.

"Oh, shall we call it off then? I'll come in for a coffee."

"No, I don't want you to catch it; I know what it can do to you." Meg also knew that being among germs was not ideal as it was possible it could result in a relapse.

"Oh, ok, well, I am not sure if I want to go by myself."

"Oh, please go; I will feel bad if you don't."

"Well, I guess I could manage it; at least I won't have anyone to keep up to."

"Yeah, right," Jenny said. "Well, have a good time." Jenny closed the car door and waved to her friend.

Meg watched as Jenny walked into the house she shared with her parents; the same house she had been longing to leave for quite some time now. Then it hit her - why on earth didn't she think of it before? Jenny could move in with her! It would be great having her in the house and she couldn't deny a little help with the outgoings would be a great help.

"How could I be so stupid?" she said out loud, hitting the steering wheel in frustration.

She must remember to mention it to Jenny the next time she saw her. It really would be perfect. The two got on so well and Jenny had been desperate to move out for ages.

Meg drove happily to the sports centre, music blaring out as per usual.

Argrave Sports Centre was the largest in the area, with an Olympic-sized swimming pool where many a future champion had trained. The gymnasium was more than adequate and the sports hall housed many a basketball match. Meg often stopped off after her swim with Jenny to watch the guys in action, Meg for the match, of course, but Jenny had her eye on one player!

Meg paid her money and walked into the newly redecorated changing rooms which, in themselves, were quite a spectacle.

"Too posh for the likes of us," Meg had often said.

She changed into her costume and went into the pool area. It was a little quieter than usual, which pleased Meg, as she wouldn't have to dodge anyone!

She swam a few lengths on her front and then turned to do the backstroke. No sooner had she set off than she clashed heads with someone else.

"Oh sorry!" she said, as she turned round to see who she had hit.

"My fault; I am so clumsy," came the reply. The victim was a young man who could do nothing but smile at Meg who couldn't help but return the gesture.

"Don't I know you from somewhere?" he said.

"That's an old one!" she replied.

"God, sorry, I didn't mean it like that, but really, your face is familiar; give me a second - it will come to me…" The man thought for a minute much to Meg's amusement.

"Got it; you sometimes come and watch the basketball!"

"Yeah, so?"

"I am in the team! I am there playing more often than not; do you like basketball?"

Meg thought that a rather obvious question. Why would she watch nearly every week if she didn't!

"Done it again, haven't I? Of course, you like it; why else would you watch?"

"Quite!"

The two swam out of the way of the angry faces staring at them, stood in the middle of the pool. After reaching the side of the pool, they talked for a few minutes and then Meg, looking at her somewhat wrinkled fingers, decided that it was time to get out!

"Can I meet you in the bar after you are dressed?" he asked her.

She blushed a beautiful crimson.

"I don't even know your name and you are talking about seeing me when I am dressed…!"

"Oh, sorry, I didn't mean it like that! I, I am just so hopeless at this."

"At what?"

"Chatting people up."

"So, you ARE chatting me up?" Meg couldn't help but say.

"Well, of course, who wouldn't?"

Meg blushed yet again; she wasn't used to this kind of attention.

He spoke to her, fumbling his words, for a few moments longer and then asked, "So, can I see you in the bar after?"

"I don't know, and I still don't know your name!"

"Scott," he replied.

"I am Meg."

"Hi! There, we have been introduced; now will you meet me?"

"Persistent, aren't you?"

"I guess, well…?"

"Ok, I guess so."

They both left the swimming pool and went to their changing rooms. As Meg stood under the shower, she wondered if this was really a good idea. Should she tell him about the MS? That would probably frighten him away. But was that such a bad idea? Was she ready for another relationship?

She had felt differently about Matt, when the potential arose for a relationship with him, even if it hadn't turned out the way she had hoped! He had already known her and somehow, she could cope with having a relationship with him, but this was different; she wasn't ready for a relationship with someone new.

As she wiped the water away from her face, she thought, 'Hold on, this isn't a relationship; we are just having a drink.' She stepped out of the shower and got dressed, thinking about Scott.

He was waiting for her in the bar when she arrived. She hadn't realised how good-looking he was in the swimming pool, nor how stunning his eyes were, large blue eyes with the longest lashes she had ever seen. He didn't seem that tall in comparison to the others standing at the bar, but since Meg was rather petite, as she walked towards him, he still towered above her.

"Hi," she said nervously.

"Hi, almost didn't recognise you with your clothes on!" He chuckled rather loudly for Meg's liking!

"Thanks! Embarrass me, why don't you?"

"Sorry, couldn't resist!"

Scott bought Meg a drink and they found a table. As soon as they sat down, Meg felt she was being interrogated, being asked questions left, right and centre, some of which, she wasn't ready to answer. She felt rather uncomfortable.

"…Where do you work? Do you keep fit other than swimming…?"

Meg decided she couldn't start a relationship on lies so she just spoke up in the middle of the interrogation.

"I have MS!" she blurted out.

"Oh, I am sorry, I have made you feel uncomfortable with all those questions, haven't I?"

"Well, yes, but you weren't to know!"

"Actually, I had an idea."

"How come?"

"Well, I liked you from the first moment I saw you so I kept looking at you, limping sometimes, sometimes you looked ok, rubbing your arms, I don't know, I put two and two together and, for a change, I obviously got four!"

"Well, good for you, now you can leave, knowing that you are clever and that you guessed right!" Meg was rather curt with him.

"Look, I am sorry. I didn't mean it like that. Please don't be like that with me. I was just concerned when I saw you in obvious pain!"

"Look, I am sorry, I just wasn't prepared for this kind of situation. I have been with someone for a long time and we broke up recently. I have not really been out with anyone since the diagnosis and the break-up. I didn't know how to handle it all."

"There is nothing to handle; just be yourself. You seemed alright!" Scott was trying to lighten the situation.

"Look, I am really sorry, I am just not ready for all this. I am sorry I have wasted your time." Meg's eyes filled with tears and she walked briskly out of the bar, leaving Scott bewildered.

She was more confused than ever as she drove home from the sports centre. She hadn't expected to have someone interested in her. Now she had told Scott what was wrong with her, she knew that would be the end of that. She couldn't have anyone putting up with the trauma of looking after her for the rest of her days. She couldn't risk them turning on her the way Tim had done. Scott seemed too nice to do that but she couldn't risk it. Besides anything else, it really wouldn't be fair to him.

Meg hadn't really thought about having a relationship. She was too involved in everything else. She would have to find a way to let anyone who did appear to be interested in her know that SHE wasn't interested.

Chapter 23

Meg drove to work the following day, missing her talks and laughter with Jenny. Her new hours meant that she could no longer share the driving and come to work with her friend. She really needed to talk to her about it, to get her opinion. It would have to wait.

At the next available opportunity, she told Jenny what had happened.

"Oh dear, you are in a mess!" her friend said, still full of the cold.

"Tell me about it; I don't know what to do."

"Well, let Scott decide."

"What do you mean?"

"Well, like you say, he had already suspected that you had MS and he still wanted to go out with you."

"Yeah, so? He might have guessed but that doesn't mean he knows all about it."

"Maybe, but I am guessing that he does, and that hasn't put him off, despite your ugly mug and lack of personality!"

"Ha, ha, thanks, mate!"

"At least it made you smile! Look, why don't you go swimming without me again and speak to him, give him the opportunity to decide what he wants to do."

"Makes sense, I guess, but I don't really want to go on my own."

"You'll be fine!"

"Ok, if you say so."

"Yes, I do; don't write yourself off so easily!"

Meg smiled warmly at her friend. She was very lucky to have her around.

She suddenly realised that she hadn't mentioned her ideas about Jenny moving in with her.

"Are you still fed up at home?" she asked Jenny.

"Subtle change of subject! Avoiding the issue…"

"Well, are you?" Meg didn't see it as changing the subject; she just wanted to discuss the matter whilst it was fresh in her mind before she forgot. Unfortunately, this was something which she seemed to be doing an awful lot of these days.

"Of course I am, what's new?"

"Pussycat!"

Jenny rolled her eyes at her friend.

"Well, I have been thinking…" started Meg.

"Careful!"

"Shut up and listen!" Meg teased. "I get fed up being on my own. I need help with the costs of the house and the cleaning…"

Meg went on to explain how much trouble she was having keeping up with everything. She explained everything in great detail, without actually saying what she wanted or what her idea was. She appeared very nervous, which made her slip up with her words. She was trying to say things too quickly, getting all tangled. Jenny looked very bemused by the whole thing.

"So, to cut a long story short…" Meg continued.

"Too late!"

"I wondered," Meg ignored Jenny's facial expressions and comments. "And I will change my mind if you don't behave!"

"For goodness' sake, girl, spit it out! I can't take the anticipation!" Jenny squealed, hoping she had guessed what Meg was about to say. Other people in the large staff room were now starting to look.

"I wondered if you would like to move in with me."

"Hmmm, move in with the woman I have had to put up with for the last thousand years; let me think about it!" But Jenny could not hide her delight at the suggestion. Her face shone with excitement; her beautiful large eyes brightened. She stood up and danced around the staff room like a little schoolgirl waking up on

Christmas morning to find she had just received the present she had always wanted!

"I'll take that as a definite maybe then, shall I?" Meg was a little embarrassed at the attention being drawn to them.

"It's a YES!" Jenny rushed back to where Meg was sitting and gave her a big hug.

"Steady, people will talk!" Meg joked.

"Let them, it will give them something else to gossip about!"

No time was wasted as the next few days were spent moving Jenny's belongings into her new home.

"All my worldly belongings!" Jenny joked as she stepped out of the hire van.

By the end of the day, Jenny was moved in. Still living with her parents, she didn't really have much to move in. They were both exhausted but happy with their achievements.

They were both lucky it was Saturday, as they were talking until at least three am! Actually, Meg was doing most of the talking. She was expressing deep concern about other people's opinions of her.

"When are you going to learn not to give a damn about what other people think?" Jenny said, relaxing on the sofa, feeling very much at home in the living room.

"I am sure we have had this conversation before; change the record, will you?" she continued.

"Yeah, I know, but I can't help it; I wish there was a way of letting people know what it is really like for me, without preaching or worrying that people will think all I talk about is the MS."

"Well, funny you should mention that because I have been thinking about it for a few days now."

"Oh?" Meg was intrigued.

"Yeah, well, everyone seems to know someone with MS but they still don't really know anything about it. So, I think you should get your story published."

"My story?"

"Well, maybe not your story, but some kind of story to raise the awareness of MS. From what I have heard, the reason people have a difficult time believing that you are ill is because you look so great, and you don't always have problems. Sometimes, you have a problem like with your walking, and then a few minutes later, you are walking fine!"

"But that is all part of it," Meg protested, feeling like Jenny was her enemy.

"I know that! You don't have to explain yourself to me, but if you got something published, more people would know it too, and maybe they would understand a little more!"

"You have it all worked out, don't you?"

"Well, what can I say? I care!" Jenny looked at her friend with obvious concern.

"I know you do and I am so lucky to have you as my friend. I really ap… appre…, oh, for God's sake, I appreciate it!"

"What are you on, girl? Spit it out!" Jenny said, giggling.

"It's not funny. I can't help it. I have noticed I struggle with my words sometimes when I am …" Meg drifted off the conversation, forgetting what she was saying.

"When you are tired."

"Yes, what?"

"You struggle with your words when you are tired?" Jenny offered help to Meg who was starting to get a little agitated at her problem. She was oblivious to half of the conversation she was having. Many people had made it worse by laughing when she got her words jumbled up, not believing it was the fatigue that was causing it.

"Ok, so then, Miss Organised," Meg began, trying to forget the problem, "I suppose you have even picked out which magazine I should write to, to publish the story?"

"Well, it just so happens…" Jenny stood and produced a magazine from her bag.

"This one appears to appeal to a wide audience so I think this is the one!"

"Right! Ok, Einstein, anything else?"

"Actually, yes! Maybe you could also contact the staff magazine and get your story in there too!"

"Wow, now that WOULD be making a statement!"

When the two finally parted company to go to bed, Meg found she couldn't sleep; not that it was something unusual, but her mind was racing. She was turning ideas over and couldn't get them out of her head.

The next morning, the air was crisp. Frost sprinkled on the now dying plants. The cul-de-sac looked very cold but beautiful. As Meg brushed her hair, she watched as neighbours walked by with their dogs, everyone clad in various winter fashions. One couple particularly amused Meg; not only were they wearing matching sweaters and hats, but their standard poodle was also sporting the same sweater!

Meg walked past Jenny's room to wash. Hearing no sound, she went quietly downstairs and set the coffee maker going. She prepared a tray for her friend with croissants, coffee, juice and strawberries. She walked slowly and carefully up the stairs and knocked on Jenny's door.

"Come in!" came the sleepy reply.

Meg walked into the messy room with the tray.

"Good morning!" she greeted her. "Welcome to your first morning in your new house."

"I am honoured!" said Jenny, rubbing her eyes and stretching her arms. "Sorry about the mess - I'll have it cleared up as soon as I can!"

"Don't worry about it! I think we have a busy day ahead of us so eat up and get dressed!" Meg instructed.

"Yes, Ma'am; what are we doing?"

"You ask that, in this mess?"

Jenny smiled at Meg as she left the room, allowing her to eat breakfast.

Meg went downstairs to eat her own. While she waited for her friend, she picked up a pen and paper and wrote down some ideas for her story to the press!

Soon after, Jenny walked down the stairs to join her friend, refreshed from the shower she had taken but still feeling a bit of a headache.

"How much did we drink last night?" she asked Meg.

"Who cares? Why, are you suffering?" Meg's voice was bright and breezy!

"Yes, and you aren't! Typical, you have always been able to hold your drink!"

Meg just winked at her friend! If the truth were known, she hadn't drunk nearly as much as Jenny simply because she COULDN'T take it anymore! It seemed to trigger all kinds of symptoms off!

"So, what's the plan, Meg, my friend?"

"Well, I thought we could decorate your room and make it more your own."

"WE are going to decorate?"

"Of course, with a little help from my dad! It shouldn't be too difficult."

"Ok, great!"

A few hours later, they pulled up outside Meg's parents' house.

Meg walked down the path, followed closely by Jenny. Jack was in the kitchen, rummaging through the huge fridge.

"Hiya, greedy!" she greeted her little brother as she crept up behind him. Little was really the wrong word - he towered above her, but then he had towered above her for some time. However, he would always be her little brother!

"Hiya, skinny!" he replied in his usual jovial tone. "Hi, Jenny."

"Hi, Jack, how are you?"

"Hungry!"

"How is Claire?" Jenny asked him.

"Great; she's in there actually!" Jack pointed towards the living room door.

Neither Jenny nor Meg had ever met Claire. Meg was very keen to see if this young woman met the high standards she had set for her. After all, she had to be something special to be acceptable. Jenny and Meg looked at each other, raised their eyebrows and raced to the living room door to catch sight of Claire! What they saw was an attractive young woman, neither slim nor fat, talking to Meg's mum.

She had shoulder-length light brown hair. She had beautiful hazel eyes. Whilst she wore no make-up, she still looked very attractive. She smiled warmly, standing to greet Meg who returned the beam. Somehow, Meg could tell from the way she smiled and carried herself that she seemed a nice, kind person.

"You must be Meg," she said.

"How did you guess?"

"You are the spitting image of Jack."

"Oh, thanks, and I thought you seemed nice! This is my friend Jenny."

"Hi, Jenny. How are you?" Claire had a beautiful spoken voice.

"Fine, thanks!"

"Well, my brother certainly knows how to pick them!"

"Thanks, I think!" Claire responded.

The decorating plans went to pieces as Meg and Jenny spent the rest of the day chatting to Claire, finding out they had met at college and were in a couple of the same classes. She seemed really nice.

"You'll all stay for tea, won't you?" Evie yelled out from the kitchen.

Meg was startled at the time when she looked at her watch. She looked at Jenny to see if she wanted to stay. Jenny nodded in approval.

"I always did love your mum's cooking," she commented.

"That would be great, Mum," Meg called out, going into the kitchen to see if her mum needed any help. When she was told none was needed, she returned to the living room to find her father had finally sat down from doing all sorts of jobs around the house.

"Actually," Meg began, "it was you we came to see!"

"Why, what do you want?" her dad joked.

"Why should I want something? I just might have wanted to see my lovely Dad."

"Now I know you are after something!" David smiled.

"Ok, then, I am."

"A-ha!"

"I wondered if you could help us decorate Jenny's room."

"Jenny's room?"

"Oh yes, didn't I tell you? I asked her to move in with me?"

"That's great, hon!" Her father knew it would be a great help to Meg, having someone else around the home, and who better than Jenny?

"Hmmm, I don't know if I can fit you into my busy schedule… tomorrow ok?"

"Fantastic! We will help, of course!"

"You'll do no such thing! You just keep the coffee flowing! I am not having you making yourself ill over wallpaper."

Although Meg knew he was right, it still irritated her that she wasn't able to help.

Her father could guess the meaning of the look on her face.

"Besides," he said, "I don't want any of it to be upside down!"

The following day, they went shopping for wallpaper, and after a long and painful debate, the decision was made! The wallpaper was on the walls in no time, thanks to David, and Jenny had bought herself some wardrobes and a couple of shelves. Within the week, the room looked great and was now officially Jenny's.

"I am so glad you are here," Meg began. "I am only sorry I didn't think of it before."

"Well, I am here now and we are going to have fun together, I just know it!"

"I have been thinking about what you said about the magazine and I think you are right."

"Great; do you need any help?"

"Well, no, I have already prepared something so your opinion on it would be enough, if that is alright?"

"Sure, go ahead!"

Meg found the piece of paper with the jotted notes. She sat down and began to read, with Jenny listening intently.

At the age of 24, I was diagnosed with Multiple Sclerosis. I was thrown into turmoil.

At the time I was diagnosed, I thought the way I was told

was terrible; it seemed to be slipped casually into the conversation. I later realised there could be no easy way of breaking that kind of news to somebody.

Although I had guessed what was wrong with me, I still had no idea what the illness was about. Few people do, but many know people with the illness. Multiple Sclerosis is a chronic progressive disease of the nervous system, where the protective layer around the nerve, called the myelin, is severed, kind of like a rope that frays, thereby cutting off transmission of messages from the brain to the various parts of the body. This means that certain activities are not always possible, such as walking, talking and various other activities, which many people take for granted. Sometimes, the same symptoms come back to haunt people time and time again, and sometimes, they will suffer a symptom once and maybe never again.

There are various types of Multiple Sclerosis; the one that I suffer from is called relapsing-remitting; this means I have good times and bad times. Sometimes I can carry out my daily activities like other people, but other times, I cannot even get out of bed as the illness is so bad. One of my greatest passions is writing, but I cannot always do this as my hands do not allow it. Even as you speak, I am not writing this article; I am speaking through a specialised microphone connected to my computer. I am just getting used to this, but I have to admit, it is fun.

No one is really sure how the illness starts. There are many theories, such as a virus, stressful situations; some even say it is the environment in which we live. It is still unclear; this could explain why there is no cure as yet, however, I am forever hopeful.

The biggest problem I constantly face, aside from the illness itself, is other people's attitudes, due to the fact that a lot of the time, I look like a healthy young woman. I get the constant *comments - "But you look so good!" Yes, I am fortunate in that I am not always in a wheelchair, but this doesn't mean I do not suffer. Fatigue is my main symptom, but people have no idea what fatigue really is. They just say, "You just get tired?" No is a simple answer to that one - fatigue and tiredness are two entirely different things. Tiredness is maybe when you may do a little bit too much, whereas fatigue is when you don't have the energy to do even the simplest of tasks like reaching for your drink.*

The treatment is another battle. There is a drug called beta interferon, but this drug is very expensive and is only prescribed to a limited number of patients. Unfortunately, I am not one of them.

Life is a constant struggle but I am fortunate to have the best, most understanding parents anyone could wish for and I have a fantastic friend who has always been there for me and she still is. I was due to get married a few months ago but my husband-to-be decided it was not the life for him. However, I try to keep optimistic, which is a struggle sometimes, especially when some people just do not understand. Therefore, I am writing this article in the hope that more people will understand the illness and will appreciate that just because people are not in a wheelchair, Multiple Sclerosis still affects many people in many different ways. Please try to help them even if it's only to lend a sympathetic ear.

Thank you.

Meg sat back, exhausted, as if she had forgotten to breathe during her recitation. She looked up at Jenny for her opinion.

"So, what do you think?"

"Hmm, it will do, I guess!"

"It will do? IT WILL DO! It took me ages to do that!"

"I am teasing; it is perfect!"

Meg wrote off to the magazine and was delighted to find she didn't need the reserve list; they got in contact with her and even called to take her photo.

She hoped that when published, the magazine would help others with MS by letting people know what it was like. She was sure other people would have the same worries about friends' and family's attitudes. Hopefully, this would achieve something.

She didn't have to wait too long. As luck would have it, the magazine had a space in their next issue. Meg bought it and was delighted with the final article. It was a double-page spread with not only Meg's words but also those of a doctor. Giving the medical information highlighted the severity of the illness even more. It certainly had some effect as one afternoon, whilst Meg was in the supermarket, the cashier kept looking at her with apparent perplexity. While Meg was packing away her shopping, the cashier, whose nametag said Lucy, spoke.

"You are the girl in 'Today's Woman' magazine, aren't you?"

"Yes."

"It was a great piece; my sister has MS and was particularly delighted that MS had finally been tackled from that angle."

"Well, thanks!"

"She has a lot of the same problems, particularly with other people and their attitude, and I am sure your article has helped."

"Good! That was the idea."

Meg was delighted. If the piece had reached one person and had such an effect, then it had been worthwhile.

Chapter 24

It was Thursday once again. Jenny and Meg had missed one week at swimming. Meg was very apprehensive about going again and meeting up with Scott. Jenny had spent the entire day trying to convince Meg, yet again, that it should be up to Scott to decide on their relationship, and that she shouldn't take that choice away from him by avoiding him.

"You do like him, don't you?" she asked.

"Yes, I do, very much."

"Well, let's go then!"

Off they trekked to the sports centre and after they swam, they walked up to the sports hall to watch the basketball team.

They found a couple of seats and sat down. Meg noticed Scott straight away. He looked very unhappy and his heart didn't seem to be in the game. He kept gazing around the seating area. Meg felt guilty at once. A few minutes later, Scott looked up again at the seating and saw Meg. He beamed with delight. There was a definite spring to his step for the rest of the game; he scored a few baskets and seemed like a different person.

"Welcome back, Scott!" one of the team players said.

Scott just smiled and turned again towards Meg and waved, brushing his hair from his face.

"He probably won't even want to talk to me," Meg said to Jenny after waving back gingerly.

"Are you kidding? Look at him; you have made his day!"

"I'll be back in a sec," Meg heard Scott shout to his teammates.

He jogged up to where Meg was sitting and said, "Hi!"

"Hi."

"Look," Scott continued, "I am sorry if I made you feel uncomfortable the other week. I was worried last week when you didn't show. I only wanted to go out with you! Blew it, didn't I?"

"Hold on; I should be the one apologising. I acted inexcusably. I had no right to speak to you like that."

She smiled at him.

"Ok," he said, "I have an idea. We both seem to have got off on the wrong foot, so what say we start again?"

"Hooray!" Jenny exclaimed, listening to their conversation.

"Hi, my name is Scott!" he greeted Meg with a cheeky smile.

"Hi, I am Meg and this is my friend Jenny!"

"Nice to meet you both! Listen, Meg, I was wondering, maybe you would like to go out for a drink sometime this week with me?"

"That would be nice."

"Saturday, at the Conservatory, perhaps?"

The Conservatory was a trendy new wine bar that had opened not too far away from the sports centre.

"That sounds nice; how does 8 pm sound?" she offered.

"Ok. Shall I pick you up?"

"I think you already did that," Jenny joked, delighted that the two had arranged a date.

Meg gave Scott the directions for her house and then left with Jenny to let him finish his game.

Scott was true to his word and picked Meg up on the following Saturday. He was dressed casually in a light blue shirt and his jeans. His scent was very appealing. Meg herself had spent ages in her bedroom, pondering over what to wear. She had driven Jenny insane, flitting in and out of her room in various outfits, asking her opinion. Meg had finally opted for her first choice, a short dress which was a black, sleeveless polo neck top with a grey stripe at the bottom. They both enjoyed a pleasant evening, chatting about everything from pop music to annoying little brothers.

Meg's life appeared to be getting back on track. She seemed to be in remission except for the odd symptom. She mentioned this to the neurologist, who said it was to be expected. Sometimes, symptoms lingered on and didn't go away. Unfortunately, that was just how it was. He was, however, delighted that she had slowed down, as it was obviously having a positive effect on her life.

"I am glad you have finally listened," he said. "It's just a shame it has taken so long. But surely, you can see how much it is helping you? I am sure you could slow down even more but this is a start. It's about time you got used to the idea that you aren't the same person you were a few years ago. I know you are young and it is difficult to accept, but you have to. You don't have the same limits or energy as before. The medication can only do so much; the rest is up to you. Don't set yourself large goals. This doesn't mean you have to stop living. I am sure there are things you can enjoy doing." Meg agreed, telling him about her swimming and the little bit of writing she was doing.

"Oh, yes, I saw the piece! I was very impressed." He was also delighted about the swimming. It had been a very positive appointment.

Meg had even heard that Matt, whom she hadn't spoken to for such a long time, was also doing well. He had found himself a new love. She phoned him to see how everything was going and was delighted to hear how happy he appeared to be.

It had now been nearly 6 months since the breakup with Tim and she appeared to be well and truly over him. She rarely mentioned his name, and if someone else did, she didn't break down in tears anymore. She had been seeing Scott for a few months now. Everyone really liked him, particularly Meg's parents. He seemed so understanding with everything. In the short time they had been together, they had become very close. Meg had met his parents and had immediately got on well with them. They knew how much Scott thought of her and were delighted at how their relationship was going. Much to Meg's joy, they thought very highly of her. The four of them went out for dinner on many occasions. The added bonus, however, was how well the respective parents got on with each other. This was something unfamiliar to Meg, as Tim's parents had never spent much time with her own. Nevertheless, many dinner parties were had between the two couples. The topic of conversation each time was, naturally, Scott and Meg!

Christmas was, yet again, just around the corner. The year had flown by, considering everything that had taken place.

Jenny and Meg were spending Christmas with their own parents and had been busy buying presents. Meg, in particular, had been rushed off her feet. She had been baking Christmas cakes and mince pies, and the house had been given a good tidy, ready for the decorations. Jenny had offered to help with all of it but Meg had refused, saying she had much more time to do it.

She decided to throw a party between Christmas and New Year, mainly to celebrate how good she was feeling and how much her life was improving. She refused to buy any ready-made party foods, wanting everything to be homemade. She hadn't realised what a mammoth task arranging a party really was. It was all worthwhile though, she thought, as everyone commented on what a lovely evening it was and how delicious the food was.

All her family was there, including Jack with Claire, of course. Jenny had invited her family and was surprised to learn that her brother had said goodbye to his girlfriend and was doing better at school.

Matt was there alone; his friend had been invited but Matt didn't really feel ready to go so public. Scott was there. All in all, it had been quite a night. The tree and all the decorations looked beautiful, as did the buffet. Meg had taken extra care just to give it that little extra special touch.

It was a cold winter's night. The wind whistled through the trees, playing a haunting melody. All the friends and family were huddled together near the fire, laughing and joking. Traditional music played in the background along with some modern hits. Jack had been particularly amusing on the Karaoke machine, thinking he was Frank Sinatra, much to the delight of Claire. He could actually carry a tune. She did manage to turn the tables on him though as she sang, shocking everyone with a beautiful voice.

"You really have picked a winner!" Meg said to Jack. "You are a very lucky young man."

"I am the lucky one," Claire said on hearing the two talking about her.

Soon after, people could see that Meg was beginning to tire, wobbling around the room. Finding it difficult to string together a coherent sentence, she remained quiet.

"I think it is time we were going, love," Evie said, walking up to her daughter. "It has been a wonderful evening; you have done really well. I am proud of you!"

"Thanks, Mum, but you d…d…don't have to…"

"Don't have to what, love?"

"Huh?" Meg didn't even realise that she had stopped mid-sentence.

"You were going to say something."

"Was I?"

"It doesn't matter, Meg. We are tired, and anyway, it's late!"

The other guests took their cue and within half an hour, they had all left.

"Something I said?" Meg asked Jenny as she flopped on the sofa.

They both retired to their rooms and were asleep in no time.

Meg awoke the following morning to be greeted by Jenny carrying a mug of coffee and some toast.

"Did you sleep like that?" Jenny asked.

"Like what?"

Jenny pointed to Meg's body, which was still fully clothed.

"I must have just fallen asleep as soon as I got here!" To be truthful, Meg didn't even remember coming up to bed.

"Well, I guess we have a busy morning of clearing up so I will just get a shower and be with you!"

Jenny protested, raising her hand. "No, you will not! You stay here, get into your nightshirt and I will clear up. You need to rest."

"Are you trying to tell me what to do?"

"No, but you have been so busy these past few days with this party that the least I can do to thank you is to clear up."

Meg didn't like to admit it, but she was so exhausted and decided that Jenny was right. She stood up and got into her nightshirt and got back into bed. This task in itself was taking all of Meg's energy. It didn't help matters because she didn't seem to have the full use of her legs. She fell asleep, and, a couple of hours later, had a bath and went down to join her friend.

"Did I shout at you? I am sorry!"

"No worries!" Jenny reassured her friend. Meg looked around the room to see that Jenny had pretty much done all the clearing up. Meg helped her put the last few things away and was exhausted after only helping for five minutes. She dropped to the sofa as Jenny brought them both a drink.

A couple of hours later, lunch comprised of the party's leftovers, which turned out to be quite a selection of delights!

Meg tried to get up to clear away the dishes when she had finished eating. She found it very difficult as her legs gave way, causing her to tumble over onto the floor. She had no feeling in her legs. Jenny panicked, rushing straight to her friend to offer assistance.

"What can I do?" she asked.

"Give me a new pair of legs!" Meg tried to joke. "I don't think there is anything you can do. I am sure it will wear off."

Jenny looked anxious.

"Maybe you could do one thing for me…"

"Name it!"

Meg asked her to lift her leg and then let go to see if Meg could hold it up on her own. As she expected, as soon as Jenny let go of her leg, it came crashing to the floor like a lead balloon.

"I am so sorry, did I hurt you?"

"I didn't feel a thing." Meg couldn't hide the fear. It showed in her face. The look of sheer horror, as there was no feeling whatsoever below her waist.

"I am calling the nurse," Jenny announced.

Meg managed to convince her friend otherwise, after all, what could she do?

"I have just been too busy, overdoing things as usual!"

Jenny helped Meg sit back on the comfortable sofa rather than the hard laminate flooring on which she was sprawled. She put on Meg's favourite film and instructed her to lie back and enjoy the film, but to call her if she needed anything.

By the time the film had finished, Meg was sure her legs would be fine. She had regained some of the feeling in them. She decided against trying to test out her theory by walking. Instead, she let Jenny make them both another drink.

Jenny was more than happy to look after her friend. She felt terrible at having let her do all the work for the party. Meg had insisted on doing everything, telling Jenny she really needn't feel bad. She was still upset, however, that it had taken something like this to slow Meg down, but the last thing Meg needed was to be told this. She didn't need to have someone tell her that the reason this had happened was that she never listened to people and carried on as if there was nothing wrong with her. She needed a sympathetic ear. Jenny only had to think how she would feel in her friend's position. It had to be so difficult for her, to learn to adapt to a different lifestyle knowing she couldn't do a simple task, which everyone else could do without a problem.

Jenny decided that maybe Scott would be the person to cheer her up, so she called and asked him to come over and he was only too happy to oblige, sounding just as concerned as Jenny about Meg.

As she put down the telephone, she heard Meg call to her.

"Yes, ma'am?" she called, walking into the lounge and performing a little curtsey.

"You wouldn't make me a cuppa, would you?"

"Yes, milady!" Jenny winked at her friend and did as instructed.

Scott arrived a few moments later with a bouquet of flowers.

"For the patient," he said, smiling. He leaned over to kiss Meg's face, which had brightened up considerably at the sight of Scott.

Fortunately, Scott managed to convince Meg that maybe she was having a relapse, especially when she opened up and told him of the other problems she had been having. Her memory was so bad that she was writing all of the symptoms down! She read out the list… her hand got tired soon after writing or doing something, her fatigue was worse than ever. She had pins and needles all down her right side. Her balance was terrible… the list went on…

Scott was rather annoyed that she hadn't spoken out before. He was appalled that she had endured such pain and discomfort without telling anyone. Meg had the simple reply to that one - she hadn't wanted to worry anyone or, even worse, have people get annoyed that she was doing nothing but talk about her illness. However, Scott would hear of no excuses and telephoned Meg's nurse. She told him that Meg must ring the hospital.

Upon doing this, she was instructed to make her way to the hospital, where she would be seen by her neurologist. As fortune would have it, he was on the hospital ward, doing his rounds.

Scott and Jenny helped her into the car and Scott drove them all immediately to the hospital, taking her wheelchair. He sped her up to the ward like a racing driver. Meg was glad of the lightness he made of pushing her, as she was having a hard time dealing with it.

They waited on the ward for the neurologist. Meg was getting more and more upset by the minute; tears were starting to form on her face.

"Come on, now," Scott said, gently trying to comfort her as the tears ran down her face.

"But what are they going to do?" she asked between sobs.

"I don't know, sweetie, but whatever it is, we will get you feeling better soon."

"I really should go and telephone your mum and let her know what is happening. She will never forgive me if I don't!" Jenny offered.

"Yeah, thanks, I would appreciate that."

Jenny smiled and hugged her friend before disappearing down the corridor, dodging to avoid the busy nurses bustling up and down in their smart uniforms.

Scott took Meg's hand in his own and gently touched her hair with his other. Although still short, her hair was beautiful and soft and shone in the winter sun.

"Don't cry, baby; we'll get through this together. You know I am here for you, don't you? Anything you need just tell me; I will do anything you want."

"One thing."

"Name it!"

Meg paused for a second, then continued, "Don't resent me for any of this."

Scott looked puzzled at the request.

"Never! Why should I resent you?"

Before she had the chance to answer, he brushed her hair away from her face and brought her closer. He gently touched her lips with his and gave her a soft warm kiss. There was so much feeling in that kiss and their lips stayed together until they were interrupted by a small cough. They hadn't heard the footsteps walking towards them. Meg looked around and was somewhat embarrassed to see her neurologist.

"Sorry," she said, somewhat red-faced.

"No need," came the reply. "Now then, what's been happening with you? I understand you are having a difficult time."

Meg explained all her symptoms to him and he seemed genuinely concerned, much more so than when they had previously met. She hadn't noticed how kind his face looked, how gentle and soothing his voice was and how much he really seemed to care. He was particularly concerned about the lack of coordination and asked her to try walking in a straight line, heel to toe. She could barely walk at all, let alone in a straight line.

The neurologist helped her sit back down at the side of Scott, who held her hand. The neurologist needed no more convincing. He knew what he needed to do.

"I can help you with the coordination, I am certain. I think it is about time for more steroids."

"Great." Meg remembered how they made her feel before when she was taking them!

"Did they help you before?"

"I guess so. To be honest, I didn't know if they did or if I was just feeling better anyway."

The doctor knew it was more than likely the steroids that had made her feel better, but not wanting to upset her, he said, "Probably a bit of both."

She was obviously still having a difficult time understanding the grave nature of the illness. The doctor checked the notes to see that it was over six months since she had her previous course. He was a little disappointed that they had not lasted any longer. He really didn't like giving them too often, but he knew it was the only course of action he could take.

"It says here in your notes that you have finally listened and slowed down a little from your old self; is that still the case?" he asked.

"Fat chance!" Scott began. "She still refuses to listen. She has been rushed off her feet organising a Christmas party, refusing help from anyone."

The neurologist sat beside her and said, "I don't mean to worry you, but if you don't slow down, your MS is going to progress, maybe so much that we can't help you as much. Don't go mad thinking that we can mend you if you get ill. We shouldn't really have to give you the steroids so often; they should work for a lot longer than they are doing. I think you are giving them far too much work to do."

Scott was as disturbed to hear all this as Meg.

"Now, are you going to listen?" he asked softly.

"Ok." In her heart, she finally gave in, admitting defeat. She certainly did not want the MS to get any worse than it already was.

And so, once again, Meg found herself with the drip containing the steroids, pumping into her arm. After 3 days, she was finished and feeling worse than ever.

Scott had taken the week off work to take her to hospital and he insisted on looking after her. She really wasn't sure if she was comfortable with the arrangement. She didn't like him seeing her like this. A lot of people had commented previously that they were surprised she felt so ill after the steroids; it was only medication, after all! But how would they like to be sat with a needle in their hand pumping into their veins for 3 days? She wasn't going to get all upset about what other people thought anymore, though. Vanessa had admitted, when they had met, that she had felt the same way.

Scott was there for her, 24 hours a day, comforting her when she couldn't sleep, another unfortunate side effect of the steroids that only a few understood.

Her mum did, though, and she didn't have to endure the steroids, so why couldn't other people? The truth was, her mum had endured the suffering nearly as much as Meg had, from the last course of steroids.

Meg had a long spell away from work this time, as the steroids seemed to be taking longer to have a positive effect on her. Even when she did return to work, she struggled immensely.

One particular day, Anita approached her to have a word. She took Meg to the little office to the back of the room and spoke to her.

"I am not going to waste time; I am just going to get to the point. We think maybe work is too much for you and maybe you ought to give up."

Meg was appalled at the suggestion.

"Give up?"

"Yes, we can see that you are wasting away here. Maybe you would be better off at home, then it wouldn't matter if you were feeling ill, you could just sit down and take it easy. You wouldn't have to struggle on like you do. We are all very proud of you for trying so hard to cope, but we feel you are making yourself so much worse."

Meg thought about it for a few seconds. Deep down, at the bottom of her heart, she knew it was the right thing to do and that what Anita was saying made sense. There was only one problem -

"What about the money? I can't afford to not work."

"We have a pension scheme that includes this sort of thing. It's not a great amount of money but I think you will be fine."

She watched Meg ponder over the suggestion.

"I'll leave you to think it over for a few days."

Meg watched as Anita left her in the small room.

She talked it over with her parents later that day and was not surprised at their response. They were in full agreement with Anita.

"You know it's the right thing to do, Meg," her father had said.

"I guess so, but what will I do with all my time?"

"Have some fun; get your life back. You will be able to do the things you haven't been able to," her mum suggested.

Meg left them later that evening and, once again in her life, she was facing confusion. Having to give up work at such a young age… One strange thing annoyed her about the whole thing. When she met someone and they asked her what she did for a living, what would she say? It wasn't even as if she looked disabled or ill which would probably stop people from asking.

She spoke to Scott about it, and he was very supportive. He really made her see that it was probably for the best.

A few days later, she saw Jenny and she had some good news for her.

"You have a computer, right?" she asked.

"You know I do, why?"

Jenny went on to explain about a website for people with MS and was surprised to hear she had never checked it out before.

"I guess I just didn't want to see what other people were like and how bad it could be."

"Well, apparently it is really good."

Meg wasted no time and checked out the website. It was a great help to her as there were regular chats, which she participated in. She was relieved to see other people really knew what it was like for her and the group was very supportive. The only problem she found was that it was an American-run group so the chats were late at night. When she mentioned it to the group, they said they didn't have many chats at a better time for her, so why didn't she start up a group of her own?

Her time was pretty much filled with this from then on, and she found herself contributing more and more to the website, doing more for them. For the first time in a long time, she felt really good about herself.

The website didn't totally fulfil her life or take away the anguish of the illness, but it certainly helped, and took care of a lot of the boredom she suffered. She found comfort in listening to people talking to her and asking for her advice, advice that she was qualified to provide, given that she knew exactly how other people felt.

Her only real problem now was Scott. She found herself falling for him. She was spending more time with him and thought it was unfair to him given her situation.

Chapter 25

A few weeks later, Meg was starting to feel a little better, but it seemed she still had a little bit of a problem walking. She had remembered what the neurologist had once said, that some symptoms may stay with her and never go away. So, she resigned herself that this was the way it was going to be. Scott was still hanging around though.

Meg still didn't feel like Scott understood everything. Why would he still be with her if he did? Maybe he thought she would be all cured now she had taken the steroids and they were beginning to take effect at long last…

Meg decided the only thing she could do, to be sure of how Scott was feeling, and to be totally honest and fair with him, was to tell him everything. So, one evening, not too long after the steroid treatment, she went to visit him at his house. She sat him down and began…

She began with the various symptoms which had led to her fears of the diagnosis. She watched as his face changed from looking simply interested to horrified when she told him of the abuse she endured with Tim, the thrown glasses, the mental torture, leaving her at the altar and then having the barefaced cheek to want to start all over again.

She told him of how the illness had changed everything in her life, of how frustrating it was to see that she was unable to do the things she once could, but that she was gradually beginning to accept it. She was starting to adjust to her new life and trying to acknowledge that maybe it wasn't worse, just different. She had tried to make the most of a bad situation by volunteering on an MS support group on the

Internet. She had found a lot of help there and was feeling satisfaction from helping others with their MS.

But Scott's face really changed when she told him she had resigned herself to a life of solitude. She didn't want to put someone through the torture of the MS, having to push her around in a wheelchair for the rest of their lives. She didn't want to have to subject a man to the unpredictability of the symptoms, not knowing from one day to the next how she was going to feel and having him resent her for it.

When Meg had finally finished, she looked at Scott, waiting for his response. His face said all she thought she needed to know. He looked absolutely horrified. When Scott didn't respond immediately, Meg took the initiative to speak and make up his mind for him.

"It's ok," she began. "I understand. I can see what you are thinking, so you don't have to say anything. I can see that you don't really want the responsibility of caring for me. I…"

"Mind if I say something?" he interrupted. He looked at the sad, lost face, her slender figure looking frailer than ever. She looked so vulnerable. He smiled at her warmly.

"You are a kind and very loving person," he told her, "so I can't…!

"You can't lie to me and lead me on by carrying on with the relationship; it's ok." Meg's face looked even more heartbroken than ever. Although she admitted that she had decided it wasn't fair to have a long-term relationship with Scott, Meg couldn't deny she had fallen for him, big time. She hadn't even felt this way about Tim. All this taken into consideration, this was a very difficult conversation for Meg.

"Can I speak now?" Scott winked at Meg.

"Sorry!"

"Do you promise not to interrupt me?"

"Yes, sorry!"

"In all the time I have known you, I have never had trouble shutting you up. I thought you were a quiet person!"

"Sorry!" Meg couldn't think of anything else to say.

"Ok," Scott finally began. "Here goes - I never believed in love at first sight until I met you…"

Meg rolled her eyes but tried to look serious when she received a warning glare from Scott.

He continued, "You seemed like such a happy person. You are beautiful and kind and your bravery in coping with all of this is endearing. You are everything I could want in a partner. The fact that you are ill is a small setback. If we stick together, we will get through it all. I know it is an unpredictable illness but I know more about it than you think. Deep down, I know you love me and I love you. Believe me, Meg, we can get through this. We will enjoy our good days and struggle through the bad ones. If you are worried that I will ever resent you for any of this, then you really don't know me as well as I thought you did. I could never, ever resent you or treat you the way Tim did. Don't you see? I love you too much for that. So much so, I intend to marry you…"

Meg's jaw dropped to her knees.

"Go back a step; did you say marry?"

"You heard. Will you marry me, Meg Walker?"

The tension could be cut with a knife. The atmosphere was so quiet you could hear a pin drop; even the birds seemed to have quietened. After a long pause, Meg replied, "Scott, I really can't do it, it is just not fair to you. I am carrying too much baggage, too many scars."

Scott simply replied with a smile, his eyes twinkling at her.

"Why are you smiling? What is so funny?"

"Do you know that is what Multiple Sclerosis means?"

"Means what? What are you talking about?"

"Multiple Sclerosis means Many Scars. When are you going to accept that I am not going to go away? I love you, scars and all. I have always loved you and I have always known about your illness, so please get it into your thick skull, I am not Tim!"

Meg looked apprehensive.

"Ok, I believe you," she said reluctantly.

"Do you love me?"

"Scott, I love you more than I can explain. I love you more than you will ever know, which is why…"

Scott raised his hand to prevent her from continuing.

"So. what is your problem then? Marry me…"

A huge smile formed on Meg's beautiful face as she uttered one simple word -

"Yes."

Acknowledgements

Firstly, I would like to thank Sophie at Publishing Push for all your help and guidance. You helped make the whole process a little less daunting. And a huge thanks to Audrey for all your help and to Christine for all your hard work proofreading!

Nicola, my best friend. Thank you for giving me that little nudge and for telling me that if I can do it, I should do it.

To my family, thank you for all you have done and continue to do for me. You have no idea how much I appreciate you all.

But mostly, thank you to my amazing son, Alex. Thank you for looking after me more than I wish you have to.

Finally, Steven, my husband and soulmate, thank you for putting up with me for so long. I love you "Always and Forever".

I am donating £1 of my earnings from every book to my local branch of the MS society.

Printed in Great Britain
by Amazon

80557581R00150